T

**DICK SNOW:** The ~~mountain man carried a rare-barreled~~ caplock shotgun-rifle combination. He used it for hunting down trail dinners and—on occasion—hunting down men. . . .

**CHARLEY ROGERS:** The bright-eyed boy had lost his family and learned the ways of the Cheyenne. Now he was leaving his Cheyenne village, on his way to becoming a man. . . .

**NELL JOINER:** A local saloonkeeper was trying to steer Nell into prostitution. But in Dalton, Colorado, the still-beautiful woman was clinging to memories of her husband's gold strike, and to her hopes. . . .

## Praise for R. C. House's
### *Trackdown at Immigrant Lake*

"A vintage Western! House captures that time after the Civil War when bold men ventured westward to seek their fortunes. In House's book, you can smell the burnt powder, taste the trail dust. He knows his guns; he knows the West. This is a superb entertainment, fast-moving, studded with characters plucked from our bloody past and kept alive on the printed page. One of the best traditional Westerns I've read lately."

—Jory Sherman, Spur Award-winning author of
*The Medicine Horn*

ACIE CASEY: The prospector had survived a war and a hard life in the hills. And in the middle of a rainstorm he could whip up the best meal you'd ever tasted. . . .

BARNEY WISNER: He was Acie's fellow veteran, friend and partner. Together they'd pulled through some hard scrapes—but none harder than this. . . .

ELK LEGGINS: The Cheyenne chief was a man of compassion and wisdom. He knew the boy he called "Cha-lee-rah-jaw" had to seek out his own people, and he asked Dick Snow to show him the way. . . .

## Praise for R. C. House's
### *Trackdown at Immigrant Lake*

"*Trackdown at Immigrant Lake* crackles with excitement. . . . From start to finish, this book draws a reader into the vortex of the action. R. C. House creates memorable characters, and you'll be sorry to see them go when the last page is turned."

—Fred Bean, author of *The Last Warrior*

SIMON PARSONS: The thin, mercurial outlaw didn't hesitate to steal a treasured keepsake from a boy—and then use it to plot his next crime. . . .

DAVE DEWEESE: He kept his gambler's suit in his saddle-roll and waited until his next chance to lie and cheat. And with his sapphire-colored eyes, he could make anyone believe any lie he told. . . .

## Praise for R. C. House's
### *Trackdown at Immigrant Lake*

"House's work gets better with each book. *Sudden Gun* was terrific. *Trackdown at Immigrant Lake* is even better."
—Dale Walker, *Rocky Mountain News*,
President of the Western Writers of America

"*Trackdown at Immigrant Lake* moves rapidly. . . . With the death of the incomparable Louis L'Amour, there is a need for somebody to fill the vacuum. One of the established writers who will claim his share of the range is undoubtedly R. C. House."
—Don Coldsmith, Spur Award-winning author of
*The Spanish Bit Saga*

**Books by R. C. House**

Spindrift Ridge*
Requiem for a Rustler*
Warhawk
Trackdown at Immigrant Lake*
Drumm's War
The Sudden Gun
Vengeance Mountain
So the Loud Torrent

*Published by POCKET BOOKS

# R.C. HOUSE

# SPINDRIFT RIDGE

**POCKET BOOKS**

New York  London  Toronto  Sydney  Tokyo  Singapore

An *Original* Publication of POCKET BOOKS

POCKET BOOKS, a division of Simon & Schuster Inc.
1230 Avenue of the Americas, New York, NY 10020

Copyright © 1993 by R. C. House

All rights reserved, including the right to reproduce this book or portions thereof in any form whatsoever. For information address Pocket Books, 1230 Avenue of the Americas, New York, NY 10020

ISBN: 0-671-76044-0

First Pocket Books printing November 1993

10  9  8  7  6  5  4  3  2  1

POCKET and colophon are registered trademarks of Simon & Schuster Inc.

Cover art by David Henderson

Printed in the U.S.A.

Kind permission was granted to use portions of *Everything Comes To He Who Writes*, written by Robert Dyer, copyright © 1992 by Robert Dyer and published in *The Tombstone Epitaph*.

# SPINDRIFT
# RIDGE

The soft chatter of a chilling rain on the tin roof of the Golconda Hotel helped lure Deweese out of the warm gauze of sleep. He felt snug under the clean sheets and dry blankets, his body heat reinforced by the woman asleep beside him. Her musky scent wafted up to him from under their covering.

One eye slitting drowsily, the other, it seemed, still asleep, Deweese cautiously edged away a hand that had rested on the velvet-skinned form beside him through the night and absently palmed a stubbly chin. His eyeballs felt morning-after dry, reminding him of night-before drinks; he blinked to clear the thickness of sleep in them and to refresh his waking eyes.

His body was close enough to touch hers but didn't. Her warm back was to him, a tantalizing wealth of clean chestnut hair spilling over her pillow.

What was her name? Martha? Already he'd forgotten. No, that was too common for a whore. Maribelle? That was closer, but not it yet. Wait, he thought. Michelle! That's it; her name's Michelle. Good name for a whore, he thought; probably not her real one.

Outside the room's double-hung window sash and its thin, grimy wisp of curtain, his waking ears tuned to the muted rattle of a buckboard or two from the street below, along with the soft plop or muddy suck of hooves in the oozy mire of Golconda's main street. The town, too, had come awake. Beside him, the woman stirred. From the light seeping into the room, Deweese judged they had slept about ten hours.

On the verge of waking, she rolled in her sleep to face him. As she turned, an arm inched over in spite of the blankets' weight and crept across Deweese's naked hip. In a gesture of the ease she felt with the man who had loved her so completely and so well in the dark hours, her soft hand slid down his buttock to rest there affectionately. Deweese accepted the touch without moving.

A murmur of contentment tinged her waking voice. "Dave?" Her words came to him in a whisper. "You awake?"

"Yeah," he responded. "About three minutes."

"What time is it?"

"Time for us to get out of here, I suppose."

"Not yet, Dave." She slid closer to him. "There's always a little more time. And it won't take long. Let's." Michelle's body performed suggestive movements against his.

"I wish we could, Michelle," he said, mildly protesting. "But after last night, hon, I'd better ride on. I don't know how long I'll be welcome in this town."

"I've got some money, Dave. Just stay with me, please? Long as you don't care how I make it, it'll take care of both of us. They'll forget about it as long as you don't gamble."

2

Money! Deweese thought fast. It was the first time the girl had mentioned it in their two passionate days—and even more passionate nights—together in Golconda.

Michelle had stood behind him when one of the more shrewd poker players had discerned a small perforation on the corner of an ace. Despite Deweese's protests that the card had been marked long before he bought in, he was ordered out of the game. In truth, a tiny, pinlike projection on the palm side of his ring had done it.

Deweese's winnings and his stake were confiscated, and it was suggested that Golconda was no longer a healthy place for him.

He edged his nude form closer to the woman beside him in an intimate gesture intended to demonstrate the sincerity of his affection for her.

"No," he said. "After last night, they won't let me stay. I did not cheat. I'm a professional gambler. I don't need to cheat."

"I know, Dave."

"But they still want me out of town."

"Take me with you, Dave."

Trying to appear impulsive and emotional, Deweese took the woman in his arms, their bodies touching full-length. It was not prelude to anything physical; his reassurance would sway her thinking.

"I'll come back for you, Michelle. Or I'll send for you. I haven't wanted to tell you until now . . . about me."

"What, Dave?"

"So many fortune hunters. A man has to be careful.

Until these last few days with you, I haven't wanted to tell anyone. Now, maybe I can."

"Is there something wrong? Something I hadn't ought to know?"

Deweese chuckled. "No, dear heart, nothing like that. I've got to get to California. My uncle's quite ill. He has a gold claim, a good one. I'm to take over the operation in return for looking after him. Six months at the outside and I'll be a wealthy man."

"Then why can't I go with you now?"

"There's a lot of rough country, and I've got to ride it all the way. The stage takes too long. I'll write you every day, Michelle. I promise." Deweese hesitated. "There is something, maybe, that you could do for me. I hate to ask it."

"Anything, Dave. Anything. Just ask."

Deweese paused again. "No! Hell, no. I can't do it. It goes against everything I stand for. It's the reason I was in that card game in the first place last night when they claim I cheated. I'm nearly broke. I hoped to win enough to grubstake me for the rest of the trip. They took everything I won . . . and the money I brought to the table. I don't know how I'll get to California now."

"Do you need money? Is that what you're trying to tell me?"

"It's ungentlemanly of me, Michelle. I can't. I just can't."

Her voice turned eager, a good sign to Deweese. "I've saved nearly seventy-five dollars."

Feigning gratitude, Deweese brought his arms tighter around Michelle's waist. "Well, it surely would help me get there sooner and get started. I'm anxious to be on the road. If anything were to happen to my uncle, the law or the crooks could very well find a way to take over his claim and leave me flat. There are no legal papers. Just Uncle Ben's word. I've got to get there, and right away. If you could spare the money, I suppose we could look on it as an investment in *our* future."

"I saved for a trip to Kentucky to see my folks and the old home place again."

Dave kissed her lightly. "Michelle, in a few months, when I've made my fortune, I'll send you home. And this time you'll go in high style. Your former profession will be behind you. You'll go back to home and family as wife of the successful owner of a gold mine!"

Deweese felt a shudder of joy ripple through Michelle's body.

He brought her into intimate contact with him. "Maybe," he whispered, "there is time for one more after all. Kind of seal the future and our coming good years together." She trembled again in joy.

Later, in the afternoon, as the night's storm clouds were replaced by cottony cumulus under the sweep of a vast turquoise sky, Dave Deweese rode away from Golconda with seventy-five unexpected dollars in his money belt. This balanced the fifteen he'd lost in the poker game.

He grinned to himself. "Farewell, Maribelle. Or was it Martha?" He chuckled aloud, remembering his early morning confusion. He regarded the clouds again, resembling billows of snow-white fleece.

"Fleece! It's beautiful!" he emoted. "Yeah, that's me. Fleece the unsuspecting. It's beautiful!"

Deweese nudged the horse into a faster pace, his

face toward the waning sun. He patted his waist and his bulging money belt with glowing satisfaction. Prosperity was a very comforting proposition.

Scarcely fifty miles away, out on the sprawl of an endless and trackless prairie, the same rain that drummed on the Golconda Hotel's tin roof to coax Dave Deweese from sleep turned breakfast into a less-than-pleasant experience for a trio of westbound travelers.

But if anyone could make the most of a bad situation, it was these three.

Making camp on the trail was difficult at best, Barney Wisner mused. Through squinted, seasoned eyes, he watched his prospecting partner, Acie Casey, busy at his cooking fire. The tiny blaze was protected from the drizzle by the overhanging shelf of a slanted and projecting rocky outcropping they'd come across during the gloomy afternoon before as day gave way rapidly to murky night.

About three feet high and nearly as wide at its narrowest point, the overhang kept dry a scattering of dead wood that somehow had migrated there over the years. To the prospectors and their plainsman companion, Dick Snow, this roughly lateral rift had all the warmth and welcome of a St. Louis mansion; it had been that kind of a dismal day.

While Casey prepared a dry cooking place under the shelf, Wisner and Snow carefully gathered and stacked the wood to keep it dry and handy to Casey's fire. With the wood picked up, the soft, dry gravel shielded by the overhang was sufficient for them to sleep out of the wet, rolled up snug in their thick and warm buffalo robes.

While Barney rooted around in the dry gravel unearthing rocks that could turn a sleeping burrow into a torture rack, Snow, resembling a brown and furry mountain, shrouded as his tall, ample form was in his robe, scouted the sodden plains around the camp for meat. A pair of cottontails, foraging despite the cold, oozy damp, fell under the sights of Snow's unerring two-shoot rifle.

Snow's weapon was a wonder to Wisner, with his keen appreciation for mechanical things. A two-barreled caplock gun, its top bore was rifled for a .50-caliber patched ball, the bottom one a shiny-smooth tube taking buckshot and wads for small game and birds on the wing—occasional delicacies for men bored with a steady diet of venison, elk, or buffalo.

This morning, huddled in the rain under their robes, Snow and Wisner crouched patiently as Casey, hovering over the fire, poked his big cooking fork at the second rabbit Snow had brought in the evening before.

Casey was never without his collection of bottled herbs, spices, and seasonings, some of which he had sprinkled over the roasting meat. He had spitted their breakfast rabbit on a long stick, propping it at an angle over the fire so that the cooking juices dripped off the lower end. He collected the savory sauce in his small cast-iron spider skillet to baste the rabbit as it cooked.

The smells drifting to the nearby nostrils of Wisner and Snow set the men to drooling.

Snow cocked his head and squinted an experienced eye skyward. "She'll let up midday, I'm thinking. About got the rain out of her system." Dawn's light allowed vision to an awesomely distant horizon; above it, clearing, thinning clouds could be seen to the west.

Viewing it, Snow humped his shoulders to bring more of the buffalo robe's warmth around them and clutched it closer to his chest against the drizzling rain and cold.

"How much more of a ride, Dick? Till we're with your friends," Wisner asked, himself a humped mound of thick brown buffalo fur. All three wore the robes like capes, their heads hooded against the cold as well.

"Another sleep. Won't be as annoying as last night with the rain over. Midday tomorrow or thereabout. Old Elk Leggins and his Cheyennes have summered there—a pretty cottonwood grove—along Amity Creek as long as I can remember. His people have summered at that place for generations. We ought to hit Amity Creek right where they are, give or take a degree north or south." Snow spoke the language of a man concerned with points on the land and with distances and directions and travel time and the most efficient means to get there.

Casey secured the rabbit from slipping by stabbing the succulent meat with his long cooking fork. Their breakfast was ready. His sharp Green River knife separated the well-cooked game an inch or so below the front shoulders.

The tiny, brittle rabbit bones, broiled to softness, parted or yielded easily under the knife. Casey divided the lower section down the backbone, speared a half along with a hind leg, and offered it to Barney.

Wisner eagerly snagged the meat off the fork and abruptly began to juggle it in his hands like a roasting ear of corn. "Jee-zuss, Acie! That's hot!"

Casey smirked at him from under the brown and furry edges of robe framing his face. "You wanted it raw and cold, you should've told me so." He speared the lower half to present to Snow, reserving the less desirable front legs and shoulders for himself.

"Ain't complainin'. Ain't complainin'," Wisner said, peeling back his lips to avoid blistering them as he ripped hungrily at the hot, seasoned, and tender meat with bared teeth.

Snow also gnawed cautiously on his portion, moving a searing morsel gingerly around in his jaws, careful not to burn his tongue or the roof of his mouth.

"I swear, boys," he said, swallowing and aiming his teeth at a second bite, "I don't mind travelin' with you fellas one bit. Been a long time since I've had better trail vittles. Here we are cookin' in a rainstorm, eatin' somethin' you only eat when you're right up against it. So it's done to a turn and better seasoned than Maw's Sunday chicken dinners back on the farm! I'm here to tell you, Acie, I don't know how you do it."

"When you're miserable with the weather or lack of proper game," Casey said, "it's all the more reason to take the time and the pains to fix it better than ever."

"Most folks," Barney put in, "ain't great shakes at trail cookin' to start with. They hit a muddy pocket like these last few days and just crawl in some place, make a cold camp, and sit there miserable and disgusted, gnawing cold jerky and damning God and the Congress for their aches and pains. Not that way with Acie and me; we eat better on the bad days."

Casey grinned and twisted a tiny foreleg to spin off in his grip. He bit into it like a miniature drumstick. He spoke around a small bite. "You got to learn how to get by out here. Sure I cook good. Learned by myself, and I try harder than most. Barney does just about the rest of layin' up a camp and makin' it easy for us. I tell you, Dick, old Barney here could find dry wood and kindling down on the bed of the Platte at high flood and make us a soft, shady spot on a rockpile!''

Barney grinned sheepishly. ''Lucky, I guess,'' he stammered.

''I believe he could at that,'' Snow said. ''Speakin' of makin' a good camp and eatin' right, I hope to see proper game today or in the mornin'.''

''I got nothing against this here hare,'' Barney said, sucking the last of the meat off his collection of tiny bones. ''But I'm with you, Dick. A good roast of venison or buffalo would sure fit my fancy 'long about suppertime.''

''I suppose I was thinking along those lines, too,'' Snow said. ''But more that it'd be the proper thing for us to haul in a good bait of fresh meat for the women in Elk Leggins's camp to cut and dry for jerky or pound for pemmican. We don't have much else to offer in return for their hospitality.''

Acie pivoted away from the fire to face his companions as he wolfed down his short front half of the rabbit. ''That sounds like nothing more than common consideration for a host. How long do you figure we lay over with your friends, Dick?''

''Maybe three, four days. I haven't seen old Elk Leggins in maybe five going on six summers. There was a time I lived with them most of a year.''

''Good people, then, I take it,'' Barney put in.

''Indians are most all good people, Barney,'' Snow said. ''But their ways maybe seem strange and sometimes warlike to us. The Cheyenne, for instance, have their enemies in other tribes, traditional enemies. Elk Leggins doesn't go looking for trouble, but if it comes his way, he and his braves face it like men.''

"How's he around white men, Dick?'' Acie asked.

"Strange ones, not like you. Strange to him, like Barney and me.''

"Bein' friends of mine'll be enough for Elk Leggins. You got no cause for concern, Acie. So far, compared to some of the other villages and branches of the Cheyenne, he's been lucky. Spared any confrontations, you might say. But it's been a while since I've seen him. With our kind coming in like locusts over the land, putting down corner markers and calling everything inside theirs, and layin' railroad track and runnin' furrows over the grasslands, it's hard to say how long old Elk Leggins will be able to turn the other cheek.''

"It'd be nice if they could all live in peace,'' Acie said solemnly. "Lookin' around here, it seems there'd ought to be land enough for all.''

"Nice isn't a word you hear all that much among our kind coming out here, Acie,'' Snow commented. "And some of our red brothers aren't that *nice* either.''

"Ain't that the way it is?'' Barney put in. "There's always the good and the evil. Love and hate constantly at odds. All a man can do in this life is toe the mark the best he knows how and, as Acie says, try to live in peace. Life's a hard enough road without cluttering it up with meanness and spite.''

Snow sat a long time pondering Barney's words. His prospector friend made sense. "If more felt that way,'' he said, sighing, "I suppose I'd never have to worry that old Elk Leggins might be forced to take the war trail. If that day ever comes, I'll be one of the world's saddest men. There's no fairness when men of peace and decency have their backs pushed against the wall and have to come out fighting.''

Acie Casey turned philosophical, too. ''Maw always warned me never to think that ever'thing in the world was going to be fair. A man can live as close to the rules as he knows how and try to be a friend to all he meets, and life can still kick him in the teeth.''

Snow whistled a soundless sigh of resignation or understanding. Again he studied the sky. ''If we get going soon,'' he said, ''we'll ride out of this spell of weather faster. If you look yonder, the blue sky is headed this way. If we ride for it, it'll get here sooner.'' The three bustled about, breaking camp and loading their horses.

Over where the sky was blue, thirty and more miles west along Amity Creek in his summer camp, Elk Leggins paid little heed to blue skies; his thoughts were cloudy. The hospitality of his village was being abused by a band of white men who had worn out their welcome several days before. Still the unwelcome guests showed no sign of leaving.

## ❧ 2 ❧

Goes Slowly, a head man of Elk Leggins's village, intruded on the chief's dark thoughts with the suggestion of a walk and talk along Amity Creek. Elk Leggins surmised correctly that Goes Slowly desired to talk away from the ears of the Simon Parsons party that four days before had ridden into the Cheyennes' hereditary summer village.

The seven white men had been welcomed, fed by the women of the village, and provided warm, dry sleeping places in lodges of families away hunting. Elk Leggins had been wary enough of the complete strangers not to bed them in family circle lodges. Now, more than ever, he was pleased with that decision.

When the first morning came and the visitors were fed again, they made no move to leave. Day merged into night and back again, and still the white men made no signs of leaving.

Simonparsons, as their leader came to be known to Elk Leggins's people, was a pinched-up, tall, and gaunt man with a pinched-up reedy voice, and a behavior that might be regarded as pinched-up as well.

His men's voices blared louder than was necessary, a trait that rasped on the ears of the normally quiet-spoken Cheyenne. The men were boisterous and swaggering, and after three days they moved about as though they owned the camp and the villagers were there at their sufferance.

Elk Leggins realized something had to be done when he became aware that the strangers' annoying presence was causing impatience and dissension and angry outbursts among his people. The white strangers had disturbed the peaceful, harmonious rhythms of village life and work; Elk Leggins sensed that the very air was filled with a heaviness, an invasion of personal and community spirit, a harshness—not unlike sound—that even the ear could sense.

"When will the white men leave?" Goes Slowly asked, as if reluctant to get to the root of his concern immediately. The two village leaders were well beyond earshot of the camp, resting in the shade of a monarch cottonwood, its spreading limbs shrouded in the thick, verdant leaves of late spring.

Beside them Amity Creek, wide and deep enough for fast movement, flowed silently or warbled as it passed over gravel bars or large stones. As if in accompaniment, the light breeze of morning worked through the leafy thickness over them and in nearby trees, whispering sounds of calm that the two men had been familiar with even in their boyhoods.

Elk Leggins knew that the setting should have permitted peace and calm to enter his heart; at this particular moment, it did not.

"It would not be proper to ask," Elk Leggins responded. "Simonparsons had made no words to tell

14

me of their leaving. I have very few of the white man's words left anymore that were taught me by Dick Snow. I have not thought to ask Cha-lee-rah-jaw for such help; he is a boy. Simonparsons knows nothing of our tongue."

"They are no longer good visitors," Goes Slowly pronounced, his face grim and disapproving. "They enter a man's lodge without hailing and without being bidden. They move about blind to custom or tradition in the lodge. They handle things without asking and treat special belongings crudely. They have done other unpardonable acts."

Elk Leggins studied the weather-lined face of Goes Slowly; they had been friends since boyhood. "Is there something I have not heard, Goes Slowly?"

"Brother, no one knows better than you how much I honor an enemy who can sneak into my camp and steal my horses without even disturbing my sleep. In turn, if I am clever and fortunate, I can steal his horses in the same way, and he respects me. If I am foolish in making noise and I am caught, I may be humiliated or I may be tortured. Or I may be killed and scalped. It is our sport, a game, a gamble. That is the way."

"The men of Simonparsons do not respect the way?"

"When I welcome a man to my lodge, even a white man who I have learned many times may be my enemy, it is the way of our people, our village, that I light the pipe and spread the robe of friendship and peace for him as a friend. These men I do not understand. The one of Simonparsons with the dirty long hair and face and the long nose entered my lodge unbidden, but I welcomed him. He handled special belongings no man but I may touch. Still I did not object. I tried to understand his ignorance of our ways. I tried very hard to remember your words of calm and patience, brother. But I still do not understand these people and their ways. When he was gone, my special knife in the sheath beaded by my first wife went with him without my knowledge. This is *not* our way!''

Elk Leggins stared a long moment at Amity Creek gliding by a few inches from his moccasin soles. If only, he thought, life could be as serene and free of perplexities—for but a few moments—as the river. But that, too, was not the way.

His face, lined with the years as it was but eternally open and smiling, was more furrowed and now was clouded with a frown. ''It was worse for Red Beak. He, too, came to me with such a story. From the medicine bundle displayed before his lodge, a pouch of revered trophies of his own and of his fathers is there no more. He has come to me saying that only seven white scalps dangling from the lodgepoles would atone for the injustice. I am inclined to agree, but that, too, is *not* our way.''

Returning from his talk with Goes Slowly, Elk Leggins's troubled mind was startled by raised voices—a man's loud words in English and a woman's frantic protests in Cheyenne—a short distance away. Tracking the sound to a pathway behind the lodges, he found a Simonparsons man forcing a resisting young woman of his village toward a vacant lodge, gripping her by the arm and neck.

Elk Leggins took a few steps toward the struggling pair, words he had learned long ago from his white friend of many years rising in his throat. ''Hey!'' He shouted Dick Snow's well-remembered cry of exclamation. The man stopped in surprise, still clutching the woman.

"Stop now!" Elk Leggins commanded in more of the white man's language he had learned from Dick Snow.

Hearing the words from one he considered an ignorant and heathen savage, the man dropped the woman and strode past Elk Leggins, muttering to himself. He passed near enough for Elk Leggins to smell the sharp, rank belly odor of the white man's whiskey. That, too, alarmed him. He had heard of the fearful effects of "snakehead" whiskey on others of his people. Elk Leggins hoped to keep its evils away from his village. He felt that his visitors hadn't shared their whiskey out of their own greed for it—and Elk Leggins rejoiced.

He returned to the quiet of his lodge to ponder all these things. His woman was away. In the subdued light through the lodge skins and the unmoving, serene air within the circle of his home, Elk Leggins's mind calmed. Simonparsons held these coarse and brutal men together with his promises of opportunities for mischief; he was no inspiration to his followers, as a true leader must be. That fact, Elk Leggins mused, must offer the means of persuading Simonparsons to leave; shame or humiliate them without himself losing his dignity and stature among his people.

His meditations were abruptly disturbed by the rising shrillness of boys at their play at the edge of the cluster of lodges; boys' games were expected to be noisy, and one became accustomed to the sounds.

He could also hear the harsh and coarse laughter of white men. The boys' voices Elk Leggins now heard were different, shrieking and pleading, bringing him to his feet in alarm in the west end of his lodge and going around the fire ring to poke his head out the entry hole.

Others around him also stopped their work, shielding their eyes against the sun to look toward the sounds of the boys at play as Elk Leggins stepped into the sunlight.

Two Simonparsons men had taken the boys' ball and tossed it back and forth over the boys' heads, laughing evilly. As he approached them, the pair continued to tease and torment the boys by offering it to one of them. As a boy reached for it, the man pitched it to his partner. Elk Leggins recognized one as the dirty man with the filthy long hair and long nose that Goes Slowly suspected of stealing a treasured knife.

An uncharacteristic wave of fiery outrage ran in Elk Leggins that the boy who was the major target of their hazing was of their own kind—the blue-eyed one he had taken as his son, the quiet white child with the soft hair the color of winter-cured grass.

Memory quickly recreated for him the hot afternoon of finding the white man's wagon train drawn up and deathly still—a serpentlike thing stretched across the stark and windswept prairie's endless sea of grass. All the travelers but one had died from the trail sickness; cholera, they called it. In that momentary fragment of recollection, Elk Leggins remembered the eight-year-old survivor wandering and crying out among the dead, clutching a bauble of white woman's jewelry in one hand, a small, shiny wooden box under the other arm, while abundant tears traced small, clean channels in the grime of his grieving, forlorn face.

Elk Leggins's vast store of compassion compelled

him to ignore the threat of disease to ride into the midst of death to scoop up the little one and carry him home to his lodge. It was natural, instinctive, to Elk Leggins that the boy must have a father; this little man had none. Elk Leggins appointed himself.

Now, forcing down the anger that seethed within him, Elk Leggins clapped his hands for attention and fixed his mouth into the widest grin he could muster. He held out his hands and made beckoning gestures as if to be part of the men's cruel sport.

"Want to join us, eh, Big Chief?" yelled the long-nosed man holding the ball. "Okay. Here. Catch!" With a roar of evil laughter, he tossed the ball over the boys' heads to Elk Leggins.

Deftly, remembering his own skill at childhood games of ball, Elk Leggins snagged the sphere as it whistled to him. Hard, gravel-filled, and with a stitched-hide covering, the ball's feel and weight settled familiarly into his palm and tugged against his arm. Some things, he mused happily, don't change with years, nor are their techniques lost; there was a time he was formidably accurate with just such a ball.

He looked at the two men, looked at the one farthest from him, and made as if to throw him the ball. Instead, in the act of flinging it, he deflected his aim to hurl the ball with all his might at the long-nosed one. Not expecting it, the man was hit squarely and hard on the prominent bridge of that nose, which crunched loudly like the snap of a brittle bird bone. Blood, under pressure of the blow, gushed from his nostrils and sprayed over his cheeks.

The man immediately sank to his knees, groveling

and howling in pain and humiliation, palms gingerly cupped over his battered face.

The village boys, including Cha-lee-rah-jaw, Elk Leggins's white son, retrieved their ball after it glanced off the white man's head. They raced away, happy to be free of the torment, to find new territory to continue their game.

Behind him, Elk Leggins heard with unabashed pride the adults of his village roaring with laughter over their chief's clever trick. His villagers, he knew, were unfamiliar with cruelty—but sometimes the settling of an injustice could have its humorous side, and his people were quick to see humor when it surfaced. This was one of those times.

The second man in the cruel game of "keep-away" strode angrily to the side of his injured companion, still kneeling in the dirt, his broken face hidden by his grimy, bloodied hands. Elk Leggins, satisfied with his brand of justice, turned to go back to his lodge. In the crowd he caught sight of Goes Slowly and Red Beak standing together, their faces wreathed in smiles of delighted approval.

"That warn't a kindly thing to do," Elk Leggins heard a thin but sharply disapproving voice pronounce near him. He turned to look into the tiny piglike eyes of Simonparsons, eyes that darted and sparked in angry resentment. Parsons's gaunt, pinched-up body was cloaked in tattered buckskins that ought to have been replaced long ago.

Elk Leggins remembered enough of the white man's language to recognize Simonparsons's intent. He hadn't the English to respond and knew that even if he did, the words would be sharp-edged with anger and spite.

"I go now," he said in his crude English, keeping his voice level. He stepped around Simonparsons to make his way toward his lodge. His effort to discredit Simonparsons had failed; he, himself, now seemed the subject of embarrassment. Behind him, he heard words almost screamed. "That's right, Big Chief! Just walk off. You know what you done? You broke a man's nose, that's what you done!"

Elk Leggins heard the man's hurrying steps behind him. "You broke my man's nose, and I want to know what you're figuring to do about it. Don't play dumb with me, Injun. You know what I'm sayin'."

The unintelligible words from Simonparsons's mouth only infuriated Elk Leggins; there was no mistaking the tone. He walked faster toward his home, knowing his back was straight with his rage and that his own feet thudded angrily against the packed earth between the lodges. Simonparsons followed him into his lodge to perch belligerently on the pile of robes of Cha-lee-rah-jaw's bed.

Seething with emotions alien to him, Elk Leggins took his place at the back of the lodge and sat down; more than almost any other time he could remember, he yearned to be alone with his thoughts, to find peace and calm again, and to be able to sensibly order his mind.

"You go, Simonparsons," he demanded in halting English.

He wished he had worked harder on English with Dick Snow; even Cha-lee-rah-jaw could have helped him. But the two of them had learned to get along with a mixture of sign language, scraps of English, and considerable Cheyenne. Cha-lee-rah-jaw was an apt pupil and after five years was nearly fluent in Cheyenne. Once in a while, Elk Leggins heard the boy talk to himself in English, and, considering the words were the boy's private thoughts, Elk Leggins respected Cha-lee-rah-jaw's rights and ignored the words. Simonparsons's voice brought him back to the here and now.

"Oh, no. No, I ain't going, Big Chief. Not after what you done." As he talked, Parsons couldn't keep his hands still. He fiddled with the belongings of Elk Leggins's son tucked at the head of the bed and beside it. Elk Leggins felt the anger of Goes Slowly and Red Beak when these men handled things in their lodges without asking. He tried not to look at Simonparsons, fearing the anger in his soul would come out through his eyes, revealing a weakness in his character; Elk Leggins found nothing honorable in anger.

"What do you expect you'll do for me for breakin' up my man's face that way, Big Chief? I might look kindly on seven or eight of them good horses out there on the hill." His ever-roving hands pulled the small wooden box with the little ornate brass hinges and hasp from beside Cha-lee-rah-jaw's mound of bedding robes; it was the box the boy had held so tightly the day Elk Leggins found him. Elk Leggins had seen the stones inside and believed they were play-pretty rocks the boy had collected on the trail with his people and were somehow special to him. Boys, he knew, sometimes treasured worthless things that had meaning only to them.

Also inside was a thin, folded rectangle of paper. It had markings on it that Elk Leggins knew made it a white man's talking leaf; with such medicine, a white man could look at it and speak the words of someone far, far away. He marveled when Dick Snow told him these things. But he had not seen Dick Snow since two summers before Cha-lee-rah-jaw came to stay with him. He had no way of deciphering the markings, nor did Cha-lee-rah-jaw; he had been too small to learn such medicine of the white man before his father and mother died.

Absently making himself at home and making free with the belongings in Elk Leggins's lodge, Simonparsons raised the hasp and lid for a look inside.

"You go, Simonparsons," Elk Leggins repeated in English, staring straight ahead to avoid looking his unwanted visitor in the eye.

A gasp escaped Simon Parsons's lips, and he quickly closed the lid on Cha-lee-rah-jaw's box, looking apprehensively at Elk Leggins.

"You have stayed in my village five days," Elk Leggins said in Cheyenne, still averting his eyes. "I think it is time enough for you."

Parsons continued to hold the box, but now in a tight grip. When he spoke, Elk Leggins sensed a different, excited cadence and shrillness in his words. Simon Parsons watched him closely. "Talk to me in English, Big Chief," he said. "You know the lingo good."

Parsons sneaked another peek into the box of stones. Elk Leggins's sharp ears heard him mutter softly to himself, but he did not understand the words. Now there was a forced calm in Simon Parsons's voice.

"Doesn't know what he's got here. Ore. Rich, damned rich! And that's a map, probably." Keeping his eyes on Elk Leggins for a reaction, Parsons carefully set the box back beside the pile of robes but edged it scant inches from the slight gap below the lodge cover.

Parsons had shrewdly judged Elk Leggins's lack of reaction to his handling of the box and its precious contents, and he determined there was a risk worth taking. "You savvy gold, Big Chief?"

Elk Leggins heard a familiar-sounding word in Simonparsons's English gibberish. It sounded like "go," and it pleased him.

He smiled. "You go, Simonparsons?"

"Go?"

"Yes," Elk Leggins said. "You go."

Parsons got up at once, his eyes darting from Elk Leggins to the place where he had put the box for easy reach from the outside. "Was just fixing to do that. Don't fret about that man's face and them horses. They was wrong to tease those boys that way." Watching Elk Leggins closely, Parsons cautiously edged out his foot and scooted the small box closer to the gap at the bottom of the lodge covering.

Elk Leggins was unaware of the movement. His eyes were closed and his head inclined toward the top of the lodge as he thanked the Great Spirit for deliverance from the curse of Simonparsons.

## ⇢ 3 ⇠

**C**harley Rogers sat quietly hugging his knees—as boys like to do—in the cool morning grass and shade at the side of Elk Leggins's tepee and watched the riders approach the rambling cluster of cone-shaped lodges.

The three rode toward the village from the east over a grassy knoll beyond Amity Creek, looking in Charley's thirteen-year-old eyes like the little straw or stick dolls the Cheyenne children played with. Maybe, Charley thought at first, they were Simonparsons's men returning with his shiny wood box of glittery stones they had stolen, one of two links with his early life before he came to live with Elk Leggins.

He was sure the men weren't from Simonparsons. They rode differently, erect and proud, more the way his father and the other men from Ohio rode. Simonparsons's men slouched in the saddle, evil ominous in their bearing; hunched and gnarled, resembling the ugly gray tumorlike growths on rotting logs deep in the dank forest.

Charley noted that the three pack animals of the approaching trio jogged along behind, loaded, Charley imagined, with all manner of exciting gimcracks for trading with Elk Leggins's villagers. But then, Charley remembered, he'd imagined the same thing about the Simon Parsons bunch, and that hadn't turned out well.

The early morning sun, promising warmth, had driven the night mists before it. The lodge door faced east, and Elk Leggins should have been able to see them, too, but for his closed entry flap. Charley sat in the cool, almost chilly gray shadow of the lodge's north side for the moment, content just to watch them ride in.

The man in the lead of the approaching trio was big; the biggest man, maybe, that Charley had ever seen, including his father, whom Charley seldom thought of anymore. Charley would always remember that Dick Snow looked especially large because Charley was still growing and because Dick was a splendidly proportioned man.

Not big through the belly like some of Simonparsons's white-eyes men had been; Dick Snow was stout-built through the shoulders and neck and arms, long-legged and bronzed from the sun, and thick with rippling muscles in the thighs and legs.

As the riders neared the village, Charley Rogers could see that Dick Snow also had a face full of hair that made his head and his body look larger—and certainly more fierce. Contrarily, Charley would come to learn that Dick Snow was eternally gentle unless provoked, and then as hard to stop as a wounded buffalo. When Dick Snow shaved off all that fur, which he did after a swim the morning of their arrival at Elk Leggins's camp, his true benevolence emerged full bloom in smiling eyes and a strong, square jaw.

The trio forded Amity Creek and struggled up the gradual and grassy slope to the bluff thronged with stately geometric cones of thin, tough buffalo hide lodge skins that were the homes of Elk Leggins's people. Smoke flaps had been propped open this morning to welcome the sun and fresh air, the slender lodgepole tips projecting like fingers extended in greeting to the Cheyennes' Great Spirit. As the riders loomed larger in Charley's vision, Snow's companions, in his thirteen-year-old mind, were equally fascinating.

The look of the other two suggested attitudes like those Charley sensed in the large man. None had said a word or made a motion; despite their considerable distance, Charley sensed it. He saw it in the easy, relaxed way they bobbed and rocked in their saddles in rhythm with the horses' gait. Even at his age, Charley thought, he could tell a lot about a person in the way he rode a horse; he knew they were men who would not abuse a horse the way had seen the Parsons' men do.

Knowing these men would be altogether different from those of Simon Parsons, Charley's insides tingled in eagerness to learn who they were, where they were from, and where they were going; he also knew that when they arrived, he would hang back and not speak until spoken to. He'd learned that from his mother, a rule the young ones as well as the elders observed in his adopted Cheyenne village. Despite his complete acceptance as a member of Elk Leggins's village, Charley still knew he was different, an outsider; the feeling fostered a native shyness.

Riding beside the large man but slowed by a balky pack horse was the shortest of the three. His face, under a wide flat-brimmed hat with a low domelike crown, was full-moon round, and he had an egg-shaped body and stubby, substantial arms and legs; Charley knew immediately that he would like him and knew he would not play a cruel game of keep-away when Charley's Cheyenne friends played ball. This man looked as if he might even join in, enjoying the game as much as the Indian boys did.

On the other side of the lead rider was a slender beanpole of a man. Even at a distance, Charley could see the coarse and spiky whiskers of his bushy mustache. His eyes seemed squinted in shrewdness, and from his bearing, Charley imagined he was a quiet man who spoke little but, when he did speak, said a lot.

The tall, slender man also led a balky pack horse, its head held low, keeping its neck stretched in stubbornness.

Charley continued to lurk in the shaded sanctuary of the north side of Elk Leggins's lodge as he watched them come up from the Amity Creek swale at the edge of the camp. The village dogs, alerted by the approach of horses, ran out to make a ruckus, yapping harsh and shrill and darting at the horses' hind legs, but with enough healthy respect to stay back in case those legs came up in a kick.

Charley saw Goes Slowly and Red Beak and other village elders appear as if from nowhere to watch the riders with suspicion. Other young ones Charley's size and smaller were drawn out of lodges or from chores that could wait, to run and whoop, not taking the dim view of the visitors shared by the old men at the approach of more white eyes; bitter lessons learned from extending hospitality to the ungrateful Simonparsons men had made them cautious. The old men drew their shawl-like blankets closer around their shoulders, walking to meet the newcomers in an unhurried, measured gait distinctive to their age.

Peeking around the side of Elk Leggins's lodge, Charley watched the newcomers walk their horses through the clustered villagers. "That'd be old Elk Leggins's lodge, the one with the sun sign on it," the tall man in the lead called back to his companions, pointing. He spoke with a friendly tone, also unlike the Simonparsons men, whose words were harsh and too loud. The words Charley heard from this man were drawn out and measured, as though each one was precious, and there was a ring of seasoned wisdom to everything he said.

His companions, clearly strong in their own right, watched the big man as if to take their cues from him. Riding near Elk Leggins's lodge, the big man signaled to them to draw their horses near him and wait before getting down.

Elk Leggins, unbeknownst to Charley Rogers, was away, probably answering a call of nature; he appeared around the south side of the lodge, his face carrying the serene and content expression of the man of peace he was. With recognition of the big man, Elk Leggins lifted his shoulders, and his face lit up with an expression of sheer joy.

"The return of the prodigal!" Dick Snow whooped.

"Hello, Dick Snow!" Elk Leggins called happily in English, striding out into the open. Elk Leggins was older by far than Dick Snow, his face full of beautiful lines that Charley knew he would remember for life; three curved furrows plowed their way above his eyes, following the contour of his forehead, his long and straight black hair abundantly streaked with white. The lines at either side of his mouth were deep-set and intense, always pulled back in a smile that showed most of his well-set and perfectly clean teeth.

Benevolence reigned when Elk Leggins smiled, and his face came alive with more wrinkles and creases. Charley would also always remember the trust he had in Elk Leggins's intensely dark but gentle, deep-set eyes that had so quickly calmed him the day Elk Leggins found him wandering among the camp of the dead.

Though the Cheyenne of Elk Leggins's village did not understand Christianity, they knew of the white man's way of burying the dead in the ground instead of elevating them in trees or on burial racks. They also knew the spirits of the white man's dead would roam happy on the other side if stick crosses were driven into the ground at the head end of the grave. His vision distorted by tears, Charley witnessed it all with a hollow void of ache in his chest, his belly gripped with the nausea of an alien grief. Despite the danger of infecting his camp with the white man's sickness, Elk Leggins and his braves gave the more than twenty dead—Charley's mother and father, Frank and Mary Rogers, among them—decent burials.

Before the Cheyenne burned the wagons to rid the land of the demon that had brought this deadly scourge to the white man's wagons, Elk Leggins had seen the blue-eyed youngster struggling to save the small but heavy polished mahogany chest. His parents had prized

30

it for some reason and insisted on keeping it when other bits and pieces of their furnishings and family belongings were thrown off along the way to lighten the load over rough places and ease the strain on the oxen.

As a final gesture, eight-year-old Charley had gently taken a locket on its gold chain from around his dead mother's neck and retrieved the cherished shiny box and its collection of glittery stones from its hiding place in the wagon.

Smiling in his thoroughly understanding way, Elk Leggins bawled loudly at some of the Cheyenne braves. Charley Rogers, clutching the small chest and gripping the locket, was gently hoisted up behind Elk Leggins. Their grisly burial tasks finished, the Cheyennes fired the wagons, and Charley was whisked away, bouncing awkwardly and hugging Elk Leggins's waist, to a new life as his adopted son.

"I am glad to see Dick Snow," Elk Leggins almost recited in halting English.

"My heart rejoices to see my old friend, Elk Leggins," Dick Snow said in nearly perfect Cheyenne. Dick raised his lightly clenched fist and jerked his thumb in a sign at Elk Leggins and then back at his own chest before crossing his fists at his shoulders in a gentle hugging gesture of brotherhood and friendship: "You and I—brothers."

Elk Leggins responded with the same sign, his face wreathed in pleasure, his features wrinkled in all the right places. "You bring friends, Dick Snow," he said in Cheyenne, looking at Snow's companions. "Tell them to get down and I will have someone look after your horses. We must smoke and talk. In my lodge."

As the three dismounted, Snow motioned to the short stout man. "This man is Acie Casey," he said. Waving at the tall slender one, he added, "And his name is Barney Wisner."

"Aciecasey," Elk Leggins repeated, smiling warmly at the chubby one. "Barneywisner. Come. Join me in my lodge."

Elk Leggins made a gesture of welcome and started for his lodge entrance. He was stopped short by Dick Snow's voice. "Somethin' new's been added since I visited Elk Leggins. I see a blue-eyed, light-skinned towhead peekin' around the side of your lodge." Charley Rogers understood the words and shyly ducked back out of sight.

Elk Leggins smiled, and it was a smile of pride. "Cha-lee-rah-jaw," he said. "My adopted son of five years, since I last saw you, Dick Snow. There is much to tell you of him and of evil things that have happened just in these days. He remembers the tongue of his people, and it will be good for him to hear when we speak of these things."

In that same soft voice, rhythmic as the chieftain's chants he had raised at many a ceremonial fire since Charley Rogers came to stay with him, Elk Leggins summoned Charley to him. Charley looked suspiciously at the white men first, before edging out from behind the skirt of the lodge where he had hidden.

Elk Leggins preceded them through the lodge entry, and while the newcomers hesitated among themselves as to which of them should enter first, Charley Rogers scampered into the dimly lit, warm, and good-smelling circle of floor of the tepee he called home.

"Age before beauty," he heard Dick Snow call cheerfully from outside. "Looks like you're next, Acie!"

"Pshaw," the little fat man exclaimed. "I may be a mite older than either of you, but I sure don't particularly see any beauty trailing after me, Dick!"

As the pudgy figure of Acie Casey struggled to crouch and wiggle through the entry hole with some degree of dignity, Charley found his bed-pile of robes near the door and perched on them, again hugging his knees. Barney Wisner, followed by Dick Snow, came in, and the three clustered around the central fire ring, sitting cross-legged, facing Elk Leggins seated on his pile of robes at the rear and leaning on his backrest.

Above them, the lodge's smoke flaps were flared open, trapping a beam of pleasant morning light that centered on Elk Leggins while its periphery only touched the three visitors at the fire ring. Around them, the wafer-thin lodge skins admitted a dim, soft light. Charley still sat in the cool shadow near the door. The lodge's morning fire was reduced now to embers and gray powdery ash; a thin tendril of smoke made a comforting rising pillar toward the irregular patch of sky visible beyond the slender lodgepole tips.

Casey and Wisner stayed respectfully silent, leaving Dick Snow to open the conversation. "Your people will find a load of fresh meat on one of the horses." Then he slipped into more formal speech, with which he seemed uncomfortable. "It pleases Elk Leggins's brother to bring a gift to his old friend he has not seen for five summers." His words were a mixture of English and Cheyenne.

"My village will be especially pleased with your gift," Elk Leggins said. "The last white men to stay with us took from us and brought nothing but evil." He paused. "Six summers," Elk Leggins corrected softly, his bass voice making the words sound like a chant.

Puzzlement clouded Dick Snow's face and then cleared. "A'right. Six summers." He nodded at Casey and Wisner that they could talk, too.

"It has been five summers that Cha-lee-rah-jaw has been with me as my son," Elk Leggins said, as if by way of showing proof.

"Cha-lee-huh?" Barney Wisner's thin voice asked. "Suppose he's got a real name?"

"Charley Rogers!" the boy piped up emphatically.

The heads of the three white men spun his way. "He ain't forgot his English," Acie said. "That your name, boy?"

Charley was only a bit self-conscious after his outburst. "Yes, sir," he said meekly.

"Elk Leggins said his name the way it sounded to his ears and made it into a Cheyenne name. How'd he get here?" Dick Snow aimed his question at Elk Leggins.

"Five summers ago," Elk Leggins responded. "His people all died, maybe this many." He held up both hands, fingers extended, and shook them three times to suggest thirty. "The pox or the fever. We buried them according to white man's custom." Dick Snow interpreted Elk Leggins's Cheyenne words for Barney and Acie.

"Cholera, I'm bettin'," Barney said.

"Only the boy lived," Elk Leggins said. He reached behind him for his calumet, an ornate pipe with a long wood stem and small bit. The ancient bowl of carved red catlinite pipestone was dark in a wide band at the top from many lightings and smokings. Elk Leggins brought it out any time a special guest entered his lodge. Charley remembered that Elk Leggins had not honored Simon Parsons by smoking with him.

Without a word, he leaned forward and passed the pipe to Dick Snow for the honor of loading and lighting it.

"I'm outta weed," Snow said. "Barney?"

"Got lots," Barney said, making a grab for the pipe with one hand and dipping into a possibles bag on his hip with the other for his tobacco. Snow jerked the pipe away from his reach. "Protocol, Barney," he hissed softly. "I'm to load and light."

Barney handed his worn and smudged buckskin pouch to Snow. "Suit yourself, Dick." Snow plucked wads and strands of tobacco several times and tamped them into the bowl. He picked up a stick at the edge of the fire, blew the ember tip to a cherry glow, and, gently touching it to the tobacco, drew short puffs. In seconds he had the tobacco burning well. He handed the pipe back to Elk Leggins.

The old chief ceremoniously drew in and held four hefty puffs a moment before exhaling, holding the pipe at an upward angle. He leaned forward to offer the pipe to Barney across from him, bit first.

"Take it, Barney," Snow said softly. "Smoke like he did. Then pass it on to Acie." After Casey and Snow had smoked in turn, Snow handed the still-smoking pipe back to Elk Leggins, who tapped the bowl against his palm to knock out the dottle: He stowed it in its proper place among his personal belongings at the end of his pile of robes.

"Elk Leggins rejoices that Dick Snow and his friends have come to visit," he said in Cheyenne. "I have thought for several days now how good it would be to see Dick Snow. And you are here. Like a vision. The time has come for Cha-lee-rah-jaw to seek his own people. I ask Dick Snow and his friends, Aciecasey and Barneywisner, to help find them."

# ❋ 4 ❋

**N**othing would please Elk Leggins's brother more than to help," Dick Snow said. "But the boy's people, you say, were on a westbound wagon train? All this youngun's kin would be back east. Acie and Barney and I are heading west; to the Colorado gold fields."

"Colorado?" the boy asked. "I heard about Colorado. My folks used to talk about Colorado. I remember now. That's where Aunt Nell is."

"Aunt Nell, boy?" Acie asked. "You got kin out there?"

"Sure," Charley replied confidently. "In Colorado."

"You know in what town, son?" Barney asked.

"Only that Aunt Nell is in Colorado. I think we were going to see her in Colorado when the sickness came."

"Doesn't know the town," Dick Snow moaned. "That'll help just a whole lot!"

Elk Leggins spoke up. "More of the white man's wonders have captured Auntnell's spirit in a white man's yellow iron medicine pouch. Cha-lee-rah-jaw's mother wore it around her neck. He wears it now."

"I think he means a picture," Dick Snow said excitedly to Acie and Barney. "You got it, son?" he asked Charley. The boy groped down the front of his buckskin tunic to fish out a small but ornate gold locket dangling on a loop of sweat-stained rawhide thong. He pulled it over his head, unfastened the clasp, opened it, and handed it to Dick Snow.

"That's my mother's sister, Aunt Nell. I think her name was Joiner. She was married to Uncle Seth. I think he died in Colorado. My folks were sad a long time when Aunt Nell's letter came. Maybe it was about Uncle Seth. Then my folks sold the home place in Ohio, and we went in the wagon a long, long time before the sickness came and my folks died."

Snow gently held the tiny locket in both hands, opened like a book on the small oval daguerreotype portrait of a young, dark-haired woman. It had been carefully hand-tinted with soft, natural-looking tones. "Handsome woman," he observed, leaning toward Barney and Acie so they could see.

"Small loops of linked yellow iron held it on his mother's neck as we wear the leather thong," Elk Leggins told them. "It broke and was lost, but I fixed it with a hide strip and made sure Cha-lee-rah-jaw always wore his yellow iron medicine pouch to remember his people."

Barney took the bauble from Dick Snow for a closer inspection, turning it over in his hands under the light from the open smoke flaps. "Wait a minute," he said excitedly. "On the back here. It's engraved, and fine, delicate work it was. Gold's so darned soft! So worn I can scarcely make it out." He leaned closer to hold it in the shaft of sunlight and put his nose close to the back of the locket, squinting one eye. "Yup!" he said emphatically. "Right there's all you need to know. 'Taylor and Riley, Jewelers and Photographers, Dalton, Colorado.' "

"By golly! That'll narrow the search considerable," Dick Snow enthused. "Right near where we're headed, for a fact."

"You know that territory, Dick?" Acie asked.

"I've been there, yeah. Dalton's in the Spindrift Ridge country."

"Scratches in the yellow iron tell you where Chalee-rah-jaw's people have their lodges?" Elk Leggins was mystified. "Powerful medicine! Mother's sister's spirit is in it, and scratches tell where her village is. It's a wonder."

"Not really, Elk Leggins," Dick Snow said. "No more than your pictures and signs. You paint designs on your lodge and on your horse to tell of your deeds. Your people also draw on hides the figures of many warriors to tell of great battles or events. You make signs to me with your hands that are a special language. You also leave secret marks on the trail to tell those coming after you which way you went and when you passed this way."

"That is our medicine," Elk Leggins said. "Some medicine you understand. You or someone makes it happen. Some is beyond belief, as in the work of the Great Spirit. And with both, there is that which you see as bad, and that which you see as good."

"The Lord works in mysterious ways," Acie said.

"And what we have here is good medicine as far as helping get Charley back to his people," Barney said. "This lady lives in Dalton, or at least did when this picture was made. Good starting point. It's not far out of our way, you say, Dick?''

"I'd say not two days off our trail.''

Elk Leggins still pondered the differences and similarities in the white man's and the Indian's medicine. "Even when a man or his people strive to live in peace and harmony, dark evil may yet haunt his lodge. Such evil men were here in the past days, disturbing our people and taking things which were not offered.''

Charley Rogers understood. "Simon Parsons stole my box of stones,'' he declared angrily.

"And took a special knife and beaded sheath of my friend, and treasured belongings of another. Many men were here. One tried to take a young woman of this village. And took Cha-lee-rah-jaw's box of stones and the white man's talking leaf that was in it.''

"What's this?'' Acie asked. "Box of stones? What stones?''

"Cha-lee-rah-jaw's belongings. He wears the yellow iron medicine pouch around his neck. They might have stolen that, too. From his father's possessions he also brought the small shiny wood box full of small rocks with yellow iron lumps and small rivers that shone, but not as bright, as in the yellow iron medicine pouch. Simonparsons was excited when he saw inside the box. He took his men away very quickly, and when he was gone, the box of stones was gone, too. Before he saw the box, Simonparsons would not leave my village. Then he quickly gathered his men and rode away, even though the sun was far down in the sky.''

Snow, Wisner, and Casey looked at one another. "You thinkin' what I'm thinkin', Dick?'' Barney asked. "Charley already told us about the box of stones his folks set great store by."

"Yeah," Snow said. "Somethin's all rotten in Denmark here."

"I don't get it," Acie said.

Barney spoke up. "Just a minute, Acie. Dick, something mighty precious and tempting must've been in that box. Doesn't sound like gems or jewels. What if it was . . ." Barney paused.

"Gold?" Snow asked, his voice hushed.

"If it was, why would a man from Ohio be taking raw gold out west?"

"That's a puzzler for sure, Barney," Snow said.

Acie piped up. "Elk Leggins said something about a 'talking leaf,' Dick. What's that?"

"That's what his people call a letter or a paper with writing on it. Or maybe . . . a map! Elk Leggins, was it just scratchings on the talking leaf, or did it have pictures?"

From behind them, Charley Rogers again spoke up. "I never learned to read, but it was a letter. A letter from Aunt Nell. My mama cried every time she read it. My dad was sad when he looked at it, too. But then he got excited and said we had to go to Colorado."

His eyes bright with inspiration, Dick Snow turned to face the boy. "Now, Charley, I want you to remember real good. About that letter from Aunt Nell that was in the box. Did your dad have the stones *before* the letter came from Aunt Nell and made your mama cry?"

Charley was thoughtful for a moment; then his eyes lit up. "No! I remember now! A man came to our house and told Dad there was a box for him at the store in town where our letters came. He let me ride up behind him on Dolly when he went to town for the box. I think the letter was with it, 'cause that night Mama cried.''

"You know what a map looks like, Charley?" Acie asked.

"Sure! Dad had one in the wagon of the road to Colorado.''

"The paper in the box wasn't a map?"

"I said it was a letter from Aunt Nell. If it'd've been a map, I'd've known and said so!''

"You never learned to read, Charley?" Barney asked.

"Didn't know then and don't know now.''

Elk Leggins interrupted, his voice calm but insistent. "You will have to learn the message of the talking leaf, Dick Snow." He studied his three guests. "You must take Cha-lee-raw-jaw to find Auntnell. But first you men must track Simonparsons and make him return Cha-lee-rah-jaw's box of stones.''

"That's a pretty tall order," Barney said.

"Yeah," Acie chimed in. "He's got a bunch of men, got us way outnumbered. He's desperate enough to steal, and if it *is* gold that's involved, he'll kill for it.''

"We're missing a point here," Snow said. "We don't need to confront this Parsons at all, get it? Right now, we know almost as much as he does about Charley's Aunt Nell and the stones. Except he knows it's gold, and all we have is speculation. So what we wind up with on our hands is a race to Dalton, Colorado, or wherever we have to go to find this Aunt Nell. We have the advantage that Parsons doesn't know we're on his backtrail and closing fast. Our disadvantage is that he's driven by his greed for gold. That's what turns it into a race."

"Agreed," Barney said. "But what if he finds out about us somehow? That we're traveling with the boy. He knows about him."

"It'll be a dead giveaway," Acie said.

"You fellas gettin' cold feet?" Snow asked cheerfully. "That doesn't sound like my prospectin' pardners!"

"Wait a minute!" Acie said. "Does this Parsons know about young Charley? I mean, would he connect Charley with the stones and the letter?"

Snow turned to Elk Leggins. "He the only white boy in camp, Elk Leggins?"

Elk Leggins nodded, thoroughly puzzled. Deviousness was alien to him, and even though he liked Dick Snow as much as one of his own, the scheming and plotting going on among the white men confused the old chief. Apart from that, he only half understood their conversations in English. "Did Dick Snow see others?" he asked, trying to be crafty himself.

"That answers my question," Snow said, a twinkle in his eye as he acknowledged Elk Leggins's response. Then he spoke to the others. "If we meet this Parsons and his gang on the trail, we play dumb. If anything comes up about the stones, all we know is that we were told that the kid had a box of rocks the Cheyenne knew nothing about, but it's gone. We tell them we're off to some vague destination farther west. We're helping the boy find relatives."

"Truth be told," Acie said, "the letter—like the locket—probably tells right where Aunt Nell is."

"Or was," Barney added.

"You got a point there, Barney," Snow said. "And that's where the stew gets sticky. The letter was written more than five years ago. She could be long gone to parts unknown by this time. But this Parsons won't have any more to go on than we do. You'll have to play dumb, too, Charley. We tell this Parsons character nothing."

Charley Rogers's face pinched up in sudden anger. "Even if he asked me, I wouldn't tell *him* anything! His men were mean to us. Not only to the young boys. They stole things from our village and stayed past their welcome and lived on my father's generosity and kindness. I won't say anything!"

"You want to leave Elk Leggins, Charley?"

The youngster looked at his adopted Cheyenne parent, conflicting feelings mirrored in his eyes and his expression. "No! Never! But I want to find Aunt Nell and find out about the stones and the letter that made Mama cry. It's important to me. I'll go with you, Mr. Snow, if it will help clear up the mystery. And I'll tell her about my mama and dad. She'll feel bad, but she won't have to worry about them anymore. Then I'll come back to Elk Leggins, even if I have to find my way alone. I'll remember how we went."

"You don't have to call me Mr. Snow, Charley. It's good to be respectful of your elders, but if we're going to travel together, it's best you come to know me as 'Dick'."

"That goes for all of us, boy," Barney said, smiling. "I'm Barney, and he's Acie."

"Pleased to meet you," Acie said.

Charley Rogers pointed at each of them to reinforce their names in his mind. "Dick and Barney and Acie.

I won't forget.'' Charley grinned broadly, and Acie found himself already liking the tad and looking forward to the days ahead with him on the trail.

Elk Leggins listened to them and watched, beaming like a proud parent whose child got high marks. While he might not have understood the white-man words, he recognized their intent and was pleased.

"Well, Elk Leggins," Dick Snow pronounced proudly, "looks like you did a right proper job at what Charley's folks got nicely started—bringing up the boy."

The old chief's eyes were misty as he looked at Charley and patted the pile of robes beside him. "Come sit by me, Cha-lee-rah-jaw. You will begin your quest to become a man. When you return to me, you will be changed. With these men, you will grow, and in strong ways. But you will always be Elk Leggins's son!''

The tattered and sparse whang-fringe on Simon Parsons's buckskins fluttered angrily as he strode around the night fire haranguing his followers. Against the dark night, the dancing firelight made a sinister mask of his features, shriveled by anger and impatience, as he lectured to them before reading aloud for at least the tenth time the letter from the small box of rich gold samples he had pilfered at the Indian camp.

"Now pay attention!'' he demanded in a squeaky, insistent voice that was anything but pleasant. "I still say there's a clue in this someplace." He cranked his body around to take advantage of the firelight as he read from the oft-folded yellowing sheet. "Why the everlasting hell she didn't put where she was writing

45

from confounds me! You always do that in your letters, don't you?" He looked at Broken-Nose Tom, whose swollen eyelids still carried black-and-blue remnants of his injury. His once long, thin, graceful nose, the only noble thing about him, was now broad and flat with a stublike projection above his upper lip. Tom shrugged, bobbing his head. "I reckon," he agreed. His voice, too, had changed, its tone turned thick, raspy, and nasal.

Following Tom's lead as recognized second-in-command, others at the fire murmured meek assent. Tom basked in the false glory of power; it helped him rise above his recent disfigurement. He and Parsons held sway over these misfits and malcontents, he thought smugly, united as they were in a strangely loyal brotherhood. He studied them. To a man, they blindly and recklessly followed, despite the dangers, along paths both evil and brutal, sharing abundantly in the spoils and the booty, whether it was whiskey, women, or gold. Tom saw to it that Parsons's often clumsy leadership, his ravings and at times mindless orders and demands, met with little opposition.

"Good," Parsons said. "Then listen." He cleared his throat and began to read, pausing at difficult words.

"Dearest sister Mary, beloved Frank, and dear little Charley,

"I scarcely know where to begin these sad and desolate tidings. I fear tragedy has befallen Seth. I know it in my heart and am beside myself with concern. He was home from the ridge for a week after his first gold prospecting trip of this spring, jubilant with his discoveries. He rested a great deal from his exertions, and I nourished him. I know he did not eat properly on his gold expeditions. We talked, so happily and at length, about our golden future and about how we might soon be able to pay back, with rich interest as well as with love, your generous investment in Seth's potential as a prospector and miner. He was confident that when the Little Charley Mine began to produce—yes, Seth wanted it named for dear little Charley—we would all prosper beyond our wildest dreams. He was careful not to disclose his find here in town in fear of our lives, as well as touching off a stampede to S. Ridge and invalidating his claim. He returned to the ridge, a three-day trip, three weeks ago, for a day or two of pacing off his claim, setting corner markers, and writing his description to begin his claim patent. He is nearly two weeks overdue, and, as you know, that is totally unlike Seth Joiner. How often at the farm we all laughed over Johnny-on-the-Spot Joiner. Just remembering our wonderful times back home together brings tears! To start out to search for him myself would be foolish and futile. I am fearful of enlisting aid here, thereby risking disclosure of Seth's secret, although the safety of my dear Seth is worth all of the gold mines in Colorado; yes, dear God, even the world! The very hint of gold in this country, and they would forget forever the fate of Seth Joiner in the rush to be first to stake a new claim! No, it won't do to take up a search. Dear sister! I feel so desperately alone and so hopelessly powerless in the face of such unkind fate!!

"I return Mother's little jewel chest, the best thing I have for shipping, carefully packaged, sending an ample selection of the samples Seth returned with. It should persuade you of the potential of the claim, to which, by the way, I have memorized the clues. I know it will mean a great disruption of your lives, but I beseech you, Frank and Mary, to come to me in Colorado. It will not bring my beloved Seth home to me. That I must weather alone as I lean upon the Everlasting Arms. Come, instead, that we may see Seth's dream made reality, that our lives may at last be enriched, and that by our toil and our good fortune we may benefit others less privileged, even as God has instructed us. I need you both here by my side—desperately.

Love,
Nell.''

Parsons refolded the letter carefully and laid it atop the dozen or so pieces of quartz and granite liberally veined and studded with particles of pure gold in the highly polished wood box. ''Well, all right,'' he demanded. ''Where is this place? Who's got some ideas?''

Broken-Nose Tom snuffed loudly and coarsely several times against the drainage from his injury before he spoke. ''It's like we said before, Si. This Nell is in Colorado—''

''Or was,'' Parson interrupted angrily.

''Yeah,'' Tom said. ''Three days from some awful rich diggins on 'S. Ridge.' Whattaya make of all that, Si?''

''South Ridge, maybe? I don't know,'' Parsons said, exasperated. ''Where are these people? Frank and Mary and this 'little Charley.' Sounds like their baby.

Where'd those Indians get this stuff? Wipe out a wagon train or such?''

"Prob'ly right, Si," one of the men, known as Wild Card, piped up. "You know . . . they had that white boy they kept as prisoner.''

"Yeah, but he was a grown lad. Warn't no baby. But wait! That boy lived in the old Big Chief's tent, didn't he?'' Parsons was excited.

"You said that's where that box of ore was hid, Si,'' Tom said rapidly, but when he spoke, his voice had a whiny quality.

"It was stuck up under a pile of buffalo hides that somebody was usin' as a bed,'' Parsons added. "I bet it was that white kid! Big Chief kept him in there to keep an eye on him. But that wouldn't be baby Charley that letter keeps talkin' about.''

"When's that letter dated, Si?''

Parsons picked up the letter and unfolded it again. "June 21, 1871. Hey, that's six years ago!''

"This Nell woman was in Colorado,'' Tom said, thinking out loud. "She and her husband must've been out there a while. The last time she saw Charley may've been eight, nine years ago, Si!'' The eyes of the gang members followed them, listening as their leaders thrashed it over.

Parsons's eyes brightened. "This Charley was only a little snot!''

"That's the one, by God, Si,'' Tom enthused. "That prisoner kid of the Injuns'll know all about it! Likely he can tell us where this Nell lives, or did when she wrote the letter, and about 'S. Ridge,' too.''

Simon Parsons was excited as a schoolboy about to wet his pants. "Them Injuns didn't look like they had a gun in the place. We'll go back there, and if Big Chief gives us any backtalk, why, we'll just hold our guns to the heads of some of his precious redskins, and he'll see the light of reason right off. All I want is that boy to tell me where is it this Nell lived. If he gets muley about it, I'll break the little bastard's arm. Hahdam! We're on our way! We head back to the Injun town in the mornin'!'"

# ✳ 5 ✳

**C**harley Rogers looked back only once—from a grassy knoll three miles from the Cheyenne village that had been his home for five years. Cottonwoods broadly fringing Amity Creek formed a ribbon of jade against the rumpled and rolling expanse of golden winter-cured grass. The view was unchanging aside from an occasional rock outcropping or the blue-green, irregular clumps that were wind-gnarled piñon and juniper or low-growing dust-green sage. Seeing Elk Leggins's village dropping from sight, Charley felt a tug of an emotion he couldn't quite put a name to. A distinct feeling came over him that he had left childhood behind; Elk Leggins had said it. Cha-lee-rah-jaw would return, but he would be changed. He would come back a man, altered by the days immediately ahead and those that followed. Even in his thirteen-year-old mind—mature for its years—he knew that when he rode out, Cha-lee-rah-jaw was dead. But Charley was not so old that the awareness did not leave a lingering sadness. To make the disquieting sensation pass, Charley swung his gaze back toward the west, remembering his reasons for leaving—his aunt's softly tinted picture in the locket around his neck, and the box of stones stolen from him by Simon Parsons.

Charley studied the depth of blue sky far ahead where it mated with the land's rim—in the clear morning light, a distance so immense that he found himself nearly choking on his own breath. It stretched away so far and so vast that the sensations were the same as when he lay on his back in the grass at night trying to fathom the awesome distance to stars prickling a clear, pristine ebony dome—and nearly suffocating with the efforts and the thoughts. Even turning his head, now that the cluster of familiar yellowed, smoky-tipped cones marking the Cheyenne lodges had slipped from his vision, it was the same as far as he could see on all sides. Grass, gleaming like the streaks on the stones inside the remembered box, lifted and dipped over hollows and soft-sloping hills. Only a dutiful sun, gliding on course toward its destiny with the western rim of Charley's world, gave him any sense of direction in that world's unending, rippling golden sea.

"Choke up a bit more on those reins, Charley." Dick Snow's fatherly voice turned Charley's attention from breathtaking distances to his place on the back of a Cheyenne Indian pony. He sat a white man's saddle on the pinto mare, a gift from Elk Leggins the night before he rode out for the west with Dick Snow and Acie and Barney. He had already named her Dolly in memory of his father's horse from an Ohio childhood Charley found harder and harder to remember.

"You'll find her easier to control when the reins aren't quite so slack," Dick advised. "Not so tight as to hurt her lips with the bit. Just tight enough to show her who's in charge.'' Charley slid his left fist, lightly clenched, closer down the reins. ''That's right,'' Dick encouraged.

''I rode lots with Elk Leggins and the Cheyenne,'' Charley bragged, lying. ''But mostly bareback, with just a rope tied to the jaw.''

''When we stop for a breather,'' Dick Snow said, ''let's raise your stirrups a notch. I don't think you could rest your feet in them if you tried. I daresay before long you'll be a tall man.''

A burning, galled sensation high on the inside of his thighs already had Charley feeling that an adjustment or two would give him a more comfortable ride. He appreciated Dick Snow's concern and glowed with the plainsman's references to his approaching manhood. The feelings of missing Elk Leggins were acute; the warmth he felt with his three adult traveling companions had already begun to fill the void.

''She's a right pretty mare,'' a voice said on the other side of him. Charley turned away from Dick Snow to see the grinning Acie Casey also riding alongside. ''Elk Leggins made you a beautiful gift. You're a mighty lucky lad, Jolly Roger.''

Dick Snow smiled, his face, and particularly around his eyes, crinkling pleasantly. ''Hey, that's another good nickname for Charley. All the time Elk Leggins was calling him Cha-lee-rah-jaw something like that brewed in my head, but I couldn't quite get hold of it. He's a good-natured lad, and after he's been around us for a while, he'll begin to see the humor and absurdity in life as we do. Won't be long before his new nickname fits!''

"My name's Charley Rogers!" the young man said adamantly, managing a slight scowl. As quickly he dropped the mischief, his expression and tone turning bright as a sunbeam. "But if you want to call me Jolly Roger, that's all right with me."

"What's all that about?" Barney Wisner had ridden close.

"Aw, just passin' the time, Barney," Acie said. "We decided to give this young fella a nickname: Jolly Roger."

Barney grinned, but it disappeared quickly as his face turned serious again. "All well and good." Young as he was, Charley sensed that Barney had other concerns on his mind. "But Dick, hadn't we ought to pick up the pace? If what we think about the stolen box of rocks is true, that Parsons jasper is sure to be lightin' a shuck for Colorado, like us. We kind of obligated ourselves with Elk Leggins to track down the boy's aunt. To top it off, I think we'd ought to be finding out for sure about those rocks and what that 'talkin' leaf' is all about."

Dick Snow squinted at Wisner. "Right on all counts, Barney. But we can't expect these horses to make it all the way to Colorado at a high lope. Besides, if you were to draw a straight line on the map from Amity Creek to Dalton, Colorado, my friend, you'd find I'm leading us as near that line as humanly possible and as close as the godforsaken terrain permits. I'm guessing I know the way better than this Simon Parsons."

"I withdraw the question," Barney said irritably. "But we ride all bunched up this way, we make a grand target. This Parsons is a thief, and in my book a sneak

54

thief is nothin' more than a dry gulcher lookin' for work. I'm for watchin' close against bein' blindsided."

"I guess I stand corrected, Barney," Snow said, almost in apology. "Boys, we'd best separate a few rods apart, like Barney says. And keep an eye peeled. These little hills would be great places for them to lurk with a round in the chamber."

"If he knows we're coming," Acie said.

"I think there's an outside chance he may, Acie," Snow said, his tone turned more serious. "He might expect pursuit by Elk Leggins and at least have a rear guard riding his flanks and watching the backtrail."

"But he won't know us," Barney said. "He'd have to see the boy up close to remember him at Elk Leggins's village."

"Good point," Dick Snow said. "But we still take no chances. What I know of the man and his cronies—at least their type—he's likely to bushwhack about anyone for what they got in their pockets or in their packs, whether he knows anything about 'em or not."

"I follow your line of reasonin'," Acie said, pulling his horse away from the knot of riders. He shoved his hat brim up and began peering at the hills around them with more than passing interest.

"Let's stop and get down and rest the horses a bit," Snow said. "I need to set Jolly Roger's stirrups up a notch. He might's well be bareback for all the good they're doing him."

Acie whoaed his horse and made to get down. "Barney, you and I ought to spread out and keep an eye down the trail. I don't particularly like this, three men and a boy with maybe seven or eight cutthroats sharin' the same patch of sunlight."

Barney dropped off his horse easily, sliding his Winchester from the under-stirrup boot almost in the same motion. He dropped the reins to let his horse graze and stepped away a bit to take a relaxed but watchful stance.

"I done some fighting, too, y'know," Charley Rogers piped up in another outright lie. "With the Cheyennes. You don't need to keep speaking of me as a boy. I can hold my own. Just let me have a gun."

Charley had dismounted, and Dick Snow was already raising Dolly's stirrups a couple of notches. "I'll need my two-shoot gun if there's a fracas," he said, grinning at Charley's mock-manliness. He drew his Colt revolver to present it butt first to Charley. "I'll take a chance on you, Jolly Roger. Just don't shoot yourself in the foot nor put a window in me or Acie or Barney. You know anything about a Colt single-action?"

Charley deftly and expertly took the pistol from Snow to carefully examine it, mindful of where the muzzle pointed. "What you have here," he said with an authoritative air, "is a Colt single-action army revolver, .44-40, seven-and-a-half-inch barrel." Charley recited it as though quoting from the factory manual. "These are the grips, checkered hard rubber with the rampant colt in an oval cartouche on each. This is the hammer." He tested the hammer ear with his thumb, letting it ease back to its position over the empty chamber. "Loading gate," he said, flipping down the hinged portion of the recoil plate and snapping it into place again. "This is the six-chambered cylinder with 'five beans in the wheel.' The hammer rests on an empty chamber, the precaution of a smart gun handler. Trigger and trigger guard. Along the barrel is the ejector tube, housing the ejector rod and spring, and ahead of it the ejector head.'' He looked at Snow for approval. "How's that, Dick?''

Dick Snow was flabbergasted. "Where'd you learn all that?''

"My dad was a farmer *and* a gunsmith in Ohio. He told me all about them, and I watched him work. I can take it apart and put it back together, but I was never big enough to learn to shoot it.''

"You're nigh big enough now,'' Barney said.

Snow grinned at Charley. "Easy to see you know how to handle a gun safely. First chance we get, we'll try a bit of target practice to teach you to handle it wisely and well. For now, just keep it handy.''

"He'd better,'' Acie said, a distinct quiver of apprehension in his voice. "Look coming yonder.''

A knot of scruffy-looking riders, bunched together as Barney had warned his companions, emerged in a clot of silhouette against the sky over a distant hill and moved down toward a swale opposite where Charley and his companions anxiously watched their approach.

"Can you see, Charley?'' Dick Snow hissed. "Is Parsons the man in the lead?''

"Sure as hell,'' Charley said.

"Charley, stop swearing!'' Acie shushed, intently watching the oncoming riders. "Wait till you're bigger!''

Charley bit his lip, his eyes downcast and sullen as he looked around at his adult mentors.

Dick Snow, who was big enough, and with his mind on the immediate problem, said, "Damn! We didn't talk about what we'd do if we ran into these jaspers. Parsons'll recognize Charley for sure. All we say is that

Elk Leggins asked us to return him to the white man's world. We know nothing of lockets or boxes of stones or Aunt Nell. Agreed?''

Barney looked at Acie and Charley. "Right," he acknowledged.

"Keep it simple," Acie said.

"Charley?" Snow whispered querulously. "What's the matter?"

"The sons of bitches stole my stones," their young ward replied.

"Acie told you to can the cursing," Barney warned. "Not now."

"Yeah, Charley, don't be difficult," Snow added. "Let us handle things. They got us outnumbered about two to one or better, since one of us is a kid." Snow had perceived a trait in Charley that made him a bit uneasy. The kid spoke right up. Ordinarily, Dick Snow respected that, cheered a free, feisty spirit. But there were times when diplomacy spoke louder than truth straight from the shoulder, particularly when scalps were at risk. This was one of those times. "Mind your tongue and let us do the talking."

Charley looked at Snow warily; twice in a few minutes he'd been chided—first for spitting out some profanity, and then for being a kid. "I want my damned stones back," he said stubbornly, choosing to ignore their dislike of his profanity.

Barney intruded. "Charley, we'll get 'em," he assured. "Believe me, we'll get 'em back. Now may not be the time. Listen to Dick."

Charley simmered down, and none too soon. The riders crested the rise ahead of them, their horses at an easy walk that did nothing to ease the tense air hanging over the impending confrontation. They bore down on the four standing with the horses alongside the trail, weapons at ease but in plain sight. In a late forenoon lull, the breeze had stopped, adding to the still air hanging heavy as a cloud around them.

Simon Parsons brought his band to a halt uncomfortably close to Charley and company. Acie and Barney and Dick shifted their positions for better control.

"Mornin', boys," Parsons called cheerily in a voice annoyingly shrill. "This weather suit you?" Parsons stopped his horse even closer to where the three men and the youth stood eyeing him suspiciously.

"Middlin'," Snow answered laconically. Acie and Barney eased a few paces away, holding their Winchesters muzzles down, ready to swing them to their shoulders in a wink, watching as Parsons's riders moved their mounts up and around their boss.

"Can a man get down?" Parsons asked.

"As you please," Snow said. "We're fixing to ride on shortly."

"Where you bound?" Parsons slid from the saddle. His riders got down, too, and stood holding their horses. None of them had unlimbered a gun. Despite that, the bunch had a menacing look.

"Away," Snow said, eyes turning to the far horizon. "West. You?"

Parsons paused, pondering. "That's a good question," he said, chuckling nervously. "I guess you and us must've stopped with those Injuns back there maybe a few days apart."

"Could be," Snow allowed.

"We was planning to do what I guess you fellas did for us. Didn't seem right that young fella there bein' a white-boy captive of the Cheyenne. We was thinking to go back and, you might say, liberate him. We figured to take him on to Denver and see would the authorities want to try to find his kin.'' Again came the sheepish chuckle, like a man caught with his hand in the cookie jar.

"We heard what happened," Dick Snow challenged.

"Their side of it," Parsons said, his patronizing smirk seeking the agreement of another white man. "Ain't a liar born that could stretch the truth like them heathen Injuns."

Snow turned testy. "I'll decide for myself who among us is a heathen and a liar."

Parsons drew up both hands chest-high, defensively. "No offense, friend. No offense."

"We got to get moving anyway." Snow moved toward his horse.

"Don't rush off," Parsons said. "By the way, you fellas wouldn't happen to have a little nip about somewhere in them packs, would you?"

Snow regarded him coolly. "Ain't none of us, apart from the boy, strangers to the stuff. Can't say as I can help you, though, Mr. Parsons."

"I didn't figure you could. Thought I'd ask anyway. Me and my boys been dry for a lot of days. You know my name. I didn't catch yours."

"Snow. This here's Casey, and Mr. Wisner's over yonder."

"Pleased to meet ya," Parsons said, letting a wave at Barney and Acie do for a handshake. "Say, tell you what, Snow. We're goin' straight into Denver anyway. We'll take little Charley with us and kinda save you the inconvenience."

Snow looked at Charley, hoping he wasn't about to pop off with an unfortunate remark. "You know his name in the states?" he asked Parsons.

Parsons slipped into a toadying tone of voice. "Well, yeah. That's what everybody called him yonder in the Injun camp."

Snow guessed Parsons was lying. "They called him something else."

Parsons acted puzzled. "They did?"

Snow risked a gamble with the boy. "Let's ask him. The only language he remembers is Cheyenne. You don't speak it, I guess."

"Huh-uh," Parsons responded.

Snow's smile was fleeting. He turned his head toward to Charley; Parsons didn't see Snow's grin and sly wink. "Make up something," he said in Cheyenne dialect. "What is your name?"

"Yellow Iron," Charley responded in kind, mustering as convincing a poker face as Dick Snow had ever seen; he was proud of their young ward. The kid had wisely steered away from Cha-lee-rah-jaw.

"See there?" Snow said in English. "His name isn't Charley. The name he went by with the Cheyenne was 'Yellow Iron.' "

Parsons acted confused; he'd tipped his hand, and he had no notion how much these white men knew of the box of gold ore and the letter. "Well, I don't know," he said. "Seemed like to me they called him Charley back there. Guess I was mistaken."

"Accidents happen." Snow smiled at Parsons benevolently. He felt Charley's eyes on him. The boy spoke up in Cheyenne. "Ask him about my box of stones."

"We've got him on the run, son," Snow responded,

also in Cheyenne. "We already know a great deal more than we knew. For one thing, you must be mentioned in the letter. Else where did he come up with Charley?"

"Elk Leggins wouldn't have told him. All my grandfather wanted was for this man and his men to leave our village."

"That's what I figured," Snow said, still in dialect.

"What's all that about?" Parsons demanded.

Snow swung his gaze to the eyes of Barney and Acie, hoping to put them on the alert for possible action. He had decided to risk greatly.

"Real strange," Snow responded. "He says he was known as Charley back home in the states. The rest I don't understand. He wants to know why you stole his box of stones. That mean anything? Don't to me."

"Nary a whit," Parsons lied. Suddenly Snow realized he had the dried-out long drink of water in the tattered buckskins by sensitive places where the sun didn't often shine. The paper in Charley's box of stones—and he was convinced now they were precious rocks—mentioned him but otherwise had puzzled Parsons and company. On top of it, he or Acie or Barney could level any of Parsons's men who went for a gun. His only concern was Charley's hair-trigger mouth. He decided to risk it.

"Well, Mr. Parsons, seems like we ain't got a great deal more to discuss. The sun's ridin' tall over the sagebrush, so we'd better get a wiggle on, or we might as well camp here for the night. Naw, we'll take little Yellow Iron on with us. Seems you'll have to make your way in life without him."

"But . . . but . . ." Parsons protested.

"And another thing," Dick Snow said, a growl in

his voice. "Don't come campin' on our backtrail. It ain't going to be healthy. I know how much you fellers want to pry out of this boy what he knows about those rocks. See those two backin' my play yonder, Casey and Wisner? Don't let looks deceive you. There's two of the sharpest cutthroats in the West. You dog us on the trail, and so help me Hanna, I'll send 'em back when you're sleepin', and they'll have your throats slit before you even know they're in your camp!"

Barney and Acie picked up the cue, glowering and grimacing as ferociously as normally mild-mannered men could while each let his eyes rove over those in the circle of Parsons riders; the men looked fearfully at one another and at Parsons, who stared in unreasoning fear from Snow to Casey and Wisner and back again. Both wore sinister-looking bowies in sheaths at their hips, helping to reinforce Snow's warning. Parsons's big-as-bowls eyes registered that Snow had made his point, regardless of its truth; his spontaneous quip had had a startling effect.

"Don't get me wrong, Mr. Snow," Parsons protested. "Like I told you, we don't know anything about this boy, and we sure don't know nothing about 'stones.' It was only a hunch that his name was Charley."

"Get you wrong?" Snow asked querulously. "How could we get you wrong, Parsons? We got you right. Matter of fact, we got you dead to rights. Okay, boys, let's mount up and ride."

As Parsons stood bewildered, Snow hit the saddle in unison with his companions and started down the trail. Wisely, Acie and Barney rode on either side of Charley, protecting him from any interference.

Respectfully, almost in awe, Parsons's riders edged aside and, like the Red Sea parting, made an avenue for the four riders moving out at an easy, confident walk.

Making his way through the line of horsemen, Snow spied a tall man with long and dark stringy hair and an equally long nose that had been flattened against his face. Elk Leggins had related the incident.

Snow slowed as he passed the man. He leaned out of the saddle toward him to leer maliciously. "You ought to see a sawbones about fixing that nose of yours," he said. "You're uglier than a mud fence after a hail storm!"

# ❧ 6 ❧

As young Charley and his benefactors rode away from an uneasy truce with the Parsons cohort, another westbound rider traveled the rolling grasslands on a converging trail scant miles away.

Beneath a campfire-smudged and whiskery face and properly seasoned range clothing, Dave Deweese showed a cowboy's lean body, a strong, virile face, and sapphire-colored eyes that constantly twinkled, inspiring the trust of nearly everyone who knew them. Those eyes could reflect wisdom, merriment, compassion, sadness, or love with equal quickness and a sincerity so transparent that his motives were seldom questioned. If Deweese was challenged, those eyes could display such depths of dismay and innocence that a disbeliever or an accuser most times backed away. His eyes could contact another's with an intensity that inspired confidence, while his mouth created monumental lies.

Dave Deweese also possessed a chameleonlike ability to adapt his looks, his attitude, and his personality to any situation likely to be to his benefit or guarantee his survival. At any time, he knew, he could blend into the background, only to emerge to build trust when a lucrative opportunity presented itself. Believing that when in Rome, do as the Romans do, Dave had his traditional town outfit, his gambler's clothes, clean and folded within the bedroll tied behind his saddle. His appearance on the trackless prairies was that of a penniless, out-of-work drifter whose amiable qualities only awaited the right opportunity to come to full bloom.

Deweese, however, was more suited to town than to the lonesome back country. Though no one would know it, he was considerably less at home in those wild, silent, and wide-open spaces than among townsmen whose greed was a fertile realm he found easy to cultivate and feed on. Mother Nature, he'd learned, didn't respond favorably to a glib tongue and soft, expressive eyes.

On edge since being caught marking aces in Golconda fewer than five days before, it came as no real surprise to Deweese when he heard a rustle in the grass behind him and the crisp, metallic, and sinister chatter of a round being levered into the breech of a Winchester. His alert mind created the image of a muzzle the size of a howitzer centered on the small of his back. Prudently, he reined the horse to a halt and slowly raised his arms head-high. Taking the initiative, he slipped easily into a cowboy's vernacular.

"If you want money," he called over his shoulder, "you come to the wrong place. You might better try squeezin' juice out of a tumbleweed. I'm low on water, and nary a drop of booze. I'll share my can of beans and maybe three slices of sowbelly with you, stranger. After that there's nothin' between me and starvation this side of findin' work."

"You ain't with them three jaspers with the kid on up the trail?"

Deweese still hadn't dared to glance back at the man. "It's five days since I was in a town, and you're the first living soul I've seen. How about you put that rifle down and let me fix us something to eat? If you're worried, I'll let you hold my six-gun till I ride on. I believe like the Lord in peace on earth and goodwill toward men, brother."

"Get down," the man behind him ordered with a growl. "Keep your hogleg. Try goin' for it and you're dead meat. We'll see what Simon has to say about all this."

"Simon?" Deweese asked, easing out of the saddle and preparing to guide his horse wherever he was directed. A quick glance at the rifleman spelled hardcase to Deweese. Mean and heartless. He was a rangy, nondescript character with the look of a follower—so long as the man leading operated outside the law and blood money was easy to come by.

"Straight on there," the man commanded. "Folla that horse trail."

At the crest of a knoll a short distance from where he had been stopped, Deweese looked down into a deep and wide hollow in the land. At the bottom six or seven men clustered around a small fire of buffalo chips, eating, smoking, and talking.

"Leon's comin' in, Simon," he heard one call loudly. "Got somebody with him."

As they moved downhill toward the group at the

fire, Deweese saw another tall and rangy man in ratty buckskins crank himself up off his butt and walk toward him on long legs stiff from his crouch.

"What we got here, Leon?" he called in a high voice sharp-edged with evil.

"Caught him snoopin' around back yonder. If he's with them jaspers with the boy, he's on his way to meet up with 'em, I'm bettin'."

"That so?" Simon asked Deweese.

"I told your man when he stopped me back yonder," Deweese explained, still playing the out-of-luck cowboy role. "I'm just travelin' through, lookin' for work. I ain't seen nobody for five days, and I ain't lookin' for nobody special 'less he can give me a job."

"You ain't heard of Snow and them and a kid named Charley?"

"No, Mr. Simon, I purely hain't."

"The name's Parsons. Simon Parsons. Well, you're sure a hell of a lot worse for wear than them fellers, I'll guarantee that. And from the looks of you, shorter on rations. You don't look like one of 'em. That ain't an Injun pony you got there, and it sure looked like Snow and them traded horses at the Cheyenne camp. What name do you go by?"

"Deweese. Dave Deweese."

Parsons called back over his shoulder to the group at the fire. "Hey! Any you fellers ever seen this jasper before? Or heard of a Dave Deweese?"

The men around the fire surveyed Deweese with disinterested gazes. They chorused a "Huh-uh" and turned back to their smokes and their conversations.

"Let's us walk over yonder there and have a palaver, Dave. Leon, you go on back up on that knob and keep your gun ready and your eye skinned." Leon's disappointed expression said he had hoped to merit praise for catching an invader and had been ignored. He studied Parsons for a moment, about to say something. Then he spun on his heel and marched back up to the grassy knoll and his guard post.

Away from the gang at the fire, Parsons squatted on his heels and signaled Deweese to do the same. "You got makin's about you, Dave?"

"Ran out three days ago," Deweese lied. He seldom smoked except to carry off a guise. "Sure could stand one now."

Parsons pulled out a tobacco sack and papers and handed them over. Deweese rolled a smoke with deft hand movements. When he was ready and parked it at the side of his mouth, Parsons had a match flaring to touch to the tip. Parsons rolled and fired one for himself.

"You ain't livin' too high offen the hog, mister. I don't suppose you'd have any Old Bravemaker in your saddlebags."

"Not a drop. I could stand a bit of a nip myself."

Parsons grinned an oily grin. "Looks like we're both a bit down on our luck. But my luck's about to change." He hauled out his tobacco sack and set it between them. "Like the Injuns say, help yourself again when you're ready, Dave. About all we got is our smokes."

Deweese already had perked up at Parsons's veiled hints, but he played out his role of only casual interest. Still he decided to keep the conversation on course. "Luck ain't shined on me of late neither, Simon. I can call you Simon, I suppose?"

Parsons's grin now seemed genuine and optimistic. "Some even call me Si. I like your looks, Dave. You know anything about gold?"

Deweese quickly adjusted to his surprise and chuckled. "Nothin' except what I seen in the mouths and on the fingers of the rotten rich. Fake stuff hangin' on cheap women, such as that. Seems gold and me ain't on the best of terms the way it avoids me or slips through my fingers."

"That's too bad," Parsons said. "I still could use you."

Deweese acted as though he didn't hear. "I worked with a fella one time that'd done his share of prospecting and mining, Si. Made and lost a fortune in gold and wound up on a trail drive with me out of Abilene bound for Montana." Deweese often found himself becoming loquacious when his interest had been peaked in developing a ruse with a willing subject.

Simon Parsons watched him with rapt attention. He snubbed out his soggy stub and rolled and fired another without taking his eyes off Deweese. "Do tell," he encouraged.

"We hit it off right away," Deweese continued. "Spent a lot of time together that trip. I guess I learned a good deal about gold prospecting and mining from him." He quoted from a book he'd once read. "About lodes and placer mines and dry washing and sluicing and panning. Of adits and drilling and blasting and mucking. Told me about stamp mills and assays and tailings and vertical shafts and shoring timbers and header frames. Such as that."

"He ever say anything about Colorado?"

The expectant gleam in Parsons's eyes told Deweese

that Parsons's palaver was skirting around something big. "That's where he made his killing. If it wasn't for a woman, he'd still be on Easy Street today."

"You know whereabouts in Colorado?" Parsons's voice dripped with eagerness.

"Eddie mentioned a few places. You got any special place in mind? I might remember."

Parsons studied on something in his head for a long moment.

"How about you throw in with us, Dave? We mostly live off the land, brand and sell a few mavericks." Parsons chuckled. "Once in a while a maverick or two that managed to get too close to someone else's brandin' iron, if you catch my drift. Now and then a chance comes along for some easy money, and we all live high for a while. I take care of my men, and they stick close. Si Parsons is a man of his word."

"So?"

Parsons hesitated again, acting almost reluctant to elaborate. "You're headed west. We're bound for Colorado. We manage to eat pretty regular, though it ain't always fancy. Pay ain't quite as dependable, but if things work out, it may be plenty fancy for me and those as rides with me. What do you say? There's strength in numbers, and this is no country for a man ridin' alone."

Deweese paused, as though he, too, was thinking. "Plain to me you got something up your sleeve, Si," he said, and Parsons grinned. "You ain't about to tell me till I agree to ride with you," Deweese added. "I'm about as far down and about as far out as a man can get. Don't take any cipherin' to see I don't stand to lose much. I'll make you a deal. I'll throw in with you.

When you get right down to it, I know plenty about Colorado, and I've got friends there that know more. Your side is to tell me what this deal is all about. It's pretty plain it's about gold in Colorado, but that's like askin' where in California is the blue Pacific Ocean. Could be anywhere, and just about is."

"Right so far," Parsons said. "You're pretty smart, Dave."

"And I figure it's just not any old gold. You got a lead on something, but some of the pieces are missing. Else you wouldn't be sittin' here jawin' with me. You'd be killin' horses gettin' there."

Parsons couldn't hold it in any longer. His eyes squinted with the grandeur of his thoughts. "We got hold of some mighty rich ore samples. Pretty clear they come from some place in Colorado called 'S. Ridge.' S with a period, Ridge. That mean anything?"

"That's where you're stymied, eh? No, I wouldn't know offhand."

"You want to have a look at the ore? There's a letter in there, too, tells about it. It just don't rightly say where this ridge is or what town the letter come from. Sit tight. I'll be right back."

Parsons skipped away, astonishing Deweese at how nimble he was. He was back in no time with a small, highly polished rosewood box. Lifting the lid, he held it close for Deweese to see. "Feast your eyes on this!" Deweese saw a dozen or so small, variously sized chunks of tawny granite and glistening snow-white quartz studded and veined liberally with raw gold. "You're right," he said, purposely without emotion. "Mighty rich."

"Here's the letter that was with it. Makes mention of that 'S. Ridge' I told you about."

Deweese read the letter as quickly but as carefully as possible, making copious mental notes on names and places and events; he quickly all but committed it to memory practically verbatim. Every scrap of information, every subtlety, every nuance might be important or useful at some future time. He even analyzed the handwriting, making sure he would recognize the hand if he ever saw an example of it again. He carefully re-folded the letter and handed it to Parsons. "Interesting, Si. Mighty interesting."

"Well, what do you think?" Parsons asked.

Deweese decided to show enough enthusiasm to keep Parsons excited and talking. "I think you've got yourself a gold mine, my friend, if you can only find it. Where'd you get this stuff?"

"From an old Indian, a Cheyenne, a couple days east of here. Stupid bastard didn't know what he had. Wouldn't know gold from buffalo chips. The letter being with it, and from what it says, I'm guessing these folks were coming out from Ohio. The Cheyenne probably wiped out their wagon train, and this was some of the plunder."

"He just up and gave it to you?"

Parsons fidgeted a bit in his squat close to Deweese. He chuckled nervously. "I told you, Dave, every once in a while an opportunity comes a man's way. I took the bit in my teeth and ran with it."

"You stole it?"

"Put it that way if you want to, Dave. I figured it was only a matter of time before he'd burn the letter to start a fire and throw the rocks at nuisance camp dogs. He'd had the stuff about five years.''

"You got a point there. That's all there is to it?''

"Chapter and verse. The long and the short of it.''

Deweese made sure Parsons's eyes were locked with his. "You're holdin' out on me, Si, and it makes me wonder why.''

"How you figure that? I told you everything I know.''

"Not quite. The letter mentions a youngster named Little Charley. When I got here, you made a point of asking me if I was on my way to join up with somebody named Snow and a kid named Charley.''

Parsons fidgeted again. "Guess I disremembered that I asked you that. That was somethin' I figured I wouldn't bother you with. There's some men out there a little ahead of us. It gets kind of complicated, and maybe a little touchy. There's this Snow and a couple of jaspers named Casey and Wisner. We got to watch them, and watch them close. This Casey and this Wisner are a couple of the slickest dark-hour cutthroats this side of the Mescalero Apaches. I don't want to cross them boys! There's this lad with 'em. From his age and the date on that letter, this kid might be Little Charley. It's a long shot at best. Can't get any English out of him anymore. All he knows is Cheyenne.''

"You must've talked to 'em, Si. Why have they got the kid? Where are they headed?''

"It wasn't the most pleasant of meetings on the trail. I didn't get a chance to ask them too much. I think they're bound for Colorado, too. I don't put any stock in there being much of a connection. Those boys didn't seem to know anything about the gold.''

Deweese looked Parsons over again, a simpleton in his ragtag buckskins and his lean and long grasshopper frame. No, he thought to himself, Simon Parsons wouldn't see much of a connection.

Dave Deweese figured that he sure as hell did.

# ※ 7 ※

The western land lay hushed and dark. Only the four-legged foragers-by-night were out, poking and prodding under the thick cover of cold, damp grass; the more voracious of the predators stalked boldly and broadly in the night for prey to feed their larger appetites. The Parsons horses stirred softly, grazing, their movement curbed by hobbles. In other areas, their wild, unfettered counterparts, the deer, antelope, and buffalo, also grazed, feeding in the starkly still and dark hours, freer of dangers or alarm. Yet always, by day or night, the threat was there. Without relief, they lived lives of constant tension and eternal vigilance, the least movement sounding the alert.

The awesome distances by day had been transformed into an immense rolling black carpet stretching in all directions under an infinite ebony dome of night sky sparkling with stars and constellations. No wind, not even soft breezes trifled with the solemnity of the land; air on the chill side surrounded the Parsons campsite. Under these best of sleeping conditions, snug in his bedroll, Simon Parsons, exhausted by the rigors of the day, slept like one dead, a sleep so sound that he was oblivious to everything in the world around him. Six of the seven blanketed lumps of humanity around him also slumbered like hibernating bears.

On the knoll above the camp, the huddled form of the outlaws' sentry was shrouded in his blanket and equally silent. The guard, a short and stocky, usually genial owlhoot named Dale, sat with his knees drawn up under his blanket, Winchester leaning over his shoulder, arms on knees, head lolling on arms, sound asleep.

In the camp, slight movement disturbed one of the inert lumps positioned randomly around a ruby mound of glowing embers of night fire. A head poked out, alert, eyes and head swiveling, watching and listening. Silently he flipped aside his warm soogans and the heavy ducking top sheet and stood up carefully. Erect, he waited a long moment, listening and watching through the dark. If any of the others awakened in the next few moments, justice for Dave Deweese would be swift and execution the verdict. Breathing shallowly, ready to freeze in place at any moment, he cautiously moved through the sleeping forms.

Carrying his boots for utmost silence, Dave tiptoed away from the dim firelight. He climbed the grassy knoll quietly through the dark, only to assure himself that he'd find the man called Dale as sound asleep as those snoring around the fire ring in the hollow.

He had carefully observed the men through the long evening around the fire, noting that as nighttime dragged on, Dale was the weariest of those Parsons men assigned to night guard. When they turned in,

Deweese conditioned himself to sleep lightly. He feigned sleep at each changing of the guard to observe. Dale grumbled when he was roused for his watch to stumble away, half asleep, into the night; Deweese calculated it was nearly three in the morning.

He lay alert for another three quarters of an hour before furtively sliding out to find Dale snoozing as he had expected.

Slipping with even more stealth back into the sleeping camp, Deweese quietly but haphazardly furled his bedroll and lugged it to the grazing horse herd. He saddled his gelding and, leading it gently away, blended ghostlike into the deepening murk of dark night.

Dawn broke softly over the land like a blessing, shoving the mists and the dank chill of night westward toward a distant gray horizon. In another camp, some miles to the west, three men and a growing boy also had slept warmly and well.

Now they awakened rested and robust to a glorious morning, jubilantly ready to take on what this day had to offer: another day to makes tracks for Dalton, Colorado, to unravel the mystery of the gold and the pretty woman in the locket.

It was Barney's idea to spread their bedrolls a safe distance from their dying evening fire of fragrant downed and dried piñon and juniper wood. "If Parsons sends some of his boys to sneak in and raise a little Old Ned with us tonight, they'll be looking for a fire glow, and they'll find it. Right here."

"Only we won't be," Dick Snow agreed. "By that time, we'll hear 'em thrashing around—"

"And take evasive action," Barney interrupted. "Offensive or diversionary. Lord, I commence to sound like a damned army officer.''

"Long as we don't have to stand guard," Acie moaned. "Disturb our night's rest, and we'll be frazzled and all out of sorts tomorrow."

No disturbance had come, so Dick reasoned that their logic had been justified.

As he climbed out of his bedding, Snow pulled himself erect and stretched. Invigorated by the crisp, clean morning air, Acie busied himself over a rattling pot of coffee and a sizzling skillet of salt pork. Beans, set to soak overnight and treated by dawn's early light to Acie's spices and seasonings, bubbled in a nearby pot. White hominy grits, cooked the night before and chilled and thickened in a tin can, was cut into thin discs and set to frying in another skillet.

Snow, on his way to his morning relief, paused near the fire to savor the aromas, sniffing like a coonhound catching a scent on midnight air. "Ambrosia," he mumbled as walked stiffly away. "Pure ambrosia. Acie, you are a wizard, a first-class wizard!''

Charley, feeling the camp come awake from the snug warmth of his buffalo robe cocoon, poked out a tousled towhead as his nose, connected to a ravenous appetite, brought pleasant feelings to a boy waking up cozy and safe. The soft sounds of activity and bustle in the camp added to his lulling sense of security.

Still shrouded by his toasty bedding, he surveyed the day through sleep-heavy eyes. Life, he mused—his thinking swayed by the grown-up philosophies of his companions—was made for moments like these; it was great to get up in the morning, but sometimes it was just nicer to lie in bed.

The smells reaching his nose from Acie's cooking fire dictated otherwise; his burden of pent-up night water also cried for release, creating the need to crawl out and get going.

"Mornin', Jolly Roger," Acie called from his pots and pans, watching the boy slide out of his robe and stand up. As Snow had done before him, Charley came by the fire on his way out of camp. "Smells good, Acie," he said.

"That's what it's s'posed to do, son." With his hand-hewn wood turner, Acie flipped a panful of frying grits. Charley wavered a moment near the fire, his nose consuming the wonderful cooking smells before stumping drowsily away. "Don't go too far, laddie," Acie called after him. "I'll ring the breakfast bell before you know it."

"Not soon enough for me," Barney called from where he stood examining a pack horse for back sores or any skin or health problems. Nearby, Dick Snow checked over and rolled up camp gear. "We'll pack the horses and saddle up after breakfast," he said.

The camp sounds diminishing behind him, Charley strolled over and down behind a grassy slope. His chore done, sudden movement on the edge of his vision brought him alert with a thud of alarm. Little more than a floating speck in the immensity of distance and grass, a lone rider a quarter mile away to the east moved slowly over a far hill. Charley watched him a moment, aware that he came from the direction of the Parsons camp.

Catching himself as though coming awake, Charley scurried back up the grass-slick slope, calling out when he came in sight of Dick and the others. "Rider coming!'' he yelled breathlessly. ''From over Parsons's way.'' He raced into camp as they dropped what they were doing to grab for their rifles.

''Let me have a six-gun,'' he begged as he came up to Dick and Barney, several paces apart, their rifles at the ready. Acie had his handy, too, but rustled with his pots and pans to save their breakfast in case of a delay.

''No,'' Barney said softly, stepping away for a better view of the approaching rider. ''Let us handle this one.''

''Dammit,'' Charley said irritably, ''I'm damned near full grown.''

Barney's words had a tart edge. ''Stay back behind us, young man.''

From Charley's viewpoint, Dick sided with Barney. ''If there's any shooting, Charley,'' he said crisply, ''get down behind something and stay low. Looks like he's coming from Parsons. If I need to talk to you, we'll speak in Cheyenne. Like we did yesterday.''

Charley bristled; in his eyes, they treated him like a baby. ''I never get to do anything,'' he said angrily. ''I know about six-guns. I can hold up my end.''

''Do like Dick says, Jolly Roger,'' Acie advised, further rankling Charley. Satisfied his meal was safe, Acie checked his Winchester for a round in the breech. ''Soon as we get shed of this feller, I got a mess of hot vittles for us to tie into.'' Charley's expression said he didn't much care.

The rider came up cautiously, his hands high with the reins. His swift-darting eyes appraised the men and their ready rifles. He was careful not to make any moves that might be misunderstood. Deweese also eyed the boy, with his thatch of straw-colored hair and wearing Indian buckskins. The boy stood back among the horses sullenly watching him ride in.

Deweese's mind also worked with express-train speed. Somehow, he had to put himself between Little Charley and his protectors long enough to get the information he needed without arousing the suspicions of Snow and the others. He focused on the plainsman Snow, probably the big one with the double-barreled percussion rifle at the ready; in Parsons's camp, Deweese had heard the man called Wild Card talking about Snow and his big two-shoot rifle.

Sizing up the other two, Deweese caught himself almost smiling. Casey and Wisner, whom Parsons had warned were slippery, skilled cutthroats, flanked and backed Snow, a scant step behind, their eyes clearly squinted for effect. The pair also confirmed for Deweese his judgment of Simon Parsons as a lame-brained lout. Casey and Wisner, whichever was which, would have difficulty cutting the throat of a wounded doe. Deweese gloated inwardly; by some innate, evil power in which he took great pride, he could read a man's true character—strengths and weaknesses—by his eyes. Experience had taught Dave Deweese that he was seldom wrong.

It was time to turn on the cowboy charm. "Put up the guns, gents," he called, letting the knotted reins droop over the saddle horn. He prudently brought his arms out as he rode in, striking his most engaging smile. Dave Deweese knew that his amiable grin had brought him through situations a great deal more threatening than this one. "I'm a peaceful man."

"Then pull up and get down," the one closest to him invited, the man Deweese had taken to be Snow.

Casey and Wisner, predictably, dropped their guard slightly and moved closer to Snow. A shootist, skilled with a six-gun—which Dave Deweese readily admitted he was not—could have dropped the trio in a trice, leaving him alone with the kid to persuade by whatever expedient means were necessary, until he got the truth. His look at the cowering, sullen waif convinced him it wouldn't take much.

"We see you come by way of Mr. Parsons's camp yonder this mornin'," the tall, angular man with the spiky mustache and stubbly chin observed, almost accusingly.

"You-all'd be the ones that know him," Deweese said, walking to face them. "Yeah, I stayed with them last evenin'. Rode out before daylight while the camp was quiet. Not at all what you'd call my kind of people."

"We're just about to sit down to our chuck," the genial-looking, roly-poly one of the crew remarked. "We got an extra plate. Come on, boys," he urged, "the food's gettin' cold!"

Scraping his plate clean, Deweese almost regretted worming his way into their confidence to betray them; he had never eaten so well on the prairie. The coffee was as good as it was strong, the salt pork flavorful, and the tasty beans neither chewy nor mushy. His meal was topped off with fried grits done to a turn and sweetened with sorghum.

The kid he was sure was the Little Charley mentioned in Parsons's stolen letter sidled up to the food near the fire, silent and sullen-looking. Deweese studied him, wondering how he would manage to spend some private time with the lad. He smiled at the boy, starting to win his trust.

"What's your line of work, Mister, ah ..." the one called Snow asked him. "Apart from cowboyin', I mean."

"It's Deweese," he replied, ladling more beans onto his thin plate. "Dave Deweese." He beamed his best shy cowboy grin Dick Snow's way. "Lately it seems my line of work is bein' out of work. But you got it right. Mostly I've been cowboyin'."

"How long ago did you tie up with the Parsons bunch?" Wisner asked. His graying spiky mustache, salt-and-pepper hair, and squinted, shrewd, and calculating gaze marked Wisner as a man seasoned beyond his years; one who would bear watching, Deweese thought. The other two were more transparent; Snow, the man's man who could be a real ladies' man if he wanted, and Casey, the mother hen of the outfit, but tough to the core. Casey took life's rough weather with an iron spirit and could be depended on to land on his feet.

"Like I said," Deweese responded, "I rode into their camp last evenin'. Was invited to stay for supper, and by then it was too late to ride on. So I spread my bedroll by their fire. Does the boy there talk?"

Snow studied Deweese. "Yellow Iron, you mean?" Snow looked at Charley, sending a message of caution that he hoped the boy understood. "Oh, he'll talk a blue streak once he gets to know you. Only trouble is the only language he knows anymore is Cheyenne. Been a captive."

"Yellow Iron?" Deweese asked. "That the only

name he's got?'' He caught the boy watching him intently.

It was Acie Casey's turn to pipe up before Snow had a chance to respond to Deweese. ''I'm curious, Mr. Deweese, about what gigged you to ride on over to our camp after spending time with Parsons.''

Now it was a bemused Snow and Wisner's turn to study Casey; their chubby partner was not always so outspoken. Still, Snow thought, it cut through a lot of hemming and hawing. Sometimes strangers drifting in off the range required quite a bit of that before they opened up; shady backgrounds were often covered by sham shyness.

Deweese didn't miss a beat in responding; his engaging grin came up, and he looked Acie straight in the eye. ''I'll tell you true, gents. Parsons asked me to ride with his gang. Tried to persuade me by showing me a fancy box of rich ore samples and this five- or six-year-old letter about them.''

He was aware of the intent eyes of the three of them, even the boy, fixed on him. Feeling a sudden stab of anxiety, he hoped his involuntary grimace hadn't been noted. He had just done what he himself had so often done to others—gotten coaxed into revealing critical information to his listener; in this case, to several listeners.

He was sure of it when Barney Wisner uttered an exclamatory ''uh-oh!'' under his breath. Then, for one of the first times in his life, Deweese found himself backtracking, making alibis and excuses. ''Parsons told me an old Indian gave him the stones. I got it that he was the same Indian that was looking after the boy yonder.''

The kid leaned in, belligerent and haughty, his words blurted self-righteously before his elders could stop him. His voice reached a shrill pitch in outraged defense of his foster father.

"Elk Leggins never did no such a thing! Simon Parsons, that son of a bitch, stole that box from me, and that letter is from my Aunt Nell in Dalton, Colorado!" Like a heavy weight, it was off Charley's chest, and he leaned back. Deweese caught the look of sudden panic in the eyes of Charley's adult companions.

Deweese maintained a practiced calm while the air around them seethed with heavy silence for a long moment; the dismay Deweese saw in the faces of Snow, Wisner, and Casey was hard to disguise. Here, he thought smugly, letting the zest of sudden victory seep through him for a moment, was the missing link that put him miles and days ahead of Simon Parsons, but only a notch or two past the three he faced over his curdling breakfast plate. Deweese kept his poker face while trembling with jubilation. Dalton, Colorado! It wouldn't be hard to find.

Though he could act unruffled, Dick Snow was otherwise without a shred of guile. "See what I mean, Dave?" he stammered. "Get Charley started, and his mouth runs like a river at high flood." Deweese gloated over Snow's feeble attempt at a lie about Charley's command of English; like all sincere, genuine individuals Deweese had known, Dick Snow would never make it as a grifter and a fraud. Deweese's mind flashed on ways to get away without alarming them or getting shot.

Charley looked around at the faces of his older companions, confusion registering in his eyes. "I said the wrong thing, didn't I, Dick?"

Snow forced an understanding expression for the boy. Deweese sensed a struggle on Snow's part to keep his voice level. "No, Charley. Mr. Deweese here saw the letter, and probably everyone knows by now that your aunt wrote it from Dalton. That right, Deweese?"

Dave thought fast. Even for a man of his devious talents, it was hard to weigh all the elements that quickly. "Ah ... no. Parsons doesn't know where the letter came from."

Snow pondered it; Deweese appeared to be truthful. Nagging doubt about the man still lingered. Snow's glance at Casey and Wisner showed they were as confused and troubled as he was. Deciding, Snow spoke up.

"Time to face facts, Deweese. As long as we're the only ones to know where we're headed, I guess that means you ride with us. We'll settle your case when we get there. We sure can't just turn you loose now. You may be the most decent and honest fellow in the world, but men do strange things when gold's at stake. We're dealing with this boy's legacy, and we'll not take a chance that Charley will get cheated out of what's rightly his."

Deweese tried to turn on his most ingratiating grin. "Hell, Dick, that's been my idea all along," he said. "To tie up on the side of right. Maybe sticking with you, I'll wind up finding decent and lasting work. What more could a man ask?"

Snow shrugged abruptly, apparently relieved; Casey's expression supported Snow. Deweese tried not to read doubt in the near squint of the eyes of the one called Wisner. Charley's loud voice intruded, angrily insistent and annoyingly childish.

"I don't want him riding with us, Dick! I want it the way it was. You and me and Acie and Barney. I made a mess of everything, didn't I?" Tears welled up in Charley's thirteen-year-old eyes.

Snow found himself remembering that Charley was only a boy and tried not to be too harsh. But Charley had spilled the beans to a total stranger. He knew he had his hands full; Deweese on the one, and Charley on the other.

"Naw, Charley," he drawled, hoping his calm voice would ease the boy's qualms. "Everything'll work out okay. Everything's all right."

"No, it ain't! Ain't okay!" Charley's protest came as a screech. "I made a mess of everything. I'm goin' back to Elk Leggins where I belong. You can have all that old gold!" Charley jumped up to charge away into the rolling prairie on emotion-stiff legs.

"Charley! Wait!" Snow was right up and after him, the two of them engaged in a footrace out into the high plains. Acie and Barney—startled to the core by Charley's blurted revelations and his sudden rebellion and flight—leapt up heedlessly to follow the pair into the rolling grassland. They stopped at the crest of a nearby knoll, shading their eyes against the morning sun to stare dumbfounded as Snow raced out into the sea of waving grass in his chase after Charley. For the moment, Dave Deweese was forgotten.

Near Deweese's mount, the remuda of seven pack and saddle horses stood securely rein-tied to a long picket rope stretched between two stubby junipers, awaiting saddles and packs.

Quickly, before the nearby pair had a chance to react, Deweese's sheath knife had freed both ends of the picket rope. He leapt to his saddle, clutching the ends of the long loop. Leading a virtual horse herd, Dave Deweese disappeared over a grassy knoll as Acie and Barney spun around to witness his theft through horrified eyes.

# ✦ 8 ✦

**A**cie looked up at what was still a beautiful morning. "Strange, isn't it?" he asked of no one in particular. "A day can break as fine and splendid as this one did. Then, dammit, almost before a man can say Jack Robinson, it can turn on him with thunderheads and double lightnin' like this one did."

For want of anything better to do as the shock wore off, they clustered morosely around the dead ashes of their breakfast fire. "One thing, Acie," Barney responded, breaking into a brave grin, "my belly's still happy over them mornin' vittles. When a man's full of good grub, the world never looks quite as bleak as it might otherwise."

If any of them had regrets or reproach, none spoke of it. Still, there was sadness. Dick Snow, who hadn't said much, was absorbed in poking and prodding the ashes with a long, thin stick. Charley Rogers, sitting glumly away from them, couldn't find it in himself to be as accepting of cruel fate as Acie and Barney.

Acie felt that the boy was taking it all pretty hard.

"I'm going to say this to you, Charley." The young man's eyes came up, and he regarded Acie soberly. "You're not to keep blaming yourself. We're all at fault. You saw through him, and we fellas took his bait and walked right into his trap. We're the ones—me and Dick and Barney—that ought to be sittin' around camp with a bad case of the sad-mouth."

"Besides," Barney added, his sky-blue eyes seeking the boy's, "life has a way of coming up with situations like this, like it's the Good Lord's way of testing us and keeping us on our toes. Do you know how miserable we'd be if everything was easy as rollin' off a log?"

Dick Snow heard their words, only partly heeding them. He acknowledged having what Acie called "a bad case of the sad-mouth." Try as he might, he couldn't shake it. He looked around him, his head full of the fix they'd gotten themselves into. He'd loved this land, but now it had turned on him, threatened to destroy him. He knew it wasn't the land, but more the people in it; still, in his mind, a pall hung over his world. Anger and frustration, never boon companions, now haunted and galled him for allowing himself to be led down the primrose path by a slippery jasper the likes of Dave Deweese. He hated himself for being taken in, as well as for proving unworthy of the trust placed in him by his old friend, Elk Leggins.

Snow pulled off his hat to run his fingers dejectedly through his hair, hold his head, and study the ashes of happier times before him. Charley, too, had faith in him; it was a hard pill to swallow that over this twist of events Charley might lose the legacy that was rightly his. At a time when even small consolations became beacons of hope, Snow took heart that Deweese had without doubt also hoodwinked the despicable Simon Parsons.

"Here I am," Snow said finally. "Paid to know this country—supposed to be smart, a guide and a decision maker."

"And a damned good one," Barney assured him.

"Then how could I have been so dumb? Bought that crook's bill of goods ten yards wide and a mile long."

Acie spoke right up. "That's what we're talking about here, Dick. Deweese took us all in. We're all three at fault."

Snow looked at him. "We agreed I was to guide you and Barney to the gold country. From there, you fellas'd show me where it was and how to mine." His voice had a despondent ring, as though he still shouldered much of the burden for Deweese's cruel trick. "All this was my fault."

Charley spoke up, and Snow swung his eyes on the boy's. "I ain't heard anybody blamin' you, Dick. What are you beatin' yourself for?"

Snow straightened, his heart warmed by Charley's support. "All right," he said. "We traded our horse herd for the truth about Dave Deweese. So in at least one respect, we got the best of that bargain." His shoulders slumped, and he grimaced. "Trouble is, we've got to get to Dalton before he does. And he's got our horses."

Barney saw a grim situation that needed some faith. "On the bright side, Dick, we've got the inside track to Nell Joiner—if she's there—with her nephew, Little Charley here."

"I'm not little," Charley piped up with insistence.

92

Snow's eyes caught the boy's. "Easy, Charley. We're all on edge." He swung his gaze to Barney. "Horses, Barney, horses. He's got our damned horses, and we haven't. What we've got is three pack-horse loads of gear and four pairs of boots. If Nell's still in Dalton, that slimy son of a . . ." He paused, looking at Charley.

"Go ahead and say it, Dick," Charley encouraged, unperturbed. "Deweese *is* a son of a bitch."

Snow continued. "By the time we get there, Deweese'll have her sweet-talked into turning over control of the claim, and it'll be our word against his. And he'll have claim registration on his side. My friend, I'm sorry to be the bearer of sad tidings, but it's a long way there on shank's mare."

"You mean walk?" Barney asked dryly.

"Walk's what I mean, yeah," Dick said. "What else have we got?"

"Where's the closest place to buy horses?" Acie asked. Then he looked at them sheepishly. "Not that we've got anything to buy with."

"Best go back to Elk Leggins," Dick said. "He'd give us more."

Barney bristled, his impatience near the surface. "What'll that take, Snow? Five days? Four at the best. This ain't no time for despair. You got to think, man. Think! Time we get to Dalton, Deweese will have looted Charley's claim and be only a memory. We'll have to cache our gear around here. Besides, unless we go roundabout, we're smack dab in the path of that gang, and a man ain't in a more ticklish spot than when he's afoot against a superior force of armed horsemen."

Charley Rogers suppressed a giggle that everyone

heard, and they looked at him. His abrupt change in attitude astonished them. Despite the gravity of the situation, Snow was unable to stifle his own smirk at seeing Charley suddenly so animated. "All right," he insisted, almost gleefully, "what's on your mind, Charley?"

Charley's face was alive with mischief. "Who's got the damned horses around here?"

Acie ignored Charley's profanity. "Elk Leggins?"

Charley's eyes still danced with glee as he looked at Acie. "Try Parsons."

Barney spoke up. "Charley, I just got through telling you. We've got to walk soft and wide around that man and his bunch of bad apples. After our standoff with Parsons yesterday, and then him figuring for sure that Deweese came right over here, any man'd be a fool to go to him with hat in hand to try to swing some horse-tradin' scheme, 'specially when he's got nothin' to deal with."

"Who said anything about trading?" Charley asked it with his thirteen-year-old face agleam with his own style of demonic evil.

Acie was aghast. "You mean steal?"

Snow was caught up with Charley's brand of inspiration—or spite. "No, not steal, Acie," he said. "The military prefers to call it 'moonlight requisition.' A night patrol." He turned to his pseudo–Cheyenne accomplice, young Jolly Roger. "I lived with Elk Leggins and Goes Slowly, too, son. Have you gone on a Cheyenne horse-stealing raid?"

Charley's response was in his twinkling eyes. Even though Snow knew the boy had probably lied, Charley could be depended on to brag about more involvement

94

than he had really had. Charley said, "You're damned well told!"

"What you say, Acie?" Snow queried. He was so far at his wits' end that he felt giddy, or worse, like a drowning man grasping at straws.

"What?" their pudgy cook asked, glaring at Charley's profanity. "Steal horses? From Parsons? Is that our only alternative?"

"What else have we got?"

Barney piped up, "Count me out. The Good Book promises I'll live to three score years and ten; long as I play the cards I'm dealt."

"You sound like a poker player," Snow said, baiting Barney. "And not a very good one."

Barney was right back with his card-game logic. "I'll stand pat with the hand I've got, at least in this particular deal."

Undaunted, Snow turned serious, leaning in toward them, his voice low. Acie and Barney had to get close to hear Snow's conspiratorial whisper. Charley also bent forward to hear. "Charley's idea will work. Deweese rode out there at some unearthly hour while they all slept like statues. At great risk, I might add. So give our boy Deweese credit for that much. Parsons'll post a guard, but I daresay he'll be asleep, too. We're not going up against crafty Indians, gentlemen. We're tackling frontier lowlifes. I, for one, think we can pull it off."

Acie sent Snow a penetrating glance. "It's risky business, Dick. Risky business."

"You want to walk all the way back to Elk Leggins at Amity Creek, Acie?" Snow responded. "Or shoulder a hundred pounds of camp gear and start off hoofing it for Dalton? What other chances have we got? Dire circumstances call for drastic action.''

Seeing now the desperate nature of their predicament, Barney's compass needle swung in Snow's direction. ''Aw, hell. No sense in living forever, and then as only half a man. I'd just get grouchy and weak in the bones and the bladder like my old man did. We only need to replace seven horses. Parsons must have a dozen or more, counting pack animals. It's not like we're signing death warrants for those men. We may stymie 'em and make 'em mad, but it's not like we're going to leave them to die—like Deweese left us, totally helpless.''

''Now you begin to talk like my saddle pard, Barney,'' Dick Snow said cheerfully.

Charley, still leaning in close with a face bright and expectant, said, ''I take back what I said before. Before the horse thief came.''

Snow reached over and affectionately mussed Charley's head of flaxen hair. ''At your age, Charley, you're apt to judge your elders harshly.''

''Even though sometimes they may judge you harshly as well,'' Barney added, smiling at the boy. ''Well, Dick, you've not led us astray on this whole trip since we threw together in Independence. How do we pull off this horse-thievin'?''

''We've about got a majority vote. What say, Acie?''

''Appears to me,'' he said, his soulful eyes studying those around him, ''that we'd best get busy.'' Snow took that as Acie's affirmative vote. ''Parsons'll be along here pretty quick now,'' Acie went on. ''He'll see our predicament, and that'll spoil the whole shebang. We best get humping and hide our stuff and get out of sight ourselves.''

Charley piped up, ''Then they'll figure we rode on, probably with that Deweese.'' He chuckled, relishing the conspiracy. ''That'll be the way the horse sign reads, anyway. Parsons will never expect us to be behind him.''

Snow looked his companions over. ''We may be outnumbered, but I'd stack this crew up against Parsons and his boys any day!''

A scant hour and three quarters later, from the secure vantage point of scrubby junipers on a knoll somewhat higher and a hundred yards from the trail, Charley and company stealthfully watched as Parsons's men rode first past the ashes of their supper fire and then up to their sleeping site and breakfast fire and their cleverly disguised cache—a technique perfected by the beaver men a half century before them. They'd done it well.

''What we do,'' Barney had said, wielding their lone shovel to start a massive hole, ''is dig it deep and wide enough to hold our nonessentials. Save out what we'll need for a couple of days, probably, till we can get back. Line it and cover the gear with the buffalo robes and pack the dirt back.'' Leftover soil was carefully hauled away and spread out of sight. They tramped over the spot and rebuilt their fire on top of it to disguise their digging.

Additionally, they memorized landmarks and distance from the main trail, quizzing each other almost merrily to make sure no one forgot the clues for recovering their cache. They were still at it when they heard the riders approaching and scurried up to a prearranged hiding place from which to watch and listen.

The crystal midmorning air around them was so clear that even at a distance, they could hear the discussions and arguments as eight or nine men, all with loud voices, came up with differing opinions of the details revealed in the camp signs. Loudest above the discordant and disorganized clamor rose the cantankerous screech of Simon Parsons.

"Deweese was one of 'em. Come over here and told them other jaspers about that letter. Now they've gone. Hightailin' for Colorado."

"I still think Deweese's just a drifter," said the man with the long hair and the flattened nose, riding close to Parsons. His voice, though softer, drifted as strongly up to the quartet on the hill, only their eyes and the tops of their heads showing from under the juniper. "I don't think Deweese come over here at all, Simon. We still know more'n any of 'em, Deweese and Snow's jaspers put together."

Parsons waved one of his riders up to him. "You're good at readin' sign, Wild Card. What do you make of the tracks around here?"

Wild Card, a tall, rope-thin man on a horse, studied the camp area a long time. His stirrups dangled well below his horse's belly to accommodate his uncommonly long legs. Wild Card wore a Stetson that because of its wide brim and high, ample crown looked much too large for his head. Others of the Parsons gang had already ridden their horses all over the campsite, destroying any sign.

"They must've left," Wild Card declared. "They

went west.'' Abruptly his long arm described a wide arc, almost knocking Simon Parsons's hat off.

In little knots of humanity and horseflesh, others of the Parsons men had congregated to bicker and debate the evidence. The watchers on the hill stifled grunts of glee and motioned to or nudged one another as the muddled mass of outlaws rode out of sight, their crabby dialogues fading as they disappeared over a distant knoll.

Barney was the first to rise up from his prone position alongside the small hilltop stand of shielding blue-green juniper. ''Nothing left now but take our necessities and head out after 'em.''

Snow admired their spirit as their hike became a test of will as well as one of stamina. The trek across the high prairie after Parsons was not difficult from the standpoint of terrain; all of them however, had done nearly all their long-distance traveling by horseback. Unending miles afoot brought aches and cramps to muscles unaccustomed to such misuse. Though they went about it quietly, there was still a cheerful acceptance of the unwanted duty in the way they stepped off the miles.

Burdened by a heavy over-the-shoulder pack rigged of a strap and a packhorse pannier bag, Barney's mind stayed on the tactics of their quest as he slogged along beside Snow. ''We'd ought,'' he advised, ''to have a point man out there, a hundred yards or so, spotting what's ahead. Parsons is moving faster than we are, for sure, but they might get down for a smoke or another long palaver, or they could stop early, or any one of a number of reasons. Somebody'd ought to be out ahead to approach the rises careful-like and scout the land.''

"And take turns," Snow added, seeing Barney's logic. "The point man can also make sure we stay on Parsons's trail by following the road, such as it is, or seeing if they leave the beaten path.''

"Since I brought it up, I'll take first scout," Barney said. "Charley, my boy, here's a job where you're as good as us old-timers. You can take the second shift.'' Charley glanced at Barney with understanding and appreciation in his expression.

"Yeah," Acie cheered. "Charley's been a pretty good old soldier this trip.''

"I guess I ought to be," Charley said, feigning a grumble, but with a smile. "After all, this horse raid was my idea.''

As Barney moved out at a brisker pace than the others, Charley also stepped off at a jauntier stride. Snow and Casey fell in step with him, grinning at each other; Snow felt good despite the loss of the horses and having to become horse thieves themselves. He sensed that all of them had begun to look forward to the challenge of a sneak invasion of Parsons's stronghold, as well as to handicapping the Parsons gang in what now had become a three-way race to Colorado. More than once, Charley had brought out his urgent need to catch up with the despised Deweese and get his prized Dolly back.

Sundown overtook them without a sight of the Parsons gang; they moved well off the trail for their night camp. Watching his "customers" mow away an ample meal of his tasty flapjacks, Acie proclaimed, "Well, gents, eat hearty! An army, y'know, travels on its stomach.''

Dick Snow spoke happily around a mouthful of flapjacks. "Small correction, good friend. It was Napoleon who said it. 'An army *marches* on its stomach.' ''

"I stand corrected," Acie said, a happy grin cutting his moon face. "My apologies, Mr. Bonaparte.''

"He said something else that bears on our situation. 'All is not lost until the moment when all has succeeded.' ''

"Hell!" Barney snorted. He looked at Charley. They had come to the point where they didn't scold the boy anymore for mild profanity. "Hell, Dick, I never once in my life figured everything was lost. And I've been in a mess of tights in my time, even when most of my regiment was lost at Antietam.''

"My sentiments exactly," Snow said. "Charley weathered a hard time of it losing his folks and then learning to get along in a life totally foreign to him. But he made it, and so can we. It was tough for him. And us. We older ones came through four years of damned bloody battle lines. We came through it to face even more years in this godforsaken hostile territory, never knowing when the Indians might lift your hair or your own kind pull a gun and lift your poke after mooching free eats.''

Charley piped up, "Look what happened when we fed and trusted a jasper like Deweese. Parsons stole my gold ore, and Deweese stole my Dolly. I'm out to get both of 'em.''

Snow helped himself to another mouthful of flapjack. "No, gents, our present predicament, if nothing else, is just a normal situation for us. Our challenge is to adjust, as our friend Acie here does so admirably with his cooking in dismal conditions. End of sermon.''

After their supper and doing their best to conceal the cooking site, they moved away a respectable distance for their night camp as the long shadows of twilight gave way to deepening night. They spread their saddle blankets, brought along for bedding, and settled down.

''For what I've been through, I feel great,'' Dick Snow enthused out of the night around them. He dug in a pocket for his briar pipe and waved it at Barney, begging some tobacco. Barney tossed his sack to Dick and rummaged in his clothes for his papers. None of the men smoked frequently, but there were times when a smoke—like whiskey—gave a man ease.

''Figured when we started out,'' Snow continued, ''that by now I'd be just one step this side of death. Haven't done this much walkin' since I was a boy. Can't say, though, that Acie's flapjacks and strong coffee didn't have some effect on restorin' my soul.'' He tossed back Barney's grimy, pucker-string tobacco sack. Snow's tanned face, crinkled with contentment, lit up in the flare of his match as the tobacco in his pipe bowl took up a rosy hue.

''We must've come twelve, fifteen mile today,'' Barney said, his cigarette tip glowing bright with his words.

''That's close, I guess,'' Snow agreed, visible largely by the tobacco embers' soft reflection against his nose, cheeks, and forehead. ''What do you say, Acie?''

''Fifteen? More like seventeen.''

''Charley?'' Snow called. ''You're a good judge of distance. What do you think?''

''Felt more like twenty-five to me.''

Snow's chuckle made his pipe glow brightly in the dark. "You're close to right, Jolly Roger. Until you grow a bit more, your legs are shorter than ours, so it probably did feel like you covered more. My guess is closer to Acie's. I put it at eighteen miles."

Acie chimed in, "Just now, it's good not to be pickin' 'em up and layin' 'em down, I'm here to tell ya."

"Jolly Roger!" Snow demanded softly in the dark.

"What, Dick?" Charley had perched on his blanket, contentedly hugging his knees, quietly enjoying the company and the banter of his three mentors.

"How do we find our cache, young man?"

Charley looked around at them, all vague forms in the dark. He spoke his words like a recitation. "Start at the trail on the hilltop with a piñon shaped like a man's head. Three hundred and seventy-five paces generally east into a deep hollow. To the south are two sharp-rising hills that look like a lady's"—Charley paused with a giggle, knowing his cheeks had reddened—"you know. Dig in the exact center of the small hollow."

"Right on every detail," Snow commended. "You've got a good head on your shoulders, Jolly Roger. But now the time has come . . ."

Acie picked up the pace. "The walrus said . . ."

Dick Snow paused, reminded of their earlier conversation on quotations. "Touché, Lewis Carroll and Aciè Casey. But we've got to get deadly serious." Snow spoke with grave import as he knocked the dottle from his pipe and put it away. "If we continue walking about the same number of hours they ride, we're just going to drop farther and farther back. We can't depend on staying as strong as we were today, when the weather, thank God, was in our favor. Any day we could come up with insufferable heat or unforgiving winds, or if it commences to rain in this country . . . well, Acie and Barney remember how miserable and slowed down we were even with horses for two or three days back there a while ago."

"Dick's got a point," Barney said pensively, sucking smoke with a careful two-fingered hold on the stub of his glowing cigarette.

"I'm ready to keep going, Dick," Charley reassured him.

"Listen to him, boys. That's what we've got to do. Keep moving while they sleep. Get less rest than they do. They probably still expect that we're somewhere ahead of them on the trail, *with* horses and with or without Deweese. That's one of our few advantages."

Barney, his brain reacting faster than the conversation was going, dropped his mere ember of cigarette and spoke up. "We get tough, like fighting men. Hike an hour, rest ten minutes."

"Mornin' star to moonrise," Acie added. "Then up and at 'em!"

"I don't need sleep," Charley said bravely.

Snow studied his companions reflected in the dwindling firelight. "A while ago we talked about quotations. Napoleon had another: 'Two o'clock in the morning courage.' That's why we press ourselves until we catch Parsons. Forced marches when we'd rather sleep. Acie, Barney—you were there. Remember how it was in the war? No slacking then. Comrades could die if you failed." Snow paused. "Charley, I know all this schoolbook history is unfamiliar to you, but at the battle of the Alamo down in Texas, when everything seemed hopeless, Colonel Travis—so they say—drew a line in the dirt with his saber. He challenged any one of his one hundred and eighty-some defenders who could not face a fight to the finish to cross the line and head for home.''

Snow paused for effect, his form a mere silhouette in the waning firelight. ''No one did. We don't face certain death as they did, gents. Only defeat, if we allow it. I, for one, am ready to forge ahead to help myself to a mount and a pack animal out of Parsons's remuda, root hog or die!'

To the east, an enormous moon the color of rich butter eased itself gradually out of the black hills. A thin golden light spread over the land and over the three men and a boy relaxing on their blankets. Jolly Roger studied the moon for a few moments before rising to begin rolling up his blanket and gear.

''I'm not stepping across any surrender line, and I sure as hell am not going back to face Elk Leggins without my Dolly,'' he said.

Barney's bass voice thrummed out of the dark. ''I still don't favor thirteen-year-olds cussing, but for this one I now make an exception. Damn me, but he does talk like a man growed full-size!''

Barney roused up and followed Charley's lead in assembling his road gear. Without a word, Snow and Casey followed suit. In minutes, the four jauntily walked the ribbon of moonlight that was the trail leading to Simon Parsons's camp.

# ≫ 9 ≪

They didn't come across the signs of Parsons's night camp until nearly noon the next day. Dick Snow, his face seamed with fatigue and strain, was not encouraging. "He's pushing those horses and those men for all they're worth," he said solemnly. "We're going to have the devil's own time catching up with them."

Barney, lugging a thick pack-horse pannier jury-rigged with rope and a shoulder pad into an awkward and bulky haversack, dropped his load with an exhausted grunt. He spoke as though continuing Snow's words. "Damn, but that strap cut into my shoulder." He rubbed his sore spot. "I suspect Parsons still thinks we're out ahead riding with Deweese. Parsons is maybe figuring to ride us down, disable us, maybe permanent, and get on to Colorado without any competition."

Snow managed a grin through his exhaustion. "Remember how Parsons behaved the other day when they paid us a visit? He's got a healthy respect for the two crafty 'cutthroats' riding with Charley and me."

Acie let that one pass. "They want Charley," he reminded Snow.

The subject of Acie's remark was still disgustingly vigorous while his mentors sprawled on the ground as though they'd as soon quit right now. Charley's eyes twinkled as he stayed on his feet when the others plunked tiredly down on soft spots in the grass.

"Well, he's the one that's gonna be disabled when we catch up with him," Charley said, his words like a promise. "We're fooling him by coming up from behind. Parsons won't ever catch me! And even if he did, I'd die before I let out a peep. I'm a Cheyenne."

"Charley," Snow said, the strain evident in his voice, "will you sit down? You make me tired just standing there and walking around."

"Let's go," Charley said. "We've got to catch Parsons."

Acie spoke up, sounding irritated. "Charley, we walked all day yesterday and all last night. We'll catch up with Parsons in our own good time. Let us adults decide when to rest and when to get up and go. You fellas want me to rustle up some chuck while we're sittin' around?"

"You need a rest as much as we do, Acie," Snow said tiredly.

"Pshaw! Won't take any time at all," Acie said, boosting his round form off the grass and starting to root around in his bag of gear, a pannier lash-up similar to the one Barney carried. "I could whip up some cornmeal mush and top it off with my sorghum molasses I brought along. The change of pace'll do me good."

Snow's exhaustion brought an edge of impatience, but he blunted it. "Well, then, get that whirling dervish of a Charley to haul your water from the creek down there.''

''It's a shame lettin' all that good energy to to waste,'' Barney admitted dryly, cocking an eye at the fidgeting boy. Barney shrugged, trying to relax, as Acie dug out his battered coffeepot and offered it to Charley. ''You heard the man,'' he said. Charley saw Acie's grin. He shrugged out of his pack, a man-sized load rolled and tied in a saddle blanket and worn over his shoulder in a horseshoe shape. In it were, among other things, bridles and ropes for their captured horses.

''Right after we eat,'' he said, looking around at them, ''we've got to get going after Parsons.'' He started off with a lively step for the nearby stream with Acie's pot.

When the boy was out of hearing, Barney spoke up with a wry tone and a twinkle in his eye. ''Maybe we'd just ought to hand him over to Parsons for a day or two. Might discourage the old scoundrel from going to Colorado after all. I believe that boy would be more than a match for all of Parsons's toughs put together. He's a damned handful!''

Acie rummaged in his huge leather-reinforced pannier of thick canvas for his cooking things. ''Who was it said we'd probably have to nursemaid him all the way to Colorado?''

''That's when I took him for ordinary small fry,'' Barney said. ''He's got more sand and smarts than two his age. But he's not tedious about it. He's all boy. I see a lot of the devil in him I had in me when I was about that size.''

''Makes me think of another quotation,'' Snow said. ''I don't know if it's in the Old Testament, but the one about the spirit being tempered on the forge of adversity. Charley's risen above a lot of tough breaks in life.''

"Yeah," Barney said, "but did they have to make the fire so hot?''

"Last night, Dick," Acie said, "just before we decided on this forced-march hooey, you said something about how many more miles he had to cover because of his shorter legs than us grown-ups. All night I was almost at a trot to keep up with him.''

Snow had a faraway look. "When I have a boy, I want him to be like Jolly Roger. What happened with Deweese cut Charley pretty deep. For a while there, I think he was trying mighty hard in his own way to live it down with us. I think he got over that and took this all on as a personal crusade when I told him about Colonel Travis drawing the line in the dirt at the Alamo. Boys, I believe we've got a little fighter on our hands. It's going to be us trying to measure up to him. Not the other way around.''

"Can it," Acie hushed. "Here he comes.''

Charley labored up the grassy slope from the stream lugging the full coffeepot, his grin wide and his face flushed from the heat and the exertion.

"Frogs any good to eat?" he chirped happily, setting the pot down near where Acie worked. "Couple big old granddaddies jumped off the bank for deep water down there in a swampy place. Heard 'em when I was walking down.'' He worked his voice from deep in his throat, imitating a bullfrog. "Ha-rump! Ha-rump!''

"You sound just like 'em, Jolly Roger," Acie remarked, grinning. "We've ate worse. I've known hard times when having a bullfrog or two to fix up for supper would've seemed a delicacy. We'll worry about eating frogs some other time.''

"Mush and coffee'd ought to put the starch back in our sails,'' Barney said. "I'll get you a fire fixed, Acie.''

"Much obliged. Charley, maybe you could help Barney and rustle up some kindlin' and burnin' lengths.''

Without responding, Charley raised up from his crouch near the coffeepot and started to head off eagerly to search for firewood.

"If you boys don't mind,'' Dick interrupted. "I believe maybe I've got more important work for Charley. Sneakin' off in the dark hours after Parsons's horses is going to be a mighty ticklish affair. We'd all best be armed in case of the unexpected. I'm gonna let Charley buckle on old Sam Colt here when we raid. Just now, since we've got a few minutes, I think he'd ought to run through a couple of cylinders at some sort of target and see if I can help him develop his shootin' eye.''

Charley braked to a sudden halt, turned around, and strode briskly to where Snow was getting up. Charley watched Snow expectantly. "You'll see, Dick,'' Charley enthused. "You'll see. I'll know how to handle it proper. Can I put it on now?''

"Come on along here,'' Snow said, heading out toward the trackless prairie with Charley at his heels. He held out the heavy holstered single-action on its belt with full cartridge loops to Charley. "Now the first thing you need to do is calm down all that excitement. This'll be fun, but it's also serious business. Dead serious, and I don't mean maybe. You get rattle-headed and the deal's off. Got that?''

Charley slackened his eager pace to stay in step with

Snow, whose easy walk was little more than a loose-jointed saunter, deliberately setting an agonizingly slow pace to keep the boy in check and let him know who was in charge. Charley skipped steps as he tried to buckle the heavy six-gun rig around his middle.

Acie and Barney watched them go, nudging each other as they saw that Charley didn't seem to know where to fix his admiring glances—down at the big gun slung on his slender hip or up at Dick Snow. The man and boy disappeared over a rise with Charley asking rapid-fire questions, and Dick Snow responding calmly and methodically.

"Tell you a secret, Barney."

"How's that?"

"Dick's about as excited over teaching the boy as Charley is to learn. But he'd sure never let on to Charley," Acie said.

"You're right about that," Barney agreed. "That's part of it when a man teaches a boy. He doesn't want to act like a boy himself about it. He can't show he's enjoying himself. Too easy for the meaning of the lesson to be lost that way. Oh, he doesn't have to be mean. Just firm. The lesson gets learned when the teacher is looked up to, respected. If a kid's looking at the teacher like he's a friend and a pal, the seriousness of the message gets lost. Charley's all boy, like we said, and Dick wants him to know that handling that six-gun is anything but fooling around."

Acie had the coffee started and began measuring his corn meal and water to mix up the mush. Away from them, muffled by distance and a rolling hill or two, came the well-spaced reports of "Sam Colt" in the hands of Jolly Roger, instructed by Dick Snow.

"They're a pretty good match, Barney," he said. "Dick's eager to teach and has a lot of give, and Charley's just as eager to learn, and he'll soak up that learning like sand soaks up rain."

"There's something else about all this, too, Acie," Barney said, his voice warm with prophecy.

"What are you thinkin', Barney?"

"I doubt Dick's thought about it that way, Acie, but could be he's found that son he was talking about a few minutes ago. Aside from old Elk Leggins and his Aunt Nell, if we ever find her, Charley doesn't have much of what you'd call family. Neither has Snow. These are the years for a tad Charley's age to learn what's serious and what ain't. About seeing the humor in life but not indifferent to the serious side. How to get along with people and be a good man, good at whatever kind of work he sets for himself. He begins to find out that life ain't all bullfrogs and ballgames."

"A boy needs a mother, too, Barney. Dick could be right smart of a father, all right, but he doesn't have a wife."

"There are a lot of pretty and proper young ladies who'd take a shine to Dick Snow if he once got himself gussied up in city clothes and went to some of the right places. He could take his pick. The point is that for Dick Snow, there'll never be another Jolly Roger."

Late that afternoon, as Charley, Acie, and Barney trudged along the trail west with faltering stamina, Dick Snow, ahead at point more than a hundred yards, was seen to kneel over something in the trail and then beckon them to hurry up. As they hustled to his side, Barney spoke up. "That's what you wanted to show us? A stack of horse apples?"

"You disappoint me, Barney. These aren't three hours old. We're closing the gap."

Near them, Acie rested his hand on Charley's shoulder. "I hope all this works," he said. The boy jerked away from him, impatience searing him at the thought that Acie would doubt that their mission would succeed.

Even Charley was nearly worn out when they finally caught up with the Simon Parsons gang, his original enthusiasms blunted by nearly forty-eight hours of forced marches and insufficient rest. The only things that kept them going were the pressing necessity of getting horses and Acie's innovative and varied meals on the trail.

Charley, walking point, topped a ridge to glimpse Parsons's drag rider about to drop from sight over a dip in the road. Alarm rang through him as he remembered Acie's almost prophetic words—"I hope all this works." It had all started as a marvelous adventure; now Charley, sensing uncommon spears of irritation— at the others, at himself, and at Parsons for not stopping sooner—began to doubt they could pull it off without disaster. His head and body ached from his hours without sleep and the demanding rigors of their forced marches.

For the next two hours, they probed forward, cautiously trailing the Parsons gang. Finally, they watched from a dominating outcropping of jagged granite overlooking a broad juniper- and piñon-studded meadow the Parsons gang had chosen for its night camp.

It was still early, and Dick Snow deduced that Parsons, pushing hard for Colorado and—like the foot-slogging pursuers—running out of steam, had made camp early to suit cranky men more than to give their exhausted horses a much-needed rest.

"After all we've come through on this patrol, I'm not sure we've much of an advantage in helping ourselves to any of those sad cayuses yonder," Dick hissed as they peered down from the scrub-dotted ledge overlooking Parsons.

"Pretty sad bunch from here," Barney agreed near him. "More hosses than I calc'lated Parsons had." They were stretched out on their bellies to observe from their high vantage point, shielded by a small stand of hardy trees crowding the rim, finding purchase for their roots in the fissured rock. A soft wind constantly played and whispered through the thick green foliage and held down the heat of a sun that elsewhere might be annoyingly hot.

From below, where the breeze was surely less and the sun beat down hotter, the shrill voice of Simon Parsons rose up to them as he tried to rally his disorganized, disinterested, and frazzled flock. At this point none seemed to care to listen as Parsons strode around the camp, his head swiveling as he directed his words at anyone who'd listen. He found none but went ahead delivering some form of outlaw lecture.

His men milled around, tired in their bones or bored, inattentive to their leader as they smoked, talked, or argued over whose turn it was to cook his grub over one of several random and overly hot fires. "See there," Dick whispered, "they're loyal only because there's strength in numbers. That's what holds 'em together. Alone, half of 'em wouldn't survive a hot squaw and a cold camp. Parsons tells 'em what to do, but they only half listen." Snow swung an arm out and heartily slapped Acie, nearest to him, on the back. "Does the phrase 'motley crew' come to mind when you look down there, fellas?" he said softly. "Acie, I got to hand it to you and Barney. It never occurred to me before to say how good it is to travel the land with you two."

Barney reddened, looked down at the dirt, and self-consciously rubbed his bristly mustache with a knuckle. "Ain't nothin', Dick."

"It doesn't take any special talent, Dick," Acie explained. "Barney and I just use our heads. We divide the chores. I like the idea of cookin', and about as close as Barney wants to get to it is sittin' down to eat. Barney'll build us a fine shade arbor for hot afternoons or comfy beds with grass—what he calls 'prairie feathers'—and such as that."

"You're specialists, you two," Dick said. "No other way to put it."

"I'd sure rather ride with you than with any of them down there," Charley put in.

"Appears to me if we're goin' to go through with this horse raid—and I flat got no specialty that way—Parsons has laid out his camp with us in mind," Barney observed.

"I guess you just said what I was thinking," Dick agreed. "They've turned the horses out to graze down there at the south end, made their camp—such as it is—back up this way . . ."

"And posted the guard off there to the north," Charley added.

From their promontory, they had a clear view to a small grove at a lower elevation where a Parsons rifleman smoked and whiled away the time in the shade, looking out over the trail on which the gang had ridden in.

"Okay, Charley," Dick said. "What do you think? You've sized up the situation. Where would a Cheyenne go from here?"

From his prone position, shaded by a rimrock piñon, Charley turned his intense blue eyes from under his thatch of straw-colored hair in Snow's direction. His expression said he was both pleased and puzzled that Dick would ask him. He thought a moment before speaking.

"Seems to me, Dick, that a smart Cheyenne would go down to the far end by the horses, wait till the middle of the night, and sneak in and help himself. Their guard's up here, the horses are way down there, and the camp's in between. Deweese sneaked away from them early one morning, so those gents must sleep pretty sound. Probably the camp guard was asleep that time, too."

"Right so far," Snow interrupted, looking at the boy proudly. "You make it sound so easy. So what then?"

Charley warmed to his subject. "So we slip back, out of sight, and move out south there, past their remuda. Find a high, shady spot like this where we can keep an eye on the horses and the camp. Take turns at guard—just to keep track of things—while the rest of us get some sleep. In the middle of the night we sneak in with our bridles and lead ropes, and each of us gets a riding animal and a pack horse."

"Then it's bareback to where our saddles are cached," Acie put in, watching Charley eagerly.

"We better go into the herd two at a time. The others stand guard."

For a moment, Snow turned his attention back to the camp, the distant horse herd, and Parsons's positioning of his sentinel.

"Barney," he said thoughtfully, "you've been pretty savvy so far on our tactics. How does Charley's approach add up?"

Wisner chuckled. He studied the Parsons camp a long time before responding; the milling around down there and the apparent confusion made it look like a simple affair. Barney Wisner knew better. "About the only other way would be to somehow take out the sentry yonder and try to get the drop on Parsons's entire crew. And that'd be a case of backin' into a job if I ever saw one!"

'What do you say, Acie?" Snow asked.

"Like I said, it's risky. Real risky. But it's got to be done. I can't go much farther without a horse under me. I'm against stealing, and I know you boys are. Our backs are against the wall. In my heart, I suppose I can justify stealing from the men who stole from Charley and did other vile things in Elk Leggins's village. Gents, I believe God will forgive us our transgressions. With that said, I have only one suggestion."

Snow responded. "Which is?"

Acie grinned at Snow. "That when we get settled down yonder, we find a safe spot out of sight to build us a little fire and brew up a pot of coffee. I'll whip up some flapjacks. I've been saving an airtight can of sliced peaches in syrup for a real first-class emergency, which I declare this to be. Enough for each of us to have some for topping his flapjacks. I don't believe a man ought go horse-thievin' on an empty stomach.''

"And I declare that this reconnaissance patrol is over," Dick Snow announced almost happily. "We move now to the main attack, first taking time to rest and restore our spirits over Acie's vittles!''

# ❖ 10 ❖

"Well, I'll be damned!" Dick Snow was the first to glimpse the true character of the Parsons horse string from their position south of and close to the herd. "I *thought* he had more horses than when we had that tiff with him on the trail. Now I know why."

Barney inched up beside Dick to peer down at the animals. "Hey, fellas!" he called softly back to Acie and Charley crawling up behind them. "Look what the cat dragged in!"

"Thank God!" Acie said, scooting up beside Barney and Dick to expose only the top of his head and his eyes to peer into the vale before him. "We won't have to steal horses after all. Just claim what's rightly ours."

Charley was the last to take his position beside the older men. His delight was instant. "Dolly! They've got Dolly!" He restrained himself from yelling it.

"Easy, son, easy," Snow said. "By golly, boys, Deweese must've turned our horses loose somewhere out on the range after he left us high and dry. He's got gold, not horses, on his mind. We need only to take our horses back. We're cleared as horse thieves, you might say."

"He only stole 'em to get a head start for Dalton," Barney said.

"I think after we get our horses back, we'd ought to stampede the rest of their string," Charley said bitterly. "I don't like Parsons."

"What's to be gained by that, Charley?" Acie put in. "Once we get back in the saddle, we'll be where we were three days ago."

"But six days behind that oily character Deweese," Dick said.

"Yeah," Barney added. "He's the only one to worry about. From what Deweese told us in words and actions, Parsons doesn't know about Dalton or Spindrift Ridge. He's only got the letter and Charley's rocks that came from there, but beyond that he's the blind leadin' the blind. Deweese has the clearest shot. He has his sights on Dalton, Nell Joiner, and Spindrift Ridge, in that order."

"And don't you believe different," Acie agreed solemnly.

Charley went pale. He hadn't thought of it in quite those precise terms. "As Acie said, this horse raid has got to work . . . in more ways than one," he said. "Take Parsons out of the race and get us on Deweese's trail as quick as we can."

Barney glanced knowingly at Acie and Dick; the boy was smart. "The forge of adversity," he said.

"What's that, Barney?" Charley asked, puzzled.

"Oh, nothin'."

\*　　\*　　\*

Charley was awakened by a gentle grip and shake of his shoulder. His eyes clicked open without a word to the dim face of Barney Wisner. Overhead, as though on a black robe of soft velvet, the crisp sparkle of stars filled the night sky. "It's time, son," Barney whispered.

Charley came awake instantly. "I'm ready."

All was quiet as they eased silently through the night down a sloping hill toward the horse herd to avoid disturbing the outlaw camp, while trying to keep the horses from becoming agitated.

The horses, hobbled and grazing on the hillside, suspiciously studied the four dark figures that materialized like ghosts out of the dark around them. They sensed familiar human forms and smells, took them as natural phenomena, and went back to grinding grass and enjoying the cool night without alarm. Below them, the outlaw camp slumbered as peacefully and quietly as though it did not exist. But Snow and his companions were aware that it did exist, with a lethal, vicious, and evil presence.

Stiffened backs hunched, aching knees bent, sliding silently as prowling wolves, clutching leather bridles and rope halters, Acie and Barney quickly blended with the dark mass of grazing horses, seeking familiar animals. They could not afford to be too picky; each had to find a riding horse and a pack animal and move out of harm's way to stand guard for Snow and Charley.

Still they allowed a few moments to hunt for their own horses before taking potluck. Both were fortunate in finding old reliables, cutting rawhide hobbles, buckling on bridles and halters. Almost gratefully, they led the horses away into a night that was still black as the inside of a boot.

Coming out of the herd without sounding the alarm, Acie and Barney separated in the blackness to silently seek out Dick and Charley. Moving to his right while Acie and his trailing horses dissolved to the left to find Snow, Barney saw through the dark as Jolly Roger came out from hiding with Snow's "Sam Colt" at the ready.

Barney found his Winchester, left near Charley's stand; he kept a tight grip on the trailing reins and lead rope to a pack horse's halter. "Charley! I found Dolly," he hissed softly but proudly into the night. "You saw where Acie and I went into the herd." He whispered close to Charley's ear. "She's in a ways, down the slope on your right. You'll see her. Then you get your halter on a stout-looking pack horse and hightail it back up here to me with the two of them, *sabe?*"

Without responding, the boy dissolved into the dark with no sign of Dick Snow. Barney figured the boy knew the importance of stealth as well as speed. He'd lived and learned among the Cheyenne.

Leaving Acie to keep an eye on the outlaw camp with his ready Winchester, Snow threaded his way down to the herd, wondering why he hadn't seen Charley. A night breeze, light as a feather, toyed with his face, bringing the smell of the horses to him. Good, he thought; upwind of Parsons's camp. He was not so worried about smells as about sound.

An edge of irritation gnawed at Snow that Charley hadn't waited, or had lollygagged in starting out; on this sort of raid, keeping in touch with a partner was critical. The boy was nowhere in sight. Snow figured he'd show up soon. Pausing a moment at the fringe of the herd to wait for the boy to appear, Snow wormed his way among the clustered horses, looking for his accustomed mount as well as a stout specimen to hang his halter on.

His hunt was difficult in the dense black of night, and the horses had milled since he'd viewed them before sundown. Still, Snow took time to seek out his own horse.

Those around him remained docile, watching and not grazing. They seemed comfortable with the movement around them. Snow came abruptly alert, a tremble coursing his backbone and an itch setting into his neck hairs. Some distance away, a short man moved in the dark. Snow hadn't seen Charley; there was always a chance that someone from the camp had come up to check on the herd. Snow froze in place, his right hand easing down for his six-gun; it was gone! A panicked instant later, he remembered he'd turned it over to Charley for the time of their horse raid. He was still unarmed in the face of a possible confrontation.

The man was then blocked from Snow's view as both the intruder and the horses moved. Snow's quandary deepened as he recognized his own horse among those grazing near him. He wanted to keep track of her.

Cautiously, measuring his breath, Snow eased through the herd to determine if the figure he saw was friend or foe. If it was a Parsons man, Charley was also in here, moving around in the dark, and was in danger. Snow had to make sure nothing happened to Charley.

A short figure materialized near him, close enough

for Snow's recognition. Charley was closer than Snow had figured the person he'd seen would be; still, he reasoned, it must have been Charley moving randomly through the herd.

"Charley!" Snow hissed. "Over here." The boy moved silent as air to where Snow waited.

"Dick," he whispered. "Barney said Dolly was around here." His voice sounded frustrated, almost tearful. "I can't find her."

Snow assumed it was Charley he'd seen at a distance. All was well, but the boy had given him a real scare. "You were supposed to stay with me," he growled. "I could have shot you a few minutes ago!"

"I'm sorry, Dick." Charley spoke with a catch in his voice. "I wanted to be sure I had time to find Dolly."

Snow regretted his scolding. "We'll get her, boy," he whispered. "You just had me worried. Let me find her."

"I want to."

Snow kept his voice level. "Charley, this is no time to bicker. Yonder's a sturdy-looking one for packing. My saddle horse is right beside 'im. We'll rig 'em, and you take 'em up. I'll find Dolly and get us another pack horse and be right behind you."

For a moment, he considered asking Charley for his six-gun, but he dismissed it. Together they bridled the two nearby horses; Charley, leading them, disappeared against the dense, dark, silent hillside.

Snow continued his scout of the herd, seeking Charley's prized mare. He probed with almost painful caution through the night, deciding that once they'd secured the horses uphill, he'd come back, cut the others' hobbles, and stampede them. While the Parsons crowd scurried around in confusion, the four of them could skedaddle east, bareback, to their cache. Parsons would lose at least a day recovering his mounts.

Disturbed that Charley might not have been the person he'd seen, he kept his footsteps cautious and his movements deliberate. He yearned for the comforting weight of his six-gun rig at his hip.

Dolly, when he found her, had grazed away from the herd, watching as Snow approached. Snow's glance at the camp below assured him that all remained quiet and peaceful.

"Easy, Dolly. Easy, girl," he said soothingly as he walked slowly and calmly toward Charley's horse. "It's all right. Everything's all right." Snow spoke softly, hoping it wouldn't carry past Dolly's ears.

Snow drew close to the hobbled animal, ready with the bridle to slip the bit into her mouth and the headstall in place over Dolly's head and ears. "Good girl," he continued, reaching out for long strokes and pats of Dolly's neck under and around the mane to keep her calm and to bring up the bridle with the other. "Good girl."

Suddenly, he saw Dolly's ears stiffen in a forward thrust and felt her neck and shoulder muscles tense under his hand.

The back of Snow's head erupted in a burst of jolting pain; a flash of crisp, crackling golden light exploded in his brain. An instant later, a darkness deeper than the night plunged like a great wave to drown Snow's awareness, and he felt swept over an edge, falling down and down into an infinite black abyss.

Snow's tumbling seemed not to end; time had no

dimension. He was afloat, languid, serene, and at peace. At length, brightness filtered back, a sensation seeping in behind his clamped eyelids.

The light penetrating his gathering vision was soft and dawn-gray, rousing him to an awareness of the sky being blocked by a ring of evil faces over him. A muttering he finally identified as men's voices rose to a din to drum incessantly against ears that ached along with his head. Men circled him like hovering harpies in Snow's groggy view, their voices piercingly shrill and insistent.

Abruptly he was belly-kicked by a sharp-toed boot, the sudden stab rocketing him with a hoarse grunt to a gut-wrenching reality of pain; a gorge of sour bile choked his throat. Snow, doubled over on his side, spewed it into the dirt, a sharp, foul odor rising to sting his nose.

Darkness still stained the land, but Parsons's gang, to a man, was aroused; the light from a rekindled roaring fire reached orange-red fingers into the night. Men pressed in hungrily, glorying in Snow's misery; they eagerly watched Parsons and Tom as Snow groveled.

"Come on, Mr. Bushranger!" Annoyingly raucous words clanged brutal intrusion; Snow recognized the harsh shriek of Simon Parsons. His offensive tone pulsed stubbornly in Snow's awakening ears. "We'll be needin' some answers here! Tom! You and Wild Card there hoist him up here so I can talk to him." Rude hands and arms propelled Snow to his feet, face to face with a grimy, glowering Simon Parsons.

"You've stole six of our horses, you know that, Ranger?"

Facing Parsons on shaky legs, his head still roaring

with pain and his battered gut puckering with nausea, Snow's voice sounded weak and timid, but his words rang with belligerence. "I was goin' to run off every goddam one of 'em!"

"You were, were ya?" Parsons hauled back a punch and fired it into Snow's midsection to jar the breath out of his lungs. Snow sagged against the rough arms holding him erect. Somebody dashed water in his face, its stinging slap bringing him around. His head came up, shocked by the water's force as well as its coldness.

"Well, ya didn't," Parsons said, completing his thought. "Them other fellers help ya?"

"No," Snow gasped the word, his breathing labored, aware of every item on his inventory of pain. He felt as though he'd fallen a mile and bounced three times. "They're camped a long ways off."

"He's lyin', Simon," a voice near him chimed in. It was a stocky man about Charley's height. "The kid was in the herd with him."

This time Parsons slapped Snow's face hard with the flat of his hand, the harsh sting of it adding to the deep-seated, acute agonies in Snow's head. His arms still restrained by two of Parsons's gang, the rank odor of stale whiskey and unwashed bodies assaulted his nose to further churn a gut already squeezed with pain. Snow brought his head up angrily to confront Parsons again.

"Okay, what'll it be?" Parsons snarled. "Dale says the kid was up there stealin' our hosses. I don't like liars, Bushranger."

"Looks like you're overstocked with liars of your own standin' around here," Snow growled.

The expected violent reaction from Parsons didn't

come. "Tom," he called, "we surely need to teach our backwoodsman here some manners." Snow was abruptly confronted by the well-remembered gang member with the long nose flattened by Elk Leggins, his long hair stringy with filth. Wild Card kept Snow's arms pinioned.

"Well, well," Broken-Nose Tom snarled. "Shoe's on the other foot now, ain't it? Last time I saw you, you said I was ugly as a mud fence."

Snow glared him down. "You only got it half right. I said you were uglier than a mud fence after a hailstorm."

"By God, you do need a lesson taught you!" Broken Nose hauled back a fist to land a haymaker on the tip of Snow's chin, knocking him momentarily senseless again. His head quickly righted itself, and he shook it and blinked against the pain.

Parsons's gang crowded in, relishing Snow's beating; it rose clear in him that it was another reason for Parsons's evil hold on these men. They enjoyed human suffering, and Parsons gave them ample opportunity to witness, participate, and enjoy. Snow's seething mass of agony shouted at him to slump, to quit, but neither Broken Nose nor Parsons would ever know it. Instead, Dick Snow raised his chin and stood tall.

"Okay, Tom," Parsons's voice broke in. "We don't need to kill him just yet. We need some questions answered. All right, Snow. Where you headed with that boy, you and them two cutthroats?"

Snow, still restrained by Wild Card, wearily looked up at Parsons. "I told you. We're taking the boy to Colorado, probably Denver, to see if the law can find any relatives."

"You don't know about the gold?" Parsons grinned eagerly.

"How's gold involved? That what that box of stones was about?" Pain began to ease out of Snow, replaced by his native toughness.

"You're lyin'! You know about the box of ore samples the kid had."

"Then you know more than I do, Parsons. He accused you of stealing his box of stones. What they were, the boy, Yellow Iron, didn't know, and Elk Leggins had no notion, either. Frankly, I wish to hell I knew."

"That the Big Chief's name? We was never properly introduced."

"I can't imagine why," Snow quipped.

Parsons turned snarly again. "Mister, your time's about up. We'll punch the stuffin' out of you till you own up to where the gold is. The sooner you tell us, the sooner life'll become a whole lot easier. So, was I you, I wouldn't make so free with my lip. Except for answers."

Snow's mind, clearing from the pain of his pummeling, raced. He was in what the military called an untenable position. And in this case he had no avenue of retreat. He could only guess where Charley and the others were. Though Barney and Acie had seen a broad slice of life, he doubted either had confronted a problem with the thorns of this one. They weren't brawlers or Indian fighters. Both had survived the war and probably came out of it hoping never to see blood spilled again, and certainly not to spill it themselves. His mind ached; he was on his own in dealing with this one.

He'd offer bits of the truth, avoiding the locket inscription—which he was sure Parsons was not aware of.

"I don't know anything about gold. Elk Leggins only knew that Charley—yes, that was his name—had a box of stones he hung onto after his folks died of the cholera. The whole westbound wagon train was wiped out but Charley. Elk Leggins, my Cheyenne friend, found him and kept him for five years. That's where your party and mine came into the picture." Snow hoped that much explanation would satisfy Parsons's uncommon need for a clear track to Spindrift Ridge. Maybe now they'd turn him loose.

"What about the letter?" Parsons rammed his face close to Snow's, while Broken-Nose Tom stepped aside; Snow recoiled from the stench of Parsons's breath.

"Letter? We rode in there two days after you left. Elk Leggins was disturbed about this strange box of stones being gone; it disappeared when you did. I didn't know what to make of that, but he asked me to take the boy and see if I could find his people."

Snow sagged, limp and drained, his belly cramped, his head aching. More than two demanding days afoot on the trail with scant rest, then being knocked cold and pummeled, had taken a toll. One part of his mind dreamed of a mess of Acie's warm vittles and a soft, snug buffalo-robe burrow. But it was not to be.

"You're very convincing, Bushranger," Parsons snarled, again shoving his evil face close to Snow's. "But sad to say, there's more here than meets the eye. You ain't telling us everything."

"But I am," Snow said tiredly.

"You forget about Dave Deweese. I'm sure that slick hombre is workin' for you."

"Did you see him in my party when we met on the trail three or four days ago?" Snow felt he was bargaining for his life, and physically and emotionally he wasn't up to the challenge.

"That slimy bastard could've been scoutin' in the hills."

"Not so," Snow argued. "He only came to our camp after he left you. Gave us some cock-and-bull story about wanting to join us against you. I guess he thought if he gained our confidence, we'd tell him something he needed to know. But believe me, we're in the dark about all this. And I don't know anything about any letter."

"I ain't satisfied with all this, Simon," Broken Nose put in. "Let me and Wild Card persuade him to own up." The restraining holds on Snow's arms tightened.

"Not just yet, Tom," Parsons said, waving Broken Nose aside. "Mr. Snow's letting out a little of his story at a time."

"I've told you everything I know." Snow realized his tone was almost pleading. In his misery, it was the only way he knew to handle his dilemma. "Deweese hoodwinked us like he must've done to you. We fed him and treated him right. He thanked us by rustling our horses when our backs were turned and leaving us afoot. We've walked day and night since, trying to catch up with him. When we came across your camp and scouted your herd, we figured that Deweese had turned loose our remuda and that you, coming up behind him, rounded them up. So we slipped in to get our mounts back. That's all we had in mind."

Parsons's eyes squinted in suspicion. "Deweese didn't say nothin' about the letter?"

Snow's spirit grated with Parsons's ceaseless inquisition. He wrestled with urges to slump at Parsons's feet and be done with it; Charley's face intruded on his thoughts, and he remembered his pledge to Elk Leggins. He sensed a curious new surge of strength. "One more time," he repeated. "Nobody knows anything about a letter. I got nothing about it from Elk Leggins or Charley. Hell, they can't even read! And certainly nothing from Deweese. I only started out doing an old friend a favor in trying to find the relatives of the boy."

Parsons's voice rose shrill and insistent. "Goddammit! Deweese told you about the letter, and I know it! You're holdin' out on us, Snow!" He stepped aside. "Tom, I think I've wrung out of this jasper about everything that he's going to own up to without he's persuaded a bit more. If we're gonna find our gold in Coloradah, old Snow's gonna have to cough up more than he's told us. Need I say more?"

Dawn had grown to the full daylight that began to flood Parsons's camp, blunting only slightly his punishing predawn grilling by Simon Parsons.

"Sounds like Deweese is already ahead of us, Si," Broken Nose said, changing his tune. "We got as much out of this gent as we'll ever get. Put him away for good, I say, and get cracking on the trail, and catch up with Deweese and give him the same. Then we got us a clear track to take whatever time it takes to find out where that ore came from. Whatta you think, Wild Card?"

The skinny Wild Card tossed his head in assent.

Parsons rolled it around in his mind for a long moment. "Okay, Tom. You and Wild Card and the rest of you take him out there yonder to do it. Don't make no messes in camp. I'm goin' back to bed. Wake me up when you fellers get rigged to ride." Simon Parsons spun around and stormed away into the bright morning light.

"Come on, Bushranger," Broken-Nose Tom grunted, rudely yanking Snow away from the camp. "We got work to do back yonder."

"His final walk," Wild Card intoned unctuously.

Snow's mind raced. This was the end. Parsons was done with him, and now he'd get a bullet in the head like a crippled horse. A foolish thought prodded him to make a break for it, but he gave it up. At least running from them, he'd die like a man. To grovel and plead on his knees in the dirt before this gang of low-lifes and take a deliberate bullet between the eyes had never been his idea of a proper death. He'd pondered it often. Snow gathered himself with a deep breath. He vowed to make a break for it the moment they were a few steps out of camp.

In the instant it took Broken-Nose to yank at him and begin dragging him away into the prairie, time, for some wild reason, also took leave of reality as a web of delayed reaction centered in Snow's dulled senses. A resounding thump registered in his surprised ears as a tiny hole opened at the inner tip of Broken-Nose Tom's left brow, not quite dead-center between the eyes. Seeking the cause, Snow spied a momentary puff of white muzzle blast clinging briefly to a juniper high on a solitary hill behind him. The rifle's cracking report reached his ears.

Broken-Nose Tom was pitched away, his head snapping back with an audible crack. The instant of death brought a staggering, whirling dance of resistance before he crumpled in a writhing, convulsive heap.

Around the flailing, falling body, Parsons's men dived to prone positions in the dirt, squirming into the ground in panic. A dazed Snow stayed on his feet, rocking in bewilderment, like one upright lonesome stalk in a chopped cornfield.

"All right, you bastards!" The familiar voice of Barney Wisner split the taut silence from high on the hill, swelling Snow's breath-starved chest with a thrill of relief. "There's Winchesters aimed at you from every direction! So don't move. Snow, if you can make it, drag your miserable self up here!"

"Dick! I got Dolly!" Charley's boyish call rolled down to him. "Acie's ready to drive off their horses the minute you're safe."

Snow's legs trembled with relief and dragged with residual fatigue as he started toward the hill to Barney and Charley.

As he worked his way through the inert outlaws, Snow passed the twisted body of Broken-Nose Tom among his surviving but terrified companions, sprawled haphazardly like the aftermath of a massacre. Snow's surroundings heightened the illusion. A deathly stillness bore down along with a malevolent sun on the barren emptiness of the endless land as a soft, solemn ground wind picked up, ruffling the grass and the hair of the prone, panicked outlaws.

Snow paused beside Broken-Nose Tom. "Sorry it had to be this way, amigo," he said softly to the death-warped corpse. "You asked for it."

Snow was alerted to sudden movement. He turned

his head to see Parsons raise up on his knees from a similar prone position. "I'll get you for this, Snow," the outlaw leader promised with a snarl, right hand poised to go for his holstered six-gun. Parsons dropped suddenly as a bullet scattered shards of dirt beside him, and Snow heard Sam Colt's crisp bark from the hill.

Snow walked out of Parsons's camp erect with his pride; Charley was an apt pupil. Snow knew for certain that the boy had no notion of killing Parsons when he drew a bead on him. At that range, a six-gun was unpredictable except in the hands of a very adept gun handler.

"Fine shootin', Charley!" Snow yelled loudly, knowing Parsons and his gang could hear. "You could've killed him easy as not!" Damn me, Snow thought. The boy said he could handle a six-gun; I should've listened.

When their cache was opened two days later, and their gear laid out and sorted for repacking, Barney set aside a pair of his Levi's and a blue cotton shirt. Before they loaded the panniers for the pack saddles, Barney and Dick sought out Charley, carrying the clothes.

"Barney and I've been thinking," Dick said. "We've got nothing against Indian buckskins. But if everything works out right, we'll be getting to Dalton before too many weeks. We'd like you to try white man's duds. Want to make the right impression when we meet your aunt."

"It'd be all right," Charley said. "But they're Barney's. They'd never fit."

Barney spoke up. "We thought of that. We'll shorten the pant legs. I can take a tuck in the waist. I've got a 'housewife' in my gear, my little sewing kit with needles and thread and spare buttons and such. I can make 'em look pretty good on Charley. Might have to shorten the shirtsleeves, and I might have to figure some sort of cuff on the sleeves. Collar's a bit on the ample side, but you could leave it open most times anyway. You're filling out through the chest, so we think this riggin' ought to suit you pretty well.''

''Probably help you look more grown up,'' Snow added.

''Then what are you waitin' for?'' A smile lit Charley's face.

## ❧ 11 ❧

The westering sun had long since dropped behind the tall, sprawling Spindrift Ridge, the last vestiges of daylight leaking out to make way for a lingering twilight. Soft yellow lights blinked on in the cabins, the two saloons and a hotel, as well as the Ritz-Dalton, the town's only beanery, open for breakfast, dinner, and supper for prospectors and townspeople alike.

Lew Bricker, owner of the more prosperous of Dalton's saloons and the town's only sporting palace, the Pick and Poke, was among the Ritz's last customers of the night.

Bricker, polishing off his late supper, considered himself a big frog in a small pond—Dalton—sprawled at the mouth of Dalton Gulch, a deep and narrow pine-cloaked valley about fourteen miles long on the eastern slope of Spindrift Ridge. Bricker's fellow diners were mainly prospectors who usually cooked in their cabins—a motley assortment of squat log structures whose amenities depended on the prosperity of their inhabitants. Enough of the men, tiring of their own rude home-cooked fare or when they had sufficient gold dust, often dined at the Ritz, keeping the place busy seven days a week.

While the Ritz-Dalton's only waitress busied herself cleaning the tables, Bricker could hear Hiram, the beanery's black cook, swamper, and dishwasher, or pearl diver as he called himself, bustling around in the kitchen with his chores of wrapping up the day's work.

Bricker, medium-sized and stocky, with a perennial blush from sampling too much of his own wares at the Pick and Poke, eased up from his accustomed place at the small table near the window. He'd left six bits to cover his meal of roast beef, mashed potatoes and gravy heaped over sourdough bread slices, and cooked vegetables.

He ambled over to where the slim, dark-haired, still-attractive waitress mopped the tabletops with a damp rag and straightened chairs properly under the tables. His fingers identified and fished out a two-bit piece from his pocket. As he walked to the woman, he flipped the coin to land on the tabletop, spin several times, and roll flat.

Her eyes met his. They were tired, sad eyes—Bricker had always been fascinated with Nell Joiner's eyes—but the beauty that lingered in them attracted Bricker to her. Lew Bricker confessed to himself that he was bad at remembering when events took place. About the best he could recall was that Nell and her husband had showed up in Dalton maybe five or six years back. Maybe it was seven; no matter, Bricker thought.

Sam Joiner—or was his name Seth, Bricker wondered—was a fair-to-middling prospector, but a lousy woodsman. Soon after the Joiners came to Dalton, Seth had failed to come back from a prospecting trip on Spindrift Ridge. Nell had hung on in town, hoping Seth would return or that she'd get some word about his mysterious disappearance. Without funds to return to her home in Ohio, Bricker knew, Nell had taken the waitress job at the Ritz.

The beauty Bricker had seen in Nell in her early days in the Gulch had begun to fade. He was persuaded that the hard work and long hours at the Ritz were responsible. Even at her worst, Nell Joiner had an attractiveness and an endearing quality that put her head and shoulders above the tarts who occupied the cribs upstairs in his Pick and Poke saloon. Several times Nell had spurned his offers to cut her work hours and at least double her wages by joining his "harem," as he called it.

"Always a pleasure to wait on you, Mr. Bricker." Nell's voice carried the sweetness of a pleasant afternoon and the sincerity of a rose. She scooped up the quarter and dropped it in her apron pocket.

"I still hope you're considering my offer, Nell," he said. "Four or five years on this job is enough. You deserve better. I still stand behind my promises. It's a rare opportunity."

Nell smiled sweetly, disarming him. "I still don't think that's what I want to do, Mr. Bricker."

"How many times have I asked you to call me Lew? We've been friends too long. The formality is unnecessary."

Nell smiled again, tactfully ignoring his appeal for a closer friendship.

"You'd be treated proper," he went on. "Nell, I've always assured you of that. Any of those jaspers get to roughhousing you, they'll answer to me. I don't stand for any nonsense in my place."

"Once more, Mr. Bricker, I appreciate your concern. But I have no notion of entering that kind of life."

"If you still hold thoughts of going back to Ohio, I could almost guarantee you'd have enough money in a year."

A faraway look came in Nell's eyes. "I'll get back home someday."

"You may be an old woman before you do," Bricker said as he spun on his heel and headed for the door. "If you change your mind, my offer stands. At least for a while yet."

Silence descended on the restaurant's dining room with the door closing behind Lew Bricker.

Nell glanced around the room that had become as familiar as her quarters in the old cabin she'd shared with Seth. Her mind on her talk with Lew Bricker, Nell went through the paces of cleaning and wiping the tables with the rote motions of a dancing bear. Her mind was miles and years away.

Hiram stepped out of the kitchen, his white eyeballs large with deep-brown pupils against his mahogany-colored face. His features gleamed with the sweat of warm kitchen work.

"Mistah Bricker leave?" he asked in a deep bass voice.

"Just left," Nell said, continuing her work. "Probably won't be anybody else tonight, Hiram."

The soft-ticking pendulum clock on the wall read seven, well past any traditional dinner hour in Dalton. Any miners out and about would spend the rest of the evening in the Pick and Poke or at Taylor and Riley's saloon at the other end of the main street. Unlike Bricker's, their establishment had no given name; it was known in Dalton Gulch simply as Taylor and Riley's

Ambrose Taylor and Patrick Riley, Dalton's jeweler and photographer, respectively, had their professional shops together by day and ran the saloon at night, with only a bartender running things during the day. Nights at Taylor and Riley's were highlighted by an hour-long program, often of piano music, varied with occasional dance revues by traveling troupes, orations, recitations, or comic monologues, as well as short dramas, again involving touring thespians when they were in town.

Lew Bricker, on the other hand, offered the more earthy pleasures, with girls circulating among the tables or along the bar to heighten a man's enjoyment of his evening of drinking or cards. Even greater pleasures were in store for those interested in sampling the wares available for a price in the second-floor cribs of the Pick and Poke.

Bricker did well enough, but Taylor and Riley, through their combined jeweler and photographer trades, as well as being saloon keepers and entertainment impresarios, were among the wealthiest men in Dalton.

Her mind on things more significant than clearing and wiping tables, Nell remembered the tiny portrait Seth had taken of her soon after they arrived in Dalton. Riley, also something of an artist, had softly tinted the portrait before installing it in a handsome gold oval locket created by his partner, Ambrose Taylor.

With great delight, she and Seth had sent it home to her sister Mary for her twenty-fourth birthday, the same year little Charley was six. Nell sat at one of the tables, looking wistfully out the window at the gathering dusk, remembering better, happier times when the four of them—she and Seth and Frank and Mary—were together at home in Ohio.

"The dishes is 'most done, Miss Nell," Hiram said, breaking into her brief reverie. "Food's put away, and I'll get busy shortly moppin' down the place out here. All tidy for in the mornin'."

"I'll put the receipts in Mr. Green's safe as soon as I'm finished out here, Hiram. You can close up after you've swamped out."

"Yes, ma'am," Hiram agreed, turning back to the kitchen.

Six years; six long, hard years, Nell thought sadly, as she closed the day's income in the safe in the office of the owner, Alonzo "Lonnie" Green. Green and his wife, Mariposa, opened the restaurant each morning for breakfast at five o'clock. Nell and Hiram came in at ten to help with the noon dinner meal. The Greens left at one, and Nell and Hiram ran the rest of the day and evening.

Six years. Nell's mind flip-flopped again to the past. Six years and not a sign of Seth, a grave concern only intensified by the mysterious disappearance of her sister Mary, Mary's husband Frank, and their little son Charley.

Nell slammed Mr. Green's safe door shut on the collection of bills and coins taken in during the day and spun the combination dial. She retrieved her warm coat from the hall tree behind the office door and went out into the night, bound for her cabin at the end of town, uphill all the way and closest to the distant but imposing Spindrift Ridge, rising majestically at the head of Dalton Gulch.

The darkness was cool with approaching fall; Nell was glad she had brought her warm coat in the morning. She trudged the uphill slope, watching the dark pines towering over the town grow even darker.

She had run the thoughts over and over in her head for more years than she cared to remember until their very presence or appearance in her mind brought a suffocating kind of ache. There were no answers. Seth, dear lighthearted, well-intentioned, devoted Seth, gone so mysteriously on his mission to stake out his rich claim on Spindrift Ridge. She was sure he hadn't been murdered for his claim; no unusually rich strikes had been reported in the area Seth had worked. Nell still carried basic landmarks to the location in her head. Six years, she mused sadly, as the steep grade taxed her already tired legs, was a long time to grieve.

No one in town could be trusted with her secret. Word of it—if Seth's hunch was correct, and she was sure it was—would touch off a stampede into that region of the ridge. She was also certain that her interests would be jeopardized, if not lost altogether. Secrecy, so far, had been her only ally.

Besides, she'd thought a thousand times, she had no right to disclose the location of Seth's find. In her mind, the claim belonged to Frank Rogers, her sister's husband, who had put up the lion's share to finance their trip to the Colorado diggings in the first place.

At last she was home. While a dim twilight lingered on the land, the inside of her rectangular log cabin was dark as a tomb. Finding a match, Nell lit her two coal-oil lamps, with their simple glass reservoirs on tall, gleaming glass stands. She noted that the fragile chimneys were smudged and lightly discolored with smoke; they'd need to be washed in the morning. With quick work and a single lucifer match, she lit not only her two lamps but the fire in the hearth from kindling laid in the fireplace earlier.

Her fire-starting sticks, short and narrow lengths, rested in a can of coal oil close at hand, but a safe distance from the hearth—a trick she had learned from the always-imaginative Seth Joiner. Saturated with coal oil, they took flame quickly and ignited other sticks and kindling. In short order, the cabin was lighted warmly as a merry blaze danced in the hearth, and its comfort seeped into the room.

The fire's growing flicker filled the ample fireplace to illuminate the blacksmith-forged andirons and the pivoting crane from which Nell dangled her cooking pots on hooks of varying lengths to control the cooking heat. The firelight and the lamps' soft glow accented the homey touches she'd tried to bring to her shanty, the only home she had left. The room quickly filled with the fire's crackling warmth and cheerful, soft lamplight.

Time and again in this setting she remembered her last days with Seth—gay, happy, euphoric times when Seth's enthusiasm was unbounded as he declared that they'd name his mine for their nephew, Frank and Mary's son Charley. "The Little Charley Mine!" Seth had declared lustily, swinging her in a carefree dance. That night, he'd sat down with Nell for a careful, step-by-step recitation of the landmarks and location of his find high on Spindrift Ridge. Vividly, Nell remembered each clue—every key feature that for five years she had kept locked in her heart in the hope that somehow Frank and Mary would reach her.

The cabin became warm enough now that Nell no longer needed her coat. Hanging it on a peg on the back of the door, she sat down on the contoured plank seat of the balloon-back rocker—Seth's father's favorite chair—that they'd managed to haul all the way from Ohio in the wagon.

The old chair was one of Nell's last tangible links with home. In this chair she had often rocked to sleep her tiny nephew, the perfect and bright-eyed infant Charley. The little fellow could not have been more precious to her if he had been her own.

Where, Nell thought, rocking softly and watching her merry fire, was Charley now? Probably in some rude grave alongside the trail from Ohio; but, she hoped, near his parents, also probably dead. The overland trails claimed their tax in human life. After six years, the answers were obvious; she was alone.

Hearing the lulling whispers of the fire's fingers of flame and the occasional snap of sparks as she watched the tapered yellow darts lick and dance around the logs, Nell remembered those exciting evenings with the Rogerses. She and Mary would talk of baby things and homey things, and of family and their early lives together. At the other end of the sitting room of the old Joiner family farmhouse in Monroe County, Seth and his good friend and brother-in-law, Frank Rogers, huddled as they talked and pored over maps and notes, their masculine voices drumming softly but going a mile a minute.

At first, the talk of their joint venture revolved around Frank and Seth making the prospecting trip to

Colorado. When both Nell and Mary objected to such a long separation from their husbands, it was ultimately determined that Nell and Seth would go—with Frank and Mary's blessing and financial backing.

The first tangible evidence of success in their grand scheme came with the dozen or so chunks of tawny granite and snow-white quartz liberally laced with gold that Seth brought back from one of his many prospecting jaunts. In the flickering firelight of her tiny cabin more than six years later, Nell remembered it all.

Calamity followed in the wake of those first jubilant hours after Seth returned with ore from the future "Little Charley Mine." He went back to the mountains to stake his claim for registration. Anxious days, and then weeks, passed with no return of her husband and no word. Beside herself with concern, Nell cautiously asked other Dalton prospectors to be on the lookout for him or a sign of him.

In final desperation, she turned to the only persons she knew could help—and whose financial interest in the venture she was bound to protect—Frank and Mary Rogers.

Fearful lest prying eyes uncover her secret, Nell wrote a cryptic letter to the Rogerses and sent Seth's ore samples secure in her dead mother's little rosewood jewelry chest. As an added precaution, she marked "Birthday Present" on the brown wrapping paper.

Weeks later, Nell rejoiced with a letter from Mary that their preparations were under way to come west by wagon. Her heart, heavy with the loss of Seth, beat faster at the anticipated reunion with her sister and husband and Charley, now a boy of seven, nearly eight.

More months passed without word, as Nell visualized Frank and Mary plodding out the endless miles across a nearly trackless prairie, a spirit-draining, monotonous infinity she knew only too well. That summer was long as she awaited the day of their arrival. The rains and chilly winds of autumn soon drenched and whipped the tall, dark pines towering over the buildings of Dalton as they rose uphill into Dalton Gulch, and Nell was herself drenched and buffeted with new despair and apprehension.

She consoled herself that their progress had been slower than expected and interrupted by the onset of winter. She reassured herself that they had wintered over, snug and secure in some fort along the Overland Trail, perhaps at Fort Laramie or at Fort Bridger, both places she and Seth had seen on their arduous trek west.

Surely, she rationalized, the brightness and freshness of spring would bring the Rogers wagon up the long, sloping main street of Dalton as, with whoops and hugs of rejoicing, her empty heart and flagging spirits would be renewed.

When another summer was nearly over with no sign of her family, Nell realized the worst, her spirits drooping to the lowest ebb she could ever remember. Without funds to return to Ohio—and with no close family left there anyway—she was stuck in Dalton with clues to a rich gold claim that someone else would find someday. Nell found herself spending her days fighting to retain her usually open, optimistic nature against wave after wave of despondency that threatened to engulf and destroy her.

Aside from the tarts who frequented Lew Bricker's establishment, Dalton had few women—six or eight wives of miners who lived in better cabins downhill and stayed aloof from what they considered the depraved behavior of the uphill camp and its wicked saloons and dens of iniquity. These married women, Nell had learned through bitter experience, were clannish and cloistered themselves in their own worlds of domestic toil, children, and the marriage bed. Among that group, as well as with the loose women who plied their trade at the Pick and Poke, Nell was an outcast. She found herself forced into an unnatural and unwanted seclusion.

As regularly as they appeared in town, Nell searched the faces of newcomers, hoping in vain for someone she could trust. The faces she had seen reflected a singleness of purpose—that of determined greed and lust for the gold.

Nell pondered these things wistfully as she rocked and absorbed the simple warmth of her primitive home.

# ❧ 12 ❧

Lew Bricker sat alone in the Pick and Poke sampling the quality of his wares on a quiet, sunny afternoon when most of his regular patrons were up Dalton Gulch seeking the elusive dust of their dreams.

Bricker's wandering mind came alert when a well-dressed stranger, in black from his hat to his boots, rode up to the hitch rail out front, got down, tied up, lithely jumped the one tall step to the boardwalk, and strode boldly through the batwing doors.

The black-suited jasper, Bricker observed, was lean but well-built, with handsomely carved features. The stranger only glanced at Bricker as he made his way to the bar.

Bricker appraised the man as his sole customer of the afternoon. He ordered a shot, tossed it off, and called for a second to sip. His black suit could use an ironing, Bricker mused, as though it had been wrapped inside a bedroll on a ride over the plains; nothing unusual in that, Bricker noted.

The newcomer asked a question of the bartender so

softly that Bricker couldn't overhear. Cecil, the barkeep, pointed at Bricker seated across the room and
responded, "Over there."

The man wound his way through the vacant poker
tables to one nearly at the room's center, where Bricker
sat alone with his drink and half-filled bottle.

He was relatively young, Bricker observed, with a
pleasant, likable face. Bricker, who prided himself on
being a good judge of character on first impression,
figured the man was trustworthy enough; he had none
of the evil squint Bricker associated with many of the
hardcases he'd encountered in nearly ten years of
saloonkeeping in Dalton Gulch.

"The bartender tells me you're the boss man." His
pleasant voice reassured Bricker of the man's amiable,
honest disposition.

"About right," he responded. "Grab a chair and
park. What can I do for you?"

"The name's Deweese. Dave Deweese." He shoved
out his hand, smiling.

"Lew Bricker," the saloonkeeper replied, feeling a
firm and warm handshake; Bricker knew he could always trust a man with a sincere grip. Deweese sat down
across from him. "Your drink's getting low," Bricker
said. "Next one's on the house." His bar glasses held
the equivalent of a double-header, and he filled Deweese's glass without stinting.

"Much obliged," Deweese said, tipping back his
head, placing the glass rim against his lower teeth, and
deftly tossing down the contents. His voice turned
hoarse from the whiskey's burn.

"Been three weeks on the road since the last town.
I'll tell you, Mr. Bricker, prime goods such as you

dispense over your bar really hit the spot. You keep a proper saloon, that's easy to see.''

Bricker liked to think he did, too, and it was always pleasant to have his intentions confirmed. He'd already begun to like this Deweese.

"What town might that be?"

"Golconda. Due east. Across the line in Kansas."

"I've heard of the place. Never been there."

"Gambling's my game, Mr. Bricker. I had a good setup in Golconda. I did until the saloonkeeper there wanted me to mark the aces and face cards and deal off the bottom of the deck to up his share of the take. I rode out the next day. I don't hold with anything this side of dealing them all clean and off the top."

"Looks like you and I've ridden some of the same trails, Dave. The last man I had pulled his freight a couple of weeks ago, too, but for a totally different reason. Caught him notching his aces. That's not good for business. I'm not above making money the easiest way I can, but I don't favor cutting my own throat to do it.''

"Skill beats dishonesty any day, Mr. Bricker. I know my trade."

"Without a card man, I don't make much off the tables, apart from the drinks. I keep a few floozies as well, but they're a pain in the ass. My friend, whiskey and whores ain't all they're cracked up to be."

"I heard that before, too," Deweese grinned, and it was a good smile and a friendly one, Bricker thought.

"Taylor and Riley, my only competition—down the street—are always trying to undercut me. Them two artistes don't keep girls. They got a piano man and put on a show about nine o'clock nearly every night. This place clears out and is quiet as a church till about ten. Then they'll flock back in here, have one or two more, and maybe take a girl for a flop upstairs. So I suppose it averages out.''

"I can improve your business, Mr. Bricker. I run a clean game but make sure that the right people don't often leave the table unhappy. Nobody's ever left my game completely cleaned out. Friends are what make a good card man, Mr. Bricker, not enemies.''

"And keep a businessman competitive. I like your style, Deweese. Business suffered after they found that tinhorn working here in my place. You can start work tonight, but be sure you lose a few fat pots. I want those loafers from up on Spendthrift Ridge to get the idea that Lew Bricker's new card man really runs a heads-up game.''

Deweese grinned at Bricker's nickname for the ridge. "That's just shrewd business sense. You can trust me to treat 'em right, Lew.''

"Find you a room, probably at the Gulch House for now. I'd also get that suit ironed—''

"I'd planned on that,'' Deweese interrupted.

"You can probably find an empty cabin after a while and fix your own grub. Till then, you'll probably have to take your meals at the Ritz-Dalton across the way.''

"I take it that's the best chuck in town.''

"That's all there is. But it's good food. You either eat there, cook in your quarters, or go hungry. And while we're about getting you settled, you'd better know that I'll not tolerate your cozyin' up to any of the girls here for a free one once in a while. From the looks of you, they're likely to offer it. Dip it in any of 'em and you pay just like the rest. In other words, keep your nose clean.''

"Depend on it, Mr. Bricker." Deweese picked up the bottle. "My turn to buy you one." He filled up their glasses.

"Don't mind if I do," Bricker said, sipping this one. Deweese followed suit. He caught Bricker studying him.

"You know, Dave," the saloonkeeper started, "I'm gettin' a kind of notion. You're a bit of a man of the world . . .''

"I suppose I've seen my share of it."

"Some of the miners are married, with wives at home, and if you know what's good for you in this town, you don't go sniffing around after them, either. When you see the plugs I got working for me here, you might just up and swear off, too."

Deweese grinned. "As I told you, Lew, I've been around and seen my share."

"There's one in this town, though, that's fair game."

Deweese's sudden and uncommon interest puzzled Bricker, but he let it pass; after all, he thought, the lad's been away from a town for three weeks. Deweese edged his chair closer to Bricker and sat forward in it, his drink glass clutched in his hands and forgotten for the moment.

"You must have a reason for telling me this."

Bricker continued. "She's kind of, you might say, a widow of the mining camps. Her man disappeared on a prospecting trip here some years back. Life hasn't been exactly easy for her. Why she's stayed is beyond me. She could've gone back home that first year. But she hung on, like she was waitin' for somebody."

"Hmmm," Deweese murmured in rapt interest.

"Under the strain, she looks a little trailworn these days . . ."

"But still turns a man's head, I take it?" His eyes sparkled.

"And then some."

"So what's your notion? Care for another drink?"

"House buys," Bricker said, hoisting the bottle and pouring. "She's on the verge of getting long in the tooth, and the years of late haven't treated her all that kindly. That aside, if I could get that filly in my stable, I believe I could cut my losses between nine and ten every evening to Taylor and Riley's. I'd show them damned artistes and their damned honky-tonk freak shows!"

For once Deweese let his unique perception about people show. "You haven't been able to lure her in, so you'd like me to romance her into your employ?" Deweese's open, friendly face was smeared with a conspiratorial leer.

Bricker matched him leer for leer. "And have some fun in the bargain. I'll even hike your table percentages, Deweese."

"Sounds like the grazin'd be pretty rich in these pastures," Deweese said. "When do I start?"

"Meet me at the Ritz for supper at six. She hustles the grub over there."

Deweese—trying hard to contain his delight—sensed he had his answer before he asked Bricker a final question. "What, Mr. Bricker, is the lady's name?" His heart leapt with the saloonkeeper's confirming response.

"Nell," Bricker responded. "Nell Joiner."

\* \* \*

From across the dining room, Nell felt herself being warmed, if not with a few burning sensations, as the eyes of the Dalton newcomer followed her. As she bustled about the dining room, waiting on tables, she felt his eyes on her every move; when she caught his glance, she read a message of urgency in his expression.

He had taken supper with Lew Bricker, and she sensed a nervousness or apprehension as the stranger studied her from every angle. She was aware of the same good-looking man dressed in black at dinnertime the next noon. This time he came to the Ritz-Dalton alone.

She avoided going to his table to ask his pleasure from the noon bill of fare until the last minute. Approaching him, she tried to control her nervousness.

"Have you made a choice, sir?" she asked.

The eyes that looked up into hers were large and bright, honest and sincere. "Chili and corn bread," he replied with directness. "And a cup of your excellent coffee."

"Thank you," Nell said, turning quickly and heading for the kitchen to give Hiram the order. Inside the kitchen, she slumped against the wall for a moment to regain her composure.

"You okay, Miss Nell?" Hiram called from beside the stovetop, where he ladled out a good-sized bowlful of chili.

"I'll be all right," she murmured. "Thank you, Hiram. Just a bit tired this morning." As the only unmarried woman of virtue in town, she had been ogled and leered at plenty and had learned to courteously fend off annoying propositions and even offers of money for her favors.

This man's behavior, somehow, was different; in a way the mysterious intensity of his eyes were more frightening than the annoying advances of other men. Their intentions were printed plainly on their faces and in their eyes; Nell knew she could turn sweet and polite but with a firm "no" that usually ended it right there. She pooh-poohed woman's legendary intuition, but still, some small, quiet voice inside her told her that this man out there waiting for his chili and corn bread could very well represent a dramatic new chapter in her life. It was nonsense, she insisted to herself in a rational moment. Still, even though the walls separated her from him, the burning of his stare reached her. Nell trembled.

Reluctantly, she scooped up the chili bowl and corn bread plate Hiram had placed on the counter. She juggled them expertly with one hand and arm as with her other hand she caught hold of the handle of the full coffee cup, pushing away the swinging door into the dining room with a crooked elbow. Nell drew a deep breath in anticipation and for strength, mentally phrasing a few supplicating words to her Maker for guidance.

Also praying that her shaking wouldn't make her drop her load of food, Nell set the meal down in front of him and tried to smile sweetly. "I hope you enjoy your dinner, sir," she said, and she started to turn away but was stopped by his quiet voice. "Nell?"

She turned back, eyes wide. "You know me?"

"Lew Bricker pointed you out. We need to talk. Not here."

"That's—uh—quite impossible, sir."

"You don't understand, Nell. I'm from back home. Ohio. I came to tell you about Frank and Mary and Little Charley."

The light from the front windows of the Ritz swirled in Nell's vision, and she had the sensation of the room and the floor dipping and swaying around her to the point that she nearly lost her balance. She gripped two chair backs for support and drew herself up, hoping her momentary loss of composure hadn't been too evident. At least, she told herself, she hadn't shrieked or even gasped. Her wits collected, she leaned close to the stranger. "Are they all right?"

The man's face registered an openness and a compassion as he looked up at her. "This isn't the place to talk, Nell. I've so much to tell you. In private. Neither of us needs prying eyes nor wagging tongues."

Nell couldn't wait. She was prompted to walk out of the Ritz then and there to learn what word the stranger had of her family. She looked around, her mind muddled, aware of an inability to focus her thoughts. Noontime diners watched her expectantly, waiting to give their meal orders or to pay for their meals. Her confused thoughts at least centered on the reality that she must not jeopardize her job with irrational behavior.

"I . . . I can't take the time now, Mr. . . ."

"Deweese. Dave Deweese."

Coming out of the sudden shock of the stranger's revelation, Nell's thoughts became more directed. Common sense told her that if this Deweese knew anything about the Rogers family, he likely knew of the gold as well. She resolved to wait until they could speak in total privacy and confidence, as he had suggested.

"I'll be finished here soon after seven. Can we meet then?"

Deweese seemed hesitant. "I've had to take work with Mr. Bricker—I believe you know him—dealing cards at his establishment. I think he'll be agreeable if I'm not on duty tonight. I'll call here for you at seven."

Only mildly astonished by Deweese's line of work, Nell still tried to muster a smile. Deweese also probably hadn't expected to find her slinging hash. "I suppose it's not altogether improper for us to talk at my home. People here look on things differently than we did at home."

Deweese gave her a smile, and Nell was encouraged by its sincerity. "How true that is," he said. "I'll escort you home."

"I'm sorry, Mr. Deweese. I must get back to my customers."

"I'll come by for a late supper a little before seven," he promised, dropping some coins on the table for his dinner meal; she noted that he also left some extra money.

"That's unnecessary, Mr. Deweese," she said as he got up to leave.

"That's why it's my pleasure, Mrs. Joiner," he said.

In her confusion and concentration of their brief chat, Nell had failed to note that Lew Bricker had entered and taken his accustomed table near the front window. He smiled at them approvingly.

As Nell remembered Bricker's displeasure over her repeated rejection of his offers of sinful employment, the saloonkeeper's expression added to her already mounting confusion over all these sudden turns of events. Still, the overriding and paramount concern was that Dave Deweese had news about Frank and Mary.

Ignoring the customers, some of whom were sending her messages of impatience with their eyes and their expressions, Nell followed Deweese out the door of the Ritz-Dalton. She was compelled.

"I have to know, Mr. Deweese," she called softly, and he turned back toward her. "Mr. and Mrs. Rogers. Frank and Mary. What happened to them?"

"It's best if I wait and tell you tonight."

"Please, Mr. Deweese. Are they all right?"

A long moment of silence passed between them as they faced each other in the midday sunlight of Dalton's main street. He spoke with reluctance. "Ah ... if you must know now, I'm afraid I'm the bearer of sad tidings. They met with misfortune. Some years ago." Deweese turned to leave again.

Again, she called after him. "Little Charley? Their son?"

When Deweese turned back to her, his face was contorted with grief, his own tears obviously near the surface.

"All of them. Cholera. On the trail. Nearly six years ago."

Her shoulders drooping and her heart heavy, Nell went back inside. Her worst fears had been realized.

# ❊ 13 ❊

**N**ell stared wistfully from her straight chair into what should have been a cheery fire on her hearth. Just now, she found no comfort in the dancing spears of flame. Dave Deweese, handsome in his black suit, rocked slowly and thoughtfully in the cabin's high- and round-backed rocker. In the wake of his words of harsh reality about the deaths of Frank and Mary Rogers and their little Charley on the westward trail, he sat for several long minutes of silence before getting on with the details.

Nell sighed. At this stage, she knew, she was beyond grief; she'd cried enough. "It's been so long without word, Mr. Deweese, that the final truth only confirms my worst fears. What *was* frightening was that I might never hear at all. I'm beholden to you for coming all the way here to tell me. In a way, I'm relieved. I'll be all right."

"You're a very strong woman, Mrs. Joiner. I suppose I had expected you to take the news much harder."

"You said cholera?"

"We lost nearly two thirds of the people on the train—whole families, men, women and children—in about two weeks. Cholera isn't pretty when it strikes. Extreme nausea and looseness, pain and general malaise. Extremely difficult and degrading for civilized, Christian people to be so ill in barren, hostile surroundings. After a while, one is so sick, all that no longer matters."

"I'm familiar with the symptoms. Spare me the details, Mr. Deweese." Nell hadn't meant it to sound unkind.

"Forgive me. It's still so vivid after all these years. The Rogerses were so strong and patient about it. Even their little sufferer. Sick as he was, little Charley never whimpered. They had been so kind to me, Nell. Me with no family about me to share the journey with. They insisted my wagon travel with theirs. I contributed from my food supply and hunted game for their table. Mary decided early in our travels that I was to take my meals with them each day. I didn't object."

Nell bit her lip. "So like my dear sister," she murmured. "So giving, so caring."

"And loving," Deweese added. "She became like a sister even to me. She was stricken first, and Frank did what he could for her. He expressed his unbounded love for her in so many ways and with such tenderness and gentility. The next day, I think it was, Frank and Charley both came down with it. Such a bright little fellow, that Charley. My heart ached to witness his agony."

"Poor, dear souls!"

"When Frank and Charley sickened, I cared for them

all as best I could. Bathed their feverish bodies and gave them water. Their thirst was intense. It was so ungodly hot out there on the open prairie in the glaring sun, with nothing but the canvas wagon cover to shield them. There was no one else to look after them. I had rubbing alcohol among my things, and I watered it down for a cooling body wipe for them. It seemed to renew and restore their well-being for at least a few moments during their final hours.''

Nell was overcome with compassion. She reached out a hand and clutched Deweese's as it gripped the arms of the rocker. "You must have seemed an angel of mercy to my family, Dave! How fortunate they were to have you there.''

"I did what I could until I took sick, too, and had to take to my bed in my wagon. Two weeks I lay there, racked with the agonies. No one could care for me, either. They were busy looking after their own family members, many of whom lay dying. For some unaccountable reason, Nell, my sickness was mild. I guess it was a miracle I survived, but I was gravely weakened and unfit to go on.''

"You poor, dear man!'' Nell exclaimed, still gripping Deweese's hand against the chair arm. He made no move to pull away. Nell sensed these were deep, emotional moments for both of them, even though the evening before they had been total strangers.

"They were desperate days, Nell. Those men who had escaped the pestilence gave the dead as decent Christian burials as possible under those intolerable conditions. As decimated as the party was, and with the determination that we were closer to returning home than continuing to our various destinations, they decided to turn back to Ohio. I was too weak to vote aye or nay.''

"How did you know about me, Dave? Or where I was?''

Dave Deweese stared into Nell's eyes for a long moment. "I was quite close to them, Nell. Mary and Frank told me a great deal. I knew about you and Seth long before the sickness hit.''

Nell wondered how much Frank might have revealed about their quest in Colorado. "That's all?''

Dave continued. "Not quite. Frank suffered incredible pain and discomfort toward the end, but he was very lucid and in charge of his senses. He confided in me totally when he knew death was near.''

"About Spindrift Ridge?''

"And Seth's claim,'' Deweese said hoarsely and with great feeling. Nell had taken her hand away from his. Now he reached out for hers and looked deeply into her eyes. "Frank's last words to me charged me to find you and tell you what happened. You know Frank and what a pillar of strength he was in life. He measured up in death as well.''

"Dear God!'' Nell gasped, caught up in the emotion of the moment, clasping her hands with Deweese's in the cabin's soft light and locking her eyes with his, her thoughts fused on the clear revelation of the final hours of her beloved family and Frank's entrusting their secrets to this fine man who had at last found her. In Nell's eyes—at this moment—Dave Deweese represented a savior, first bringing almost divine comfort to the supreme sufferings of her beloved family on the barren plains, and now sustaining and strengthening her in her hour of greatest need as she learned the final truths. A phrase crossed her mind: heaven-sent.

"It's yours now, Nell. Completely. We ... You ... can still call it the 'Little Charley Mine.' "

A kernel of doubt intruded upon Nell's total immersion in the passions of the moment. "Dave, they died more than five, maybe six, years ago. All this time, you've known where I was."

"I told you, dear lady, that the decimated wagon train turned back for Ohio. I had everything I owned invested in my westward trip. I was so exhausted by the scourge that I wasn't myself for months, even after we got back to Monroe County."

"You poor, dear soul!" Nell's heart again melted with compassion.

"It took me that long to get my strength back and rebuild my finances to set out again. Frank, fine man that he was, entrusted me with the rosewood box of ore samples from Seth's claim. Unfortunately, I sold the gold, Nell. Had to. The money gave me a stake to crawl out of the depths of despair. Starting back with virtually nothing, it's taken these years to recover enough to return west to find you."

"My mother's beautiful jewelry chest?"

"That, from what Frank told me and from your letter that was still inside, was sentimentally precious. My cousin has it back home. I'll see that it is returned to you."

"Dave?" Nell wondered how to speak about what was on her mind. He looked deeply again into her eyes, seeking the cause of her questioning tone. "You bathed Mary's suffering body."

Deweese recoiled. "Believe me, Nell, I took no satisfaction in exposure of her mortal form, ill as she was! It was more rejoicing on my part that I was able to bring some ease to her tortured body.''

''I don't suggest that you did anything untoward. I know she constantly wore a locket I sent her with my picture. She wrote me that she would no more arise in the morning without it than take off her wedding band.''

Deweese suddenly felt himself caught in a trap. He hadn't known about the locket. ''It was never brought up. She never wore it that I was aware of. Mary always dressed very simply. Her only jewelry was her wedding ring. The locket may have been lost, or perhaps she left it behind for safekeeping.''

''It's of no great consequence. You said Frank told you about Spindrift Ridge and Seth's find?''

''Until he took sick, Frank discussed it, but in guarded terms. I was never told anything specific. When his sickness was so intense, and he knew death was near, he appealed to me that if either Mary or Charley survived, or both, he wanted me to help them find you. If all of them died, he requested I find you to tell you you were free to do whatever you wished with the claim. That's when he entrusted me with the box of ore samples.''

Nell studied her guest, remembering her futile years at the Ritz-Dalton watching for someone she could trust to help her find and develop Seth's claim. Dave Deweese had been trusted by Frank and Mary Rogers. It seemed, after all the years, that her prayers had miraculously been answered. No one, she was convinced, would ever come along so well suited to help her as Dave Deweese.

"I wonder, Dave," Nell started, still seeking the right words. After a few moments, she found her voice. "Would you help me find Seth's claim? We could file the proper papers and open a mine on the claim, and you could get men to help you. If it's as rich as Seth believed, I'm sure I could be very content with a fifty-fifty split with you. Of course, we'd have a legal paper drawn up to that effect."

Deweese paused, his mind racing; two days in Dalton, and he'd found the Joiner woman, and already she'd offered a share in the claim. As with most of his ventures, he hadn't come to Dalton with much of a plan. It was coming together almost too fast, but he didn't know how much time he had to pull it off, whatever it would amount to. He knew he hadn't much to fear from Parsons, who had little or nothing to go on in trying to find the "Nell" and "S. Ridge" of the letter. An easy three weeks or more back, he'd left Snow, the prospectors, and the kid afoot on the prairie.

He figured Parsons to overtake the four afoot and ride past them without much of a confrontation. The perfect solution would be for Parsons to kill them, thus eliminating all clues to Dalton, and continue stumbling around Colorado looking for some vague ridge rich in gold. But, Deweese knew, he couldn't count on it. Parsons—like all of his men—was an oaf and a bungler without much sense of direction, he mused, watching Nell's expectant, eager face brightened by her own firelight.

Snow and Wisner and Casey were the more formidable adversaries. As soon as they contrived some means to find remounts or somehow recapture their own horses, Snow for certain would guide them on a beeline for Dalton and Nell. The appearance of the kid would blow his story to smithereens, and he'd be forced to flee for his life.

His best plan, he realized, had just been offered to him on a silver platter. Get Nell and her clues to the treasure moving—and fast—out of town and up into the wilds of the ridge. If either Parsons or Snow got to Dalton first, their hands would still be tied without Nell to provide information. Even if they found out that Nell had left town with a recent newcomer—and they'd be sure it was Deweese—they'd still spend weeks trying to find them on that massive mountain ridge.

"I guess I can't refuse your offer, Nell. I know what that ore assays out at, having sold it myself. Let's leave right away." He assumed she'd be eager and sensed from her looks that she was already attracted to him. That always made things a great deal simpler.

"I'd have to give Mr. Green some kind of notice. I can't just up and leave him flat."

Deweese was consumed now with the urgency of getting Nell out of town. "He'll get by. So will Lew Bricker. I've only worked for Lew one night," he said. "Nell, we've both suffered and done without and waited years for this opportunity. Let's go now. Outfit first thing in the morning, get proper horses—I've still got some money—and get provisions. I'll make you up a bedroll from what you've got here. I've a rifle and a six-gun with my horse outfit at the livery stable."

"But Dave, I still think that's kind of abrupt."

He grinned at her, and he could see from her eyes that she was captivated by him. "Five or six years of waiting. That's kind of abrupt?"

"I think about the inconvenience to Mr. Green and Mr. Bricker."

"When we get back to town with our riches, we'll be able to buy and sell both of them!" Nell now caught his wave of enthusiasm. Already her eyes looked less tired to Deweese, her features less strained.

"Seth always said I had a lot of adventure in my soul," she said, getting up and standing more erect than Deweese had seen her do before. "Seth told me it was about a three-day trip. Actually, his site is on the other side of Spindrift Summit. Downslope a ways."

Deweese's heart leapt. That kind of distance only complicated any search that might be mounted by Parsons or by Snow and his friends, Casey and Wisner.

Dawn on their second day on the trail found Nell and Deweese high above the head of Dalton Gulch, in a jumble of rocky, heavily timbered slopes. They had encountered any number of intermediate foothill chains to be conquered, only to find the imposing heights of the towering crags of Spindrift Ridge still frowning down on them.

Below them, at least out in the flatlands, the sun might be insufferably hot. Up where thick-trunked pines and firs thrust tall blue-green-needled treetops toward the sun, the air was benign, balmy. A constant, soothing whisper of wind worked perpetually through higher branches, lending a sublime serenity to the land.

Their trail, wending through a brown-needled carpet and clearly marked by game and earlier travelers, threaded its way among these somber, rough-barked giants, often leading out into sprawling, flat meadows where the clear sun glinted off winter-cured straw grass.

With great peals of delight, the pair of riders often spied deer grazing in the shady patches of such places—skittish, tawny does with spindly white-speckled brown fawns pasted at their sides, or a majestic buck drinking at a brook, lifting his regal rack in curiosity as odd four-legged animals with lumps on their backs broke into the clearing.

Crystal-clear spring-fed streams of winter snow run-off often wove across these mountain pasturelands like delicate threads, offering refreshing stopping places where they could stretch their legs and relax, water the horses, refill canteens, and splash water happily on sweaty faces. Nell's spirits, nourished by her new, unbounded freedom, turned her jubilant, gleeful as a schoolgirl, the tensions of years being purged from her system as they got away from Dalton Gulch.

Deweese, too, insulated by distance and feeling more secure from pursuit by Parsons's or Snow's party, found himself with a growing and heady sense of euphoria. He almost wished it was possible to proceed with Nell's plan—stake out, patent, and work the claim, and share the proceeds. Over a very few years, he was sure, he'd become wealthy, able to move to Denver and a life of luxury. Watching Nell grow winsome and more attractive with each passing hour, he wondered if he might even marry her and at last truly settle down.

Always the specter of his pursuers dogged him, hanging over his daydreams like a dark cloud. He speculated on the time he had left before he was discovered and exposed to Nell for the cruel hoax he had inflicted on her. He pondered it, watching her back as she rode ahead and he followed, leading the pack animal, or observing her at times when they rested and talked. Others would find heinous what he'd done to this fine woman; to Dave Deweese—like others before her, affection-starved women and greedy, vulnerable men—she only represented the means to an end. As attractive as he found her, he knew he must never lose sight of his goal.

Through his foresight, they were comfortably provisioned for at least a week in the wilds; he could supplement and extend that by meat-hunting. Under the circumstances, Dave mused, the eventual riches of Seth Joiner's Spindrift Ridge find would have to be another man's fortune. He must gauge his time, taking only enough of the rich ore for a pack horse to carry, but enough to insure a hefty return with some gold broker.

When the time was right, he'd slip out of camp at night, as he'd done with the Parsons crowd. As arduous and threatening as it might be, he knew Nell could backtrack and find her way off the mountain. He would leave his victim an out.

That afternoon, having conquered the Spindrift Ridge crest and starting down the far slope, they went into camp early in trees fringing one of the many picturesque meadowlands they had seen on their trip. Nell had already pointed out one or two of Seth's landmarks. Deweese turned euphoric, hopeful that by the next midday, perhaps, he'd be at the ledge of Joiner's big find.

They had unburdened the horses, watered them, and hobbled them to graze in the meadow. Deweese had set up camp, unfurling their bedrolls on either side of a fire site; he brought in rocks to form a protective ring against setting fire to the leaves and grass.

"I'll tend to the supper tonight, Nell," he said as they rested on their respective blankets and soogans, spread on thick white canvas ducking groundcloths. He'd brought a small flask of whiskey, bought from Lew Bricker's barkeep when the boss man wasn't around. Nell declined to share his relaxing potion, so he sipped alone. Though not a confirmed smoker, he rolled a cigarette from his small shirt-pocket tin of flake tobacco and fired it, blissfully enjoying the two vices together from the luxury of his spread bedroll; for the moment, all was well in Dave Deweese's world.

"Nonsense," Nell responded. "Let me make us some coffee. We can warm over some of that cured ham, heat a can of beans, and spread some of those preserves over slices of our sourdough bread. It's still fresh."

"Nell, you're not accustomed to such long hours in the saddle. You must be tired. I'll tend to things."

"If that's your decision, Dave, so be it." She giggled, still reveling in these moments of supreme freedom with sheer joy.

Later, after their supper, Deweese rolled himself another of his infrequent cigarettes, leaned back on his bedroll, and watched his thin tobacco smoke, reflecting the fire's light, lift in a billowing pillar into the night and disappear into the dark.

He watched as the woman adjusted and smoothed her blankets in anticipation of bedtime; her lean and shapely body sent a ripple of desire through him. It had been a long time since Michelle in Golconda.

A pair of Seth's old Levi's, conforming to her hips, and a tight-fitting, faded blue work shirt left few illusions about Nell's still-lithe but ample form. Lust welled up even stronger in him. He had about decided that after she got into her bed and the fire burned low he would suggest they share their blankets, when he became aware with a spurt of alarm of a rustling out in the dark away from the fire's circle of soft, orange light reflected against the towering trees.

"Don't move, Deweese!"

A high-pitched voice snarled at him out of the night. A form materialized over him in the dwindling firelight. Caught totally off-guard, Deweese could only stare helplessly into the pair of bores of a sawed-off scattergun. He recognized the familiar tattered and grease-hardened buckskin clothing first.

Simon Parsons!

# ⤷ 14 ⤶

With a shriek of panic, Nell leapt to her feet to flee into the night, only to be driven back by a ring of armed ugly men emerging like wraiths from Hades into the light around them. "Dave!" she screamed, darting to him. Deweese rose to catch her in his arms. In terrified embrace, the two of them cringed close to their fire as the circle of grim-faced, evil men drew a tighter human noose around them.

"Let's hear you talk your way out of this one, big mouth," Parsons grunted, keeping the short barrels aimed from the hip directly at their midsections.

Nell's body was a series of convulsions in his arms; she was petrified and speechless with panic.

"Well, come on! Let's hear it!" Parsons demanded angrily, rudely nudging Deweese's buttocks with his gun muzzle.

Deweese recoiled in stark fear. "I can explain everything, Simon," he began.

"Yeah, I'm sure you can. Get started."

"This lady and I are ... prospecting."

"And I'm sure you like the prospects of your saddled pard there, big mouth. I stood out there in the dark watching you sizin' 'er up. That explanation won't do. I got a big hunch I'm lookin' here at Miss Nell, who knows all about where our mine's gonna be."

"Don't harm her, Simon," Deweese pleaded. Still encircled by Deweese's strong arms, Nell's body continued to tremble in abject fear.

"Huh!" Parsons snorted like a pig. "My boys and me been away from towns a long time. Night before last we didn't have no chance to dawdle and buy nothing at that whorehouse saloon in town. I figured in a day or so I'd catch up with you up here with your ladyfriend there. Now me and the boys won't have to pay. When I turn 'em loose to start usin' her, she'll wind up beggin' to tell us where that gold is hid long before they've had enough. Some of these fellas—most of 'em—is so starved for poontang, they gonna be back for seconds. It's likely to be quite a night. The nice part, Deweese, is that you can watch."

Nell, still silent in her terror, shrank smaller in Deweese's arms. "You wouldn't allow that, Simon," he pleaded.

"Wouldn't I? Just don't you push me, big mouth."

In his moment of stark panic at Parsons's sudden appearance, Dave had turned nearly tongue-tied. The shock of Parsons's totally unexpected appearance began to wear off, and Deweese's glib tongue came back. "I'm ready to strike a deal with you."

Parsons almost laughed aloud. "You ain't in no position to make deals, big mouth."

"No, and neither are you."

Parsons, taken aback by Deweese's arrogance, stood with his mouth open. "Whattya mean?" he demanded.

"You set those hounds from hell of yours on her like you said, and she'll lose her mind. Go crazy. Ever hear of that happening to a woman that's been gang-raped? You didn't start in this business yesterday, Parson's, of course you know. She won't beg to tell you where the claim is. First of your jaspers jumps her, and she'll get just like those people in a madhouse. She won't even be able to tell you her own name. You do what you just told me, and you'll drive out everything that's in her head. I guarantee it." He pushed the cringing, panicked woman away toward Parsons. "Here. Take her. Go ahead. Turn your animals loose on her. Yeah, I'll watch. No skin off me. Only don't blame me if the trail to that rich gold claim is swept clean by your stupidity."

"You really think so?" Parsons asked, almost meekly.

"Try me. Come on. She hasn't told me a thing. You can slice me open and plant me on an anthill, and I still couldn't give you a clue to the trail from here. What you got in this woman is your clear track to riches. And you propose to turn her into a gibbering idiot? I credited you with more sense than that, Simon."

Nell stood between them, her eyes nervously darting back and forth to the faces of the two men. She was hunched over, trembling, her overwhelming fear making a tight mask of her face. "Dave?" she asked softly, pausing as if totally bewildered about what to say next.

"Let me handle it, Nell," Deweese said quietly. "Call off your dogs, Simon," he added angrily. As far

175

as he was concerned, Parsons could have the woman—and the gold. His only hope at the moment was to get out of this with his scalp.

"I guess there must be other ways to go about it." Then he spoke up. "Back off, boys," he ordered in his squeaky voice of authority. "Party's over. For tonight. Go see to your hosses and lay your beds. You know where the whiskey is. Dave here and I got to have a meetin'."

Deweese panicked. The wrong words from Parsons and his whole fabric of deceit with Nell would be ripped apart. Parsons had the box of ore samples and Nell's letter; Deweese was also certain that Parsons knew about Charley. From here on, he'd be walking on eggshells. He was trapped between two fires. He was determined to brazen it out.

"All this talk and you showing up out here like that, Simon," he said, "has needlessly upset the lady. Let's let her get to bed, and you and I go talk somewhere else."

Parsons pondered it. "I don't think so, Dave. You made a good point about savin' her from the boys, but as for the rest of it, I'm figuring you're just up to your old tricks."

Deweese still figured his best defense at this point was a good offense. "How'd you find me?"

Parsons hunkered down close to the fire and rolled a cigarette from makings tucked inside his shirt. "You don't credit me with the sense God gave a hog, Deweese, so I'm gonna tell ya."

Deweese squatted close to Parsons. Nell stumbled to her unrolled blankets, sat down, and wordlessly buried her face in her palms. The night's moments of terror and the confusing talk obviously had rendered her unable to make sense of anything. Deweese still watched her as Parsons fired his cigarette, inhaled, and released the smoke before he continued.

"We found the horses you stole from Snow. They sneaked in one night to steal 'em back, and we caught Snow. One of them cutthroats that rides with him sneaked up in the night and shot my man, Broken-Nose Tom, and Snow got away. I think it was that skinny one, Wisner his name is."

Parsons sucked in more of his smoke and expertly flicked off a long ash with his little finger. "We figured they'd cached their stuff and walked to where we was camped. I allowed it'd be quite a trip for 'em goin' back there and then catching up again. As for you, I sent one of my boys on a good hoss down the trail after you. I figured by this time, you was working all by your lonesome and wasn't tied up with them. I figured you'd pried out of 'em, some way, who the lady was, and where she was, and that she wasn't too far from the gold. Had you eyes in the back of your head, you'd've known when Dale caught sight of you. We come foggin' up, and from then on, one of my boys had you in his sights, and the rest of us was trackin' you all the way to Dalton."

Deweese looked deeply into the fire. "It figures," he said sadly. He glanced over at Nell; she'd flopped back on her blankets but still kept her hands over her eyes and cheeks. He hoped she was oblivious to his conversation with Parsons.

"We camped below town. I had a man in there two days, hangin' back in the alleys, watchin' you. The forenoon you and the lady headed up the gulch, all geared for a long ride, I figured you'd lead us straight to the claim. Should've stuck by my guns. The boys was pawin' the air to get the lady down and start havin' some fun, and I suppose that overcome my better judgment. That's how come we come into your camp tonight.''

''Okay. What're you going to do with us?''

''You I don't care about. You change colors dependin' on the wind. Givin' me that guff about joinin' up with me and gettin' me to tell you all about the gold. Then you go slippin' away in the night like the coyote that ate the chickens and go over and sell Snow and them your bill of goods. I'm a lowlife, but dammit, I look a man in the eye with my loaded gun and tell him to hand over his wad. You're a sneak and a grifter, Deweese. Lower even than me. Right now, amigo, I owe you a debt for showin' me the reasons not to turn the boys loose tonight on the lady yonder. It could've ruint the whole shebang.''

''What's that worth, Simon?''

''It comes down to that, huh, grifter? Well, me, I figure it's worth your life. Otherwise, when we've persuaded the lady to lead us to the goods, I either put a six-gun to your head or, like you say, stake you out on an anthill. Come to think of it, to make the cheese more binding as they say, I'll give the gal to the boys close by. While you're squirmin' an' screamin', you can watch her squirmin' and screamin'. Won't none of it matter to me, for I'll be roarin' drunk, chippin' out nuggets, and stakin' out my claim!''

''You got the woman, Simon. How about I pull my freight first thing in the morning? I got a job opportunity on west of here.''

''I bet you do,'' Parsons said with a sneer. ''That's

as far as loyalty goes with you, eh, Deweese? You'd sell your mother to a whoremaster for a side of bacon. I'd keep you on to keep romancin' 'er to show us where the gold's hid. After tonight, though, her confidence in you might be a little shaky. You got 'er up here with your sweet talk. Me and my boys may have to exert a little force, but we'll get 'er there before we drive her batty. Who cares after that?''

"It's moon bright. A man can see quite a ways. If it's all the same to you, Simon, I just might roll up my bed and saddle up tonight. I could get a ways down the trail before daylight.''

"Suit yourself. I'm all done with ya. Ya headin' for Dalton?''

Deweese studied Nell's inert form, sprawled fully dressed on top of her bedroll; she appeared to be asleep. "Seems best. No way of telling what's past the downside west of the ridge, or how far. Could I ask you something else, Simon?''

"Which is?''

"How far behind you do you suppose Snow and them are?''

"Ridin' right out of the fryin' pan into the fire, eh, big mouth? Best to avoid him and them two cutthroats. They ain't going to be particular overjoyed comin' across you again. Well, now, they must've cached their gear where you stole their hosses. They must've been hidin' in the weeds, for we had to ride past 'em. Appears to me they walked the better part of three days to where they killed Tom. Two days ridin' back to their cache and two days back to where we left 'em, and us by that time four days ahead of 'em. That puts 'em a good seven, eight days behind. We got to Dalton, what? Five days ago? Goin' back down there, you could be slicin' it a little thin.''

"What else can I do?"

"It's your neck. I'd make damned sure I went through at night.''

Deweese glanced at Nell again; he would leave the lamb among the wolves, but as Parsons said, it was his neck. "Best I leave now?" he asked, more or less asking permission. Parsons dismissed him with a disgusted wave of his hand. "I need a drink," Parsons mumbled.

Minutes later, his horse saddled and his bedroll tied behind the cantle, Deweese and the animal were vague, ghostlike silhouettes against the dark at the fringes of the dwindling firelight.

As he levered himself into the saddle, Nell rose bolt upright to a sitting position on her bedding. "Dave?" she called across to his shadowed form. "Dave! No!" Her voice rose to a horrified, quivering shriek. "You can't! Don't leave me! Dave! For God's sake! *Dave!*"

As he rode into the night, he heard Simon Parsons shout, "Shut the hell up!" and the rude, snapping sound of a slap as Parsons hit the woman across the mouth. He rode until he could no longer hear the sounds of her terrified, out-of-control, near-hysterical sobs and wails.

Quickly the trees closed behind him to block the firelight; his world became a sprawl of pewter shadows created by a round, mellow moon coasting among overhead clouds. The upslope trail to the crest was a ribbon of dim light before him, and a blissful silence swirled around the lone rider.

\* \* \*

Simons Parsons heard the last of Deweese's plodding hoofbeats before slipping away from the couple's night fire to rummage through his saddlebags for his bottle, bought in a Dalton dive by the name of the Pick and Poke. When he got back to the fire, the woman had calmed her crying, and she lay on the blankets in a stiff paralysis of fright, her wide eyes watching his movements with the pleading and panicked eyes of a trapped, condemned animal.

Parsons dropped some more of Deweese's sticks on the fire and went at worrying out the cork. Silently, in the new-flaring firelight, he lifted the bottle, offering a drink to the woman called Nell. She continued to cringe mutely against her bedding, watching him.

"Suit yourself," he said, lifting it to his lips for a long pull. He swallowed and smacked around the fiery taste. "Couple of gulps of Old Bravemaker here'd sure help ya sleep, ma'am. You can relax. I ain't gonna hit you no more 'less you start yellin' again. In the mornin', I'll trade ya a fast hoss for tellin' me how to find my way to that gold. That's a better bargain than I figured on givin' ya."

He took another tall sip, watching her askance as he tipped the bottle. A short distance away in the night, his boys had whipped up a fire to celebrate their upcoming good fortune by passing a couple of jugs of Dalton whiskey and whooping it up. Sitting alone with the woman, Simon Parsons smiled at their harsh, hoarse laughter and the bellows as they outdid one another with stories or butted in, with several of them talking loudly at once.

He took another look at Nell. "You ain't much company, y'know," he mumbled at her, having himself another stiff dollop out of his bottle. Simon Parsons took pride in his ability to hold his liquor. Even felt his mental prowess was stronger after he'd had a few. He looked and listened yearningly through the night at the fire where his men caroused. He eased up, shaking a finger at Nell.

"Now, you listen here, woman, and listen good. I'm goin' over yonder and get one of my boys to sit here with ya. I give ya fair warnin'. Don't try to bolt. For if you as much as git up outa them blankets, I'll turn the whole pack of 'em loose on ya, and they're a bunch of boys who only care what a woman is built for. Your feelin's don't enter into it." He sipped another long one, his head wobbly on his neck. "An' you know wha' I mean. I figure I can still get ya ta tell me where th' gold is." Holding the bottle by the neck at his side, Parsons stumbled off into the dark toward the other night fire.

"I still think that damn Deweese was bluffin' me about losin' her mind if the boys used her," he assured himself, his voice trailing away in the distance. Nell watched his disappearing figure as she shrank down in her bedding, watching the men's giant blaze some distance away, hearing the roar of voices welling up to her from where the Parsons gang was becoming royally drunk.

Parsons stumbled up to the perimeter of men circling a huge, hot, and crackling blaze—what the folks down on the farm used to call a bonfire.

"Where'dja leave the woman, Simon?" a man asked. "Ya din't bring 'er? Aw, ha-ha-ha!"

Parsons blinked in the fire's bright blaze. "One of

you boys go back there an' stand guard over 'er. An' leave her alone!''

Another of his men at the fire piped up. ''Si, how about we just get to play with her a little bit tonight? We ain't all going to use 'er. Nothin' like that. We jes' wanna bring 'er up here by the fire an' join in the fun. Maybe jes' give 'er some kisses. I promise we won't do more than that. Right, boys?''

Drunken murmurs of assent followed the statement of the man near Parsons. ''Tell ya what, Wild Card,'' Parsons said, lifting his bottle again for a serious pull. ''You go off there an' keep a eye on 'er—but don't get on 'er . . . hee-hee—and I'll think about lettin' you boys have a li'l lovin' from 'er yet tonight. How's that?''

''I'll drink to that,'' Wild Card said. ''Shorty was tellin' about when he rode with the rebels in Texas just after the war. . . .''

''Yeah,'' Shorty continued. ''We was mustangs for a fare-thee-well! Cap'n Jenks was mightily put out when Gen'l Lee caved in back in Virginia, an' closer to home, Gen'l Price and Gen'l Buckner sold us down the river to the Yankees in N'Orleans. Cap'n Jenks was some mean hombre, an' we set out to principally raise hell in Texas. Knocked us off a Meskin town one day about dawn. What men wasn't killed, run off. We was left with a town full of them little dark-skinned, dark-eyed, dark-haired hot tamales, and there was plenty of *aquardiente* in the cantinas. We rounded up all them little Meskin kids into the church and locked 'em up, with the padre to look after 'em. We gathered and penned all the fillies in a corral and commenced goin' among 'em, cuttin' out a filly of our choice.''

"Them must've been high old times," a voice from the men ringed around the fire piped up. "What happened then, Shorty?"

"Well, Zeb," Shorty continued, "do I need to draw you pictures? We had poontang an' whiskey till it was comin' out our—"

"Wild Card!" Parsons interrupted with a roar, seeing his henchman still hanging on the edges of the firelight. "I told you to go guard the woman!"

Wild Card had hung around to hear the end of Shorty's story of raiding in Texas. "I was jus' goin', Simon," he said, and he rushed off in the dark to where he expected the woman to be crouched on her blankets by another fire. "Simon!" he bellowed through the night, his voice registering complete panic and fear.

Wild Card's tone sobered everyone instantly, none more than Simon Parsons. He raced down to the other fire. The blankets where he had left Nell Joiner were empty!

"Damn you, Wild Card!" Parsons shrieked. "I ought to blow your damn brains out. I sent you down here to mind her!"

"I'm sorry." Wild Card's voice was fawning and contrite.

"You'll be sorrier." Parsons turned back to his men, now congregated around him. "Spread out. She ain't got far. She's askin' for it, now she'll get it! First man finds her gets first crack. Now fan out, and don't come back till you've got 'er!"

# ❧ 15 ❧

**N**ell's reaction was sudden and unplanned.

The moment of Simon Parsons's dire warning and spinning on his heel galvanized her from cringing terror to strong resolve. The second his back was turned, she was ready to strike for freedom, willing to suffer his vowed consequences if caught. He'd have to catch her—and she vowed firmly that he wouldn't.

Leaping up quietly almost before her arch tormentor's shadowy form had faded from the firelight, Nell stepped into the darkness in the opposite direction, her eyes momentarily blinded by the sudden change from bright firelight to dense dark. In seconds, vague shapes of trees and natural features took form out of the night as her eyes adjusted to the moonlit landscape.

Her mind adjusted with a return to similar clarity. Once free of the starkly terrorizing grip the night's campsite and its monster invaders had on her, Nell sensed reason creeping back.

That same slowly returning reason told her that the trail back to Dalton wended its way across the dull silver pancake that was the mountain meadowland in the dim light before her. Reason also told her that when Parsons's men mounted their furious search for her, their logic would send them pouring across the same open land to the upslope trail to Spindrift Summit.

But that way lay her only hope of escape. Breathless and agitated in exertion and fear, but firm in the rightness of her decision, she hurried the several hundred yards across the open moonlit basin. Sizing up her situation as she ran, Nell was aware that even in the faint light her movement would be visible until she reached the dark sanctuary of the distant trees.

Vile masculine roars of alert and alarm shredded the night's silence behind her like thunder from Hell; new panic was a spur driving fresh energy into her legs. Quaking with her effort, but with high relief, Nell ducked into the dark shadows of pines ringing the meadow. Behind her, Parsons's bullies boiled like maddened wolves over the moon-bright land behind her. Heedlessly, she plunged deeper into the black morass of dense forest, slowed as she felt her way. This would be the wrong time for a sprained ankle from a misstep or a crippling injury in a fall.

Her mind racing faster than her footsteps, she acknowledged that she had none of the innate woods sense of a Seth Joiner. Uncannily, he had sensed his proper direction even on a heavily overcast day. In strange country, Seth had always known the right branch of a road or trail to take him quickly home without confusion. Her thoughts coming crazily, Nell was aware she didn't have such wisdom; she didn't even have a knife.

But even Seth's woods judgment had somehow let

him down in the end. Then was then and now was now, and Nell was fleeing for her very life. She'd had the good sense to keep on Seth's warm trail coat earlier in the night, despite slight discomfort from Deweese's campfire. She had no food—only a minor annoyance—and water was nearby almost anywhere on Spindrift Ridge. She reasoned as she made her careful way through the night that reaching the safety of Dalton would be no easy task. But it had to be done. Eluding Simons Parsons's animals was the major concern. It was a matter of applying what wisdom she had, surviving in a hostile land, and escaping human beasts bent on ravishing her.

Behind her came the frightening crunching, crushing stampede of men spreading out into the forest to trap her in some kind of diabolical human snare. She picked up the pace of her flight—a doe racing to avoid being dragged down and consumed by a wolf pack.

Her limited wisdom in the ways of the woods assured her that her trail to freedom ran somewhere to her left; she must stay way from it—for at least one Parsons man would hunt for her on that route. It would continue upslope to the summit; as long as her course tended upward, she could be fairly sure of her bearings.

Her pursuers were no better able to see than she; they made no attempt to disguise their frenzied search, crashing headlong through the thickets of dense night, shouting questions and orders at one another in total confusion.

Her wisdom, honed by years of grief and taking on a brutal world alone, ordained that she must soon seek out an effective hiding place. She, too, crunched and crashed through brush heaps and piles of dead, downed limbs. She climbed now, sometimes scrambling over great chunks of tumbled mountain granite rising more sharply before her, suggesting that she was close to the narrowing cleft in the land where her trail to freedom rose toward the Spindrift crest. The noises of men widely separated and moving clumsily through the forested terrain behind her rose up to her; she had stayed ahead of them. But maybe not for long.

Nell stopped a moment to catch her breath, to let her loudly throbbing heart quiet and the tension of exertion leave her legs and body. She found herself in a jumble of hillside rocks piled helter-skelter and every which way. Somewhere, tucked in among them, she was certain, was a little nook, a cave, a hidey-hole where she could curl up as Parsons's men plunged past. It was her only hope.

It was a big land, the night was still young, the bright moon hardly starting its descent; these men chasing her were little more than dumb animals themselves, with none of the keen scent or night sight of a timber wolf or other beast of prey. The going was difficult as she made her way upslope toward the crest; her pursuers would be less enthusiastic in through here. It was time, she mused, in words she'd heard men use, to "hole up."

The sounds of pursuit had diminished. She could still hear as they thrashed around and called, some moving up the slope toward her, but at distant, divergent points. Nell again allowed herself some moments of relief and temporary victory. It was only temporary; safety was still many harrowing days and untold miles on foot away over rugged, inhospitable country.

Leaning against a rock, Nell surveyed her situation.

It was time to let Parsons's men burn themselves out in a limitless rock- and tree-strewn mountainside in the dark of night searching for a needle in a haystack.

Soon, her knowledge of men told her, her pursuers would be ready to risk the wrath of Simon Parsons to turn back to the comforts of their booze, their bonfire, and their bedrolls.

Her eyes focused more clearly on her surroundings. Above her, against a rocky ledge, the giant boulders, stacked against each other, showed a roughly triangular opening. She struggled up to a granite shelf, her eyes fighting to identify an opening into possible refuge. The stone base of the hole angled downward, but there seemed space for a human to edge in. Fearful of snakes, Nell hefted a handy wedge of rock and tossed it in, hearing it bounce two or three times before coming to rest with a crackle against what seemed to be a pocket of pencil-thin brittle sticks. Hearing no warning hiss or rattle, she wriggled her way through the rude portal, sensing the opening growing larger the farther she proceeded. It ended abruptly in a wall of adjoining rock. In its crude pyramidal confinement, she could almost stand; its extended points were far enough apart for her to comfortably stretch out, with only the gravity of the down-sloped rock pushing her against the rear wall. She rested in a narrow crevice.

The twigs, rain-borne or wind-blown into Nell's crevice, crunched as she eased down. Through the odd-shaped entrance she could see a night sky speckled with peaceful, blissful stars. Nell continued to roll and twist against the pile of twigs that had found their way in, turning them into a mat of fine material that would not give her away if the invaders ventured near.

At the moment, in a heavenly silence that seemed eternal, Nell was no longer aware of the frightening sounds of pursuit.

She allowed herself the waves of relief that came with her fragile security; there was one chance in a million—no, she thought, in a billion—that any of Parsons's six or seven bungling searchers would come to this exact spot this exact night. For now, she was safe.

She lay on her bed of crushed twigs, tucking her head into crossed arms. Her thick coat and Seth's old hidelike Levi's shielded her from the prodding points of shattered sticks. Her nose was keen on the musty, woodsy smell of her security hole and the accumulation of jumbled sticks. Overriding that aroma was the clean and cool air around her. After her ordeal of terror and flight, ease flooded into her, inclining her toward sleep—despite the threats that surrounded and tortured her with thoughts of what the next hours and days would bring.

Nell had no notion how long she'd slept; she woke refreshed but alarmed with the crunching, rhythmic sounds of approaching footsteps in the night. Her illusions of security vanished with shocking horror. Breathlessly, a new panic overwhelming her as she realized the trap she was in with no escape, she listened as the steps grew louder, nearing her hideaway. Abruptly, her view of the sky was blocked by the partial silhouette of a man standing near the entrance. She shrank closer—and silently—into her hasty bed of twigs, tensing muscles against movement that would betray her. The Parsons man was almost close enough to touch.

She nearly reacted in shock to a male voice knifing into the forced stillness of her heart.

"Hey, Zeb," his voice called softly. "That you down there?"

The response was almost inaudible. "Yeah. Shorty? Where y'at?"

"Up here."

More silence ensued, but Nell heard growing sounds of a man climbing and scrambling over small rock slides up to the ledge where his companion waited.

"How'd ya git up here, Shorty?" the man called Zeb asked, parking himself on a rock outside Nell's sanctuary.

"Done a somersault, you dumb ass," Shorty responded. "You got your fixin's? I need a smoke. This is teejuss bidness."

"Here." Zeb fished out his flake-tobacco sack and papers and handed them across the entrance to Shorty, who was now seated, the two of them blocking Nell's only escape route. She lay scant feet from them, measuring her breath in short, frightened takes.

"Shee-it, Zeb," Shorty said, his face lit by his lucifer match as he fired his smoke. "Simon ain't going to find that woman in this pea soup tonight. Lawd Gawd A'mighty!"

"We'd ought to wait till in the mornin'. She ain't going to get far afoot anyhows, Shorty. She'll sure as hell try to head for Dalton. Simon just ought to post a man up there at that narrow notch the trail goes through over the top. She's got to go that way. One man could catch her, and the rest of us get some sleep."

"That's a good idea, Zeb. But don't go tellin' Simon about it. Anything that ain't his very own idea he'll find fault with, and he might just take and give you a knot on the head for bein' a smart mouth or a dumb ass or both.''

''Well, he ought to get busy an' figure something like that. All this thrashin' around in the woods ain't my idea of fun. Chances of findin' that woman are about slim to zero. She probably knows these woods like the back of her hand already anyhow.''

The woman in question, scarcely daring to breathe, listened intently.

''I think you're about right on that, Zeb,'' Shorty said. ''She ain't up in around these rocks, and that's a fact. I've been around my share. I can smell a woman from a mile away. You can take my word on that.'' Shorty rolled and lit another cigarette.

''You sure can tell some windies about 'em, I'll say that for you, Shorty.''

''You think there's any gold mine up in here, Zeb?''

''The woman must've been Nell of the letter with the box of gold ore. Old Deweese had 'er sweet-talked all the way up here, so that part of it's come true so far. The only way Simon's going to find it is to get 'er back and pry out of 'er where it's at. She's probably got it all staked out and proper claimed already anyway. Simon never asked 'er about that. We're probably wasting time up here as it is,'' Shorty continued. ''Claim's prob'ly registered.''

Nell lay in a fixed kind of shocked silence on her bed of crushed twigs. These men knew about her letter and had seen a box of gold ore—it could only be the chest she had sent six years ago to Frank and Mary Rogers. Dave Deweese clearly had lied to her every step of the way about his relationship with Frank and

Mary. Her ears had tuned sharply to a reference that Dave—the man she had trusted as her "savior," and who had so callously abandoned her to the evil Simon Parsons—had "sweet-talked" her into the mountains. Nell now despised Dave Deweese almost as much as the hateful Simon Parsons. At the same time, she wondered how many other evil, scheming men and wicked, lustful outlaw gangs knew of Seth's gold.

"Seems like I hear some of the other boys startin' back, Shorty," Zeb said, rising up and stretching and yawning. "Maybe Simon's called off the search for tonight. We'd have better luck tracking 'er sign in daylight anyway."

"Yeah, and I got a hankerin for a pull on that jug before I roll up in my blankets. Let's go."

The two men carefully picked their way off the high rocks, their movements telegraphed to Nell in the scrape of their sliding boots and grunted curses dulled by distance and dark.

Nell, her mind in turmoil but under control, nestled into what had become a familiar, comfortable and snug burrow, warmed by her body. Again she could see the reassuring realm of stars through her crude, three-sided doorway. Again a soft silence spread over the woods and rocks and hillsides around her.

Her solitary life had taught her disciplines that had been unnecessary in the relationship she'd shared with Seth Joiner. He found her way for her in trackless woods or prairies, and his adept mind, even when asleep, could wake at will at two o'clock in the morning, or at six—or even eight. In the bitter wake of Seth's disappearance, Nell had disciplined herself to set her own clock at night and wake when she willed it.

She had no watch; Seth's beautiful old key-wound silver turnip had disappeared with him. The hour, she figured, was not much past midnight. She'd sleep until two. With perhaps four hours left then till daylight, she might be beyond the narrow notch Zeb and Shorty had had spoken of as the point of Spindrift Summit and a perfect place to trap her.

She chortled smugly; they hadn't bargained on Nell Joiner!

The two gang members she'd overheard agreed on the futility of presenting such a suggestion to Parsons; still, she'd approach the high pass with great caution. She hoped that in the similar rocky jumble on the other side of the Spindrift Ridge crest, she'd find as snug and convenient a hiding place as this one to spend the daylight hours in case Parsons continued to press his search. She tried mentally to organize an escape plan. Once past Spindrift Summit and on the downslope to Dalton, her safest travel times ought to be several hours at first light before the outlaws, wherever they camped as a base to continue their hunt, were up and on the trail. She'd hide securely during whatever daylight hours Parsons's men were abroad on the land. At day's end, when they wearied of the search and went back into camp, she'd start out refreshed and renewed to continue to trudge downslope several more hours before seeking sanctuary for the night.

Once home in Dalton, she'd deal with whatever it took to track down Dave Deweese and force him to come clean with the truth of how he came to know so much of Frank and Mary and little Charley and of Seth's gold. She might have to dog his trail for days and weeks until she could find and confront him. She could do it. And she would do it.

In her dark, chilly, rock-bound burrow high on the slopes of Spindrift Ridge, Nell shook her head in amazement at the daring and uncharacteristic nature of her thoughts. In the space of a few hours, Nell Joiner realized, she had learned a great deal about herself and her own inner strengths.

When she was back in the security of Dalton, the Parsons gang would eventually leave the Spindrift Ridge country; the day might yet come when she would have the courage to outfit herself for an extended journey into the mountains on her own to discover and stake her claim to the Little Charley Mine.

Her first major objective, though, was to slip out of the evil clutches of Simon Parsons and his men, and that would not be especially easy.

Nell drifted away into a sound sleep, snug and secure in her tiny burrow, and in her vow that whatever hardships she might face, she'd yet outwit Simon Parsons and deal with Dave Deweese and his duplicity.

# ⇒ 16 ⇐

Flying in the face of Simon Parsons's advice, Dave Deweese rode boldly back into Dalton late one afternoon several days after his escape from the perils of his confrontation with Parsons and his abandoning of Nell Joiner. Intuition told him the chances were strong that Snow and his friends were still miles away on the prairie, slogging their way toward Dalton. Time might work against him, but he'd spent most of his funds gearing up for the trail ride with Nell; expedience had demanded that he leave most of his gear and provisions in the panniers he'd taken up by pack horse.

"Lost a gold mine but saved my scalp," Deweese muttered grimly to himself as his horse plodded down the gradual slope of Dalton's main street in the direction of the Pick and Poke saloon. In the final analysis, Dave Deweese was jubilant.

He had a story all ready for Lew Bricker and an appeal for a stake against future earnings—which Deweese had no notion of ever collecting. With a loan wangled from Bricker, he'd set out for the lowlands and another flight into a misty oblivion he'd sought and found so frequently in his rootless, scheming life.

Dressed again in his black gambler's outfit and cleaned up and shaved, Deweese sauntered casually into the Pick and Poke to find Bricker where he'd been that day Dave arrived in Dalton—whiling away the time at a center table with a bottle and glass.

Bricker recognized Deweese as he swung the batwing doors aside and started toward him across the saloon's plank floor.

"Well, well!" Bricker enthused sarcastically. "The return of the prodigal! We'd about given you up for lost."

"You might say I was out working for you, Lew," Deweese responded. "Can a man buy a drink in this place?"

Bricker beckoned to the bartender. "Cecil. A glass for Mr. Deweese!" Cecil headed for them with a gleaming tumbler.

In moments, Deweese had downed his first in a gulp of instant gratification and poured a second for slow sipping.

"All right, Dave. Tell me how you were out of town five days on my behalf, protecting my best interests. I hired you to run my poker tables. Five nights more that this place was like a ghost town for more than an hour while those damned artistes put on their damned peep show and siphoned off my clientele."

"If memory serves me, Lew, you also asked me to see what I could do to entice Nell Joiner to come to work for you."

"Five days? You spent five days with her for that? You'll have the goods all worn out before she ever puts on the frills and the fancies for the upstairs trade! And my good friend Alonzo Green over at the Ritz-Dalton is madder'n a wet hen that she ran out on him without so much as a by-your-leave. Five years she worked over there, dependable as a good watch. Then, poof! She's off gallivantin' with you. Lon ain't none too happy.''

"Maybe she was tired of it. She wanted me to take her up to see Spindrift Ridge, where her husband was lost years ago. I figured it would give me a chance to put in a good word for you.''

"Well, you needn't worry about it anymore. I got some fresh talent that'll put our Nell to shame. I'm all set, Dave.''

"What happened?''

"This little baggage rode in on the stage while you were out of town. A gem. Perky as a pretty valentine. From out east, Kansas maybe, where she worked last. Her name's Cora Watson. Says she knows you. I told her you'd probably be back.''

"Huh! Cora Watson? I don't know any Cora Watson.''

"She's coming down the stairs behind you. You know her best by her working name. Michelle.'' Bricker's eyes narrowed. "Also told me why you really left Golconda.'' A spurt of shock jolted Deweese; his head spun as Michelle flounced down the stairs and approached him. Jarred by astonishment, he jumped to his feet, his mind racing for an explanation to cover his lies to her and to Lew Bricker. He turned on his broadest, most engaging smile.

"Michelle! Mr. Bricker told me you were in town. How good to see you! Did you get my let—''

"You double-crossin' son of a bitch!" Michelle shrieked in long pent-up fury. Tucked behind her wrist she palmed a long and deadly needle-tipped, double-edged dagger. With a deft twist of wrist and fist, it swung out in her grip to arc upward and forward with all the thrust Michelle's petite body could gather.

With the speed of a snake's darting tongue, she lashed out.

She was so fast, Deweese didn't see it coming and hardly flinched. The hiltless, razor-edged dirk lanced through coat and shirt to slice smoothly into abdominal flesh and muscle. Its upward stab stopped when the clenched female fist clutching the knife sank the blade to its depth—and not before an inch of its sinister length had penetrated Dave Deweese's heart.

As Lew Bricker watched, horrified, Deweese—with a cough of abrupt pain and vomited blood—lurched backward, jerking himself free of Michelle's gory hand and the red-dripping knife. His eyes, popped with astonishment and sudden pain, rolled back, lids fluttering spasmodically. Hemorrhaging blood pumped by a faltering heart gushed out of the rip in his clothing as his legs folded and he crumpled.

Dave Deweese was dead before he hit the floor of Lew Bricker's Pick and Poke saloon, his death jerks smearing his thick, pooling blood on the splintered plank flooring.

The four riding up from the lowland reaches of Dalton Gulch came on easily, conserving their mounts. As measured and steady as their horses' walk was, urgency was evident in the way they sat their saddles and gripped the reins.

"Is that Dalton, Dick?" Charley cried happily.

"None but," Dick Snow yelled, riding a few paces left of the thirteen-year-old. Behind Snow, riding side by side as they urged their pack horses along with lead ropes, came Acie Casey and Barney Wisner.

"Finally," Barney shouted so Dick and Charley could hear. "First step ought to be to kill two birds with one stone. I got nothing against Acie's chuck, but I've had a silver cartwheel or two put by for some real citified food when we'd hit town."

"Well, I've been gettin' a little tired of forever fixing your grub anyway, you know that, Barney?" his plump saddle pard moaned in jest.

"First off, we'd best start asking around for Nell."

"That's your second bird, Barney," Snow said, surveying the town from their vantage point in the lower outskirts. The wide dirt street rose gradually, flanked by small, crude, low-slung gray log cabins with split-shake roofs against the towering mat of blue-green pine and spruce lifting along a craggy mountainside. A business district somehow intruded itself among the cabins with mercantile and business establishments marked by vertical board-and-batten or horizontal lapped siding, all of it rough-hewn and already weatherstained and split by the passage of several turns of the seasons.

As they progressed into the commercial section, the plop of their horses' hooves resounding on the packed dirt street, signs proclaimed the owners or the nature of the business transacted inside the buildings they passed, and they were all eyes.

"Say," Acie enthused. "This is quite a spread! Charley! See that big up-high sign? 'Taylor and Riley.' There's gilded letters on that sign on that upstairs window. 'Jewelers and Photographers.' That's where they made your locket! And see how the sign covers the saloon downstairs? They own it, too. Says 'Shows Nightly' there. We better see what that's all about before we ride out!''

"First we got to ask about Aunt Nell," Charley insisted.

"And keep a sharp eye," Barney cautioned. "We didn't see Deweese or any of the Parsons tribe all the way here."

"Yeah," Dick Snow agreed. "If they're here or been here, Lord knows what we'll find out. That's why I'm getting anxious to knock off your second bird, Barney."

"There's the beanery, Dick!" Barney called. "The Ritz-Dalton. Bet there's an two-inch-thick steak in there waiting for you!"

Impulsively, Snow urged his horse to the hitch rail in front of the restaurant. "Slick down your hair, gents," he called jubilantly, swinging out of the saddle. "Get ready to belly up to a real table again for a change!"

"I know we got urgent business that can't wait," Barney said, alighting behind Snow and tying up at the rack. "But ain't it a pleasure to see a town again? I could spend two days just wanderin' around, being inside these stores and saloons, just rememberin' how they look and how fresh goods smell and seein' the gewgaws that fetch a man's eye! The prairie has a way of gettin' tedious. A man yearns to see a town, to see people again. It's as good for the soul as a hot bath soakin' out the trail grime!"

Acie was quickly beside him. "What about Charley? How long you think it's been since he's seen a town?"

"I only want to see Aunt Nell," Charley insisted.

"We'll ask while we eat, son," Snow promised, entering the restaurant. He stopped, crouching, to button the oversized collar of Charley's blue shirt, borrowed from Barney. Snow also stroked Charley's hair to smooth it and to control a stubborn, straw-colored cowlick. They chose a table near the center and sat down expectantly. It was noon, and an old man bustled among the tables taking orders, serving food, and cleaning up after the diners. Now and then a young black man came out of the kitchen to help—but he seemed to disappear quickly. The place was in a state of great confusion. After what seemed like twenty minutes, the old man noticed them.

"I'm getting hungry, Dick," Charley complained.

"You ain't alone," Barney said. "Had I known that eatin' in town was going to be sittin' around lookin' hungry, I'd've stayed out on the flats and had more of Acie's chuck."

Finally the old man got to their table. "You got to excuse the delay, gents," he apologized. His eyes and his bearing looked very tired. "I see you're new in town. It ain't always this way around here. Our day waitress run off here a few days ago. My missus and me and the young man in the kitchen been tryin' to keep the place open from sunup to past dark. My missus ain't adjusted too well to the strain. I sent her home. Now, you see the bill of fare yonder on the big slate board. What'll it be, gents?"

Snow spoke right up. "I think we'd all go for some coffee right away, even the boy. Canned cow and sugar if you got it. Me, now, I'll take a thick, juicy steak still quivering and oozing in the middle, and three eggs, and a big heap of pan-fried spuds. And keep the coffee coming. We're good for it.''

"Sounds right to me," Acie agreed, and Barney followed suit.

"Could I get four eggs?" Charley asked. "Oh, yeah. Steak and potatoes, too, you know." He was embarrassed in his first time ordering a restaurant meal, but dazzle-eyed with the experience.

The old man began to hustle away. "Sir!" Snow called, speaking up, and the waiter—seemed to be the owner—returned to their table, wiping his sweaty hands on an already smudged apron.

"Yes, sir?"

"I know you're busy, and this won't take a minute."
'Make it snappy.''

"We're looking for someone. Maybe you know her," Dick said. "Nell. Nell Joiner?"

The man reacted as though shot. "Jee-zuss! So'm I lookin' for 'er! Where do you know Nell from? If you find 'er, tell 'er Lon and Mariposa Green want 'er back on the job. Pronto!''

"You mean she's gone?" Snow asked.

"Run off after five steady years here workin' for me! She's the reason for all this confusion. I trusted her, and she never let me down. Till now. Oddest thing to hit this town since Seth Joiner, her man, turned up missing on Spindrift Ridge. I commence to think they're strange ones, them Joiners."

"Then where is Nell?" Acie asked.

"She ain't in her cabin. I checked on that," the man said. "I suspect she went skylarkin' up in the woods with Bricker's new card man. He come back, but she didn't. Hard to figure."

Ritz-Dalton diners around them had grown impatient, either to settle their bills or to give a food order.

"I got to go now," the old man said, eyes nervously taking in a growing crowd that was also growing more impatient. Clearly, he had a problem. "As I said, gents, my name's Green. Lonnie Green. I'll get Hiram goin' on your order. If you want to know more about Miz Joiner, you'd ought to talk to Lew Bricker over to the Pick and Poke Saloon. He talked about Nell with that tinhorn gambler before the whore stabbed him dead."

Acie spoke up. "You don't mean a jasper named Deweese?"

"I guess you knew him." Green came back to the table.

Snow looked around at his tablemates, all of them with astonished expressions. He was pleased that Charley hadn't shot his mouth off.

"You mean Deweese is dead?" Barney asked, piping up in complete disbelief.

"As a doornail. I guess Deweese bilked this little girl—a new tart Bricker put on the payroll over at the Pick and Poke—out of her savings. They knew each other back east. Some town they called Golconda. When she caught up with Deweese here in Dalton, she run a long-ass pig-sticker through his vitals, and down he went. This Deweese never so much as had a chance to say his prayers. He was in here a few times. Nice fella, too. Can't see how a nice young man like that could come to such a bad end. You know what they say: Hell hath no fury like a woman scorned."

"Anybody know where Nell is?" Barney asked.

"Sure as hell don't. Deweese told Bricker he took Nell up to the gold country. He came back, but she didn't. All I know."

"What'd they do with 'er? That lady that killed Dave?" Charley asked, his eyes big as bowls.

"She'll swing, most likely, young feller. Whores ain't got many rights. Some of the boys got a look at her and figure Deweese got as good as he gave. They want 'er to stick around."

"Hey, Lon!" a voice called from across the room. "How about some service?"

"Ahh, button your lip, Arty!" Green called back. "I'll be there in a minute."

"I could've rode to Denver and back and got fed quicker," a customer nearby called.

"Hold your horses, Ted," Green called loudly. "I'll get to all of you in a minute. These jaspers know about Nell!"

"She's my aunt!" Charley piped up proudly to one and all.

"She is?" Green asked. "Then you ... you must be little Charley Rogers! Nell talked about you all the time. Which one of you is Frank?"

"None of us," Snow said. "Frank's been dead about six years."

"Well, I'm sorry to hear that. But I got to be about my business. You go over yonder and talk to Lew Bricker. There could've been foul play."

"Right after we eat," Barney promised.

"Yeah," Green said, hustling away. "I'll get Hiram to whip up your steak and eggs and spuds right away."

# ⇒ 17 ⇐

**W**ell, boys, we'll stop off at her cabin on the way out of town," Snow said as he strode out of the Pick and Poke after talking with Lew Bricker. "Just to see if there's any chance she got home. Mr. Bricker in there seems to think Deweese left her in the mountains somewhere."

"Lowlife scum," Barney muttered. "But hell, I guess he's paid his debt now." They walked back across to their horses, still tied in front of the Ritz-Dalton. Acie had caught up with them, having used his time to stop at the general store to resupply his dwindling provisions.

"Where do you suppose old Parsons fits into all this? It plagues me that we didn't see them again before we got here."

"I don't know, Acie. I just don't know," Snow said. "Right now, we need to find Nell. Mount up, boys. Her place is up toward the head end of the gulch. We'll stop there, and if she's not home, I'm for heading into the mountains right away."

"Tall, wide country up there by the looks, Dick," Barney cautioned. "How'll we ever find her?"

"Well, we sure won't do it hanging around town," Acie said, settling into his saddle. A rare impatience rang in his voice.

"We've got to find her," Charley said mournfully. "Maybe Deweese killed her."

"Deweese was a lot of bad things, son," Dick said with a consoling tone. "But I don't think he was a cold-blooded killer."

"Let's get up the street," Barney said.

Bricker had told them that Nell's cabin was the only one up that way with windows on either side of a front door. They found it quickly and confirmed it by finding a wood plate fastened beside the door with "Joiner" carefully carved in it.

"Bet that was Seth Joiner's handiwork," Dick said, getting down to rap on the door. There was no response. He went to the one window that had the curtains pulled back and, shading his eyes from the reflections on the glass, peered in.

"Lots of woman's touches in there," he said to the others, still mounted. "This is the right place. And she's not at home."

"Can I see?" Charley asked, already getting down. He went to the window.

"Okay, Dick," Charley said after a brief glimpse. While heading for his horse, he said, "Did you see that big rocking chair? I think I remember that from somewhere."

"Just now, we'd better get busy finding the woman it belongs to," Barney said. "I'm gettin' an uneasy feeling about all this. Anything Deweese was involved in doesn't particularly inspire my confidence."

"And Aunt Nell can tell me about that chair," Charley said eagerly.

Their ride up Dalton Gulch took most of the afternoon. The stream that had created the gulch tumbled out of the mountains, probably spring-fed from underground reservoirs of winter runoff. Dotting its banks were widely separated miners' claims worked by robust men, many of them bearded and in tattered clothing. With picks and shovels, a little dynamite, and with gold rockers, sluices, and pans in the stream, they dug away hillsides or probed into solid granite with adits they called "glory holes" of varying depths in their untiring search for nuggets, dust, and flakes.

On occasional inquiry, some of them recalled seeing "Miss Nell" riding up the gulch with "Lew Bricker's tinhorn" and wondering when they saw Deweese ride out alone several days later.

"I'm a man who minds his own affairs," one grizzled, talkative old prospector related when they had nearly reached the head of the gulch and their start into the true high country. "Warn't like Miss Nell to just up and leave Lonnie Green flat like that." The old timer paused again. "Strange doin's afoot ever since that tinhorn came to town. None of my affair, but a man takes note of such things. There was strange jaspers in town, hangin' around in the alleys, watchin'. Watchin' for somethin'. They'd allus duck out of sight if they saw me comin'. I kept my old pea-shooter Colt close to my bed them nights, I'm here to tell ya."

"Any idea who they were?" Dick Snow asked the

old man, but his eyes were on his saddle mates with a questioning look.

"A man that sticks his nose in the business of others is likely to get it bit off. So it ain't none of my affair. I'd've thought them other fellas down the line would've told you if you'd've asked. They know all about it too, most of 'em."

"What's that?" Acie asked.

"Why, hell! It warn't an hour after Miss Nell and that tinhorn rode through here. Here come them guys from the alleys, six or eight of 'em. Skinny bastard ridin' at the head of 'em, looked like the boss, yammerin' his head off like a screech owl. He was wearin' leathern clothes that'd seen better days. They are plumb up to no good in these mountains, I'm here to tell ya."

"Thanks, pardner," Barney said abruptly. "We best get on our way. Got a lot of riding yet. Good luck on your claim."

"Anybody messes with Old Bill Wheeler," the man called after them, "is likely to find a fight on his hands! Apart from that, I don't go messin' into other people's affairs!" Old Wheeler nearly shouted as the four riders disappeared up the trail.

"Well, don't that put a different face on things?" Acie commented when they were well away from Old Wheeler.

"That's why we didn't see Parsons on the way up here," Barney observed. "He was always out ahead of us. Still is, and what's gigging me is that Nell's up in these mountains, too."

"What gets me is how Parsons knew to come to Dalton," Acie said. "We figured all along he didn't have an inkling. Parsons sure didn't seem to have told

Deweese. It wasn't till Charley accidentally said something about Dalton that Deweese quit cozyin' up to us and run off our horses."

"Looks like an open-and-shut case to me," Dick remarked. "Parsons and Deweese must've joined forces somewhere along the line."

"Doesn't hold water, Dick," Barney said, with a calculating tone. "It only figures that Deweese talked her into showing him the way to the claim."

Snow spoke up. "And Parsons's deal was he'd come along behind, ready to move in the minute Nell and Deweese found it."

"Your bucket's still got a hole in it, Dick," Barney said. "If that was so, how come Deweese rode back to town . . . alone?"

"To file a claim?" Snow asked.

"Maybe, but not likely," Barney continued, feeling his way with his thoughts. "First, the folks in Dalton would've found samples in his gear, and it'd've been the talk of the camp. Bricker never said a word about that, nor did the old man at the beanery."

"And second?" Acie asked.

Barney studied him. "I think that's pretty obvious, Acie. Would Deweese, if he was in his right mind, walk away from a rich claim and the woman, or both, leaving everything in the hands of the likes of Simon Parsons? I'm thinking if anything, there was bad blood between Parsons and Deweese."

"You know what that old miner said," Charley reminded them. " 'There strange doin's afoot.' " He mimicked Old Wheeler's voice.

"Mrs. Joiner could be in grave danger," Dick said soberly. "Deweese is dead and can't tell us a thing.

Parsons is up here someplace, expecting us, and there's nothing he won't stop at to protect what he considers his interests.''

"The gold's important, Dick," Barney pointed out. "But what's important to us right now is Mrs. Joiner's welfare. I don't think there's any doubt he's holding her captive. We've got to figure a way to find him without him finding us first."

"And that's not going to be easy," Snow said.

The trail had taken them well above the head of Dalton Gulch, and their horses labored on the steep grades. Looking up, whenever the view was clear of trees or not blocked by lower ridges, the sawtoothed rim of Spindrift Ridge loomed over them like a craggy fortress.

"This trail," Barney said, "seems like it's going to take us at least to the top of the ridge. Not too many folks have come this way, judging its use. No telling where Seth Joiner found his strike."

"Nor where Parsons might have bushwhackers laying in ambush for us," Dick said. "I'm getting to liking this setup less and less. We're sitting ducks. We've got think about how to save our hides if we're to save hers."

"How about this?" Charley piped up. "How about we take turns? Two of us scout either side of the trail on foot for a few miles while the other two come along slow with the horses. Then we switch off, and the other two scout for a couple of hours."

"Sometimes, Jolly Roger," Dick Snow said, "you amaze me. It's dangerous. But under the circumstances, four of us riding along making perfect targets of ourselves is nothing short of pure dumb."

"Won't make much time that way," Acie put in.

"But we'll make it," Barney said. "I guess. Or is it I hope?"

"It was my idea. I go first," Charley insisted.

Dick Snow looked at Acie and Barney almost helplessly. "Jolly Roger to the rescue," he said, grinning. "Who's game to join him?"

"I'll take the right side of the trail," Barney offered.

"Walk soft," Dick Snow advised. "Keep a sharp eye. You spot anything, whistle like a bird to alert your partner, and then both of you get back here double time and report."

Acie spoke up. "One round of that ought to be enough for today. Judging from the looks of the sky, we better find us a safe place to lodge for the night before long and start out in the morning."

"But I got to find Aunt Nell," Charley insisted.

"Charley," Dick Snow said emphatically, an edge in his voice, "that's what all of us want, too. But when it gets dark, there's no point in blundering ahead. We need to go into camp, eat something, and rest. We'll be back at it first thing in the morning. Is that clear?"

Acie looked at Barney without a word; Dick Snow was right. The situation, no matter how you looked at it, was dicey.

Charley studied Snow with big eyes. "Yes, sir," he responded.

Dick Snow reached across from his horse and put a fatherly hand on Charley's shoulder. "We all want to find your aunt, son. The sooner the better. But we're not going to do it by bulling ahead and getting hurt, or worse, getting killed."

Charley acknowledged Snow with his eyes.

"Now get out there on your scout," Snow added. "But keep your eyes open."

By midmorning of the next day they were high enough to be nearing the crest of Spindrift Ridge, and Charley was again out as forward scout with a rifle at the ready. He wore his old buckskin jacket for warmth against the chill of the higher elevation. His mind's eye had an image of Barney Wisner out of sight across the trail from him, a Winchester cradled easily in his crossed arms, probing ahead like Charley for any sign of Parsons's dry-gulchers.

Dick Snow and Acie Casey brought up the rear, urging the horses slowly along the trail, hopeful that Charley's and Barney's sharp eyes would spot any lurking bushwhackers and avert a tragedy.

Charley's route ultimately took him into a small but roughly circular break in the tall evergreens. The massive monarchs circled the cabin-sized clearing like temple pillars. Over everything a hushed, cathedral-like stillness prevailed; motes and beams of sunlight slanted on an angle down through trunks, limbs, and needles to focus their dim light on the clearing.

Charley edged into the open space, his eyes drinking in the majesty of it all, and hearing high in the branches the almost sorrowful soughing of the wind combing through towering boughs.

With a sense of reverence, shadowlike in his memory of his parents, but stronger in his upbringing by Elk Leggins, Charley felt a spiritual presence pervading the almost mystic circle of slanted pale sunlight. A soft kind of peace flowed over his thirteen-year-old soul. His memory registered the sensations, hoping the day would come when he could return alone to this sanctuary under happier conditions to camp and to relive in a strengthening kind of solitude the sensations he now experienced and sought to savor—the oneness with nature or the Great Spirit or God—and find that abiding strength of spirit that he sensed now filled and nourished him.

Charley's sweet vision of peace was rudely shattered, and he came alert to a stark, frightening reality with a jolt as he saw a movement at the fringes of the clearing, a flickering of motion and color that brought a burst of alarm to his consciousness and to his sight. Reality charging through him with an energizing force, Charley whipped his long-barreled six-gun to a defensive level.

The misty, shadowy form had disappeared into the forest, or behind one of the stately trunks. Charley reacted by darting to the sanctuary of a nearby tree. His momentary enjoyment of the setting had vanished, gone like the wind. Danger and death lurked now in a depressing stillness. Charley was galvanized into intensity itself. Scarcely breathing, he poked out the long-barreled Colt and enough of his head to see and, he hoped, to be shielded from gunshots. He peered around the pine's gnarled, scaly roots. Nothing moved. He sensed, though, that another person skulked out there, occupying and invading his momentary but precious link with heaven, eternity, and everlasting power. He heard nothing—only the raspy heaving of his own lungs. Barney—across the trail from him—would obviously continue to move toward the crest, unaware that Charley was pinned down and no longer protectively flanked him.

Charley had waited too long. His heart raced with

the danger-fraught situation. It was time for decisive action. If this was part of the expected ambush, Barney was a slow-moving target, and Dick Snow and Acie Casey moving up from the rear with the horses, counting on Charley's forward-probing vigilance, were dead ducks.

He lowered his voice as much as possible against his adolescent shriek; he tried to sound as commanding as Dick Snow.

"Hold it right there!" he yelled. "There's three of us over here! We all got guns on you. Step out with your hands in the air!" He bellowed as bassly as his youthful voice would allow.

A clean-shaven long-haired jasper inched out from behind the big tree trunk. He had no weapon. At least none visible, and Charley was convinced that if the man made a false move, he could drill him easily from this range.

He wore miner's clothing and an old slouch felt hat. Though his hands were in the air, the breast pockets of his coat or shirt looked full. Troubled thoughts intruded on Charley's mind. Prevailing over his confusion was his idea of what Dick Snow would do in this kind of situation.

"Walk across to me!" he commanded, trying to sound like Snow, and stepping out into the clearing's meager shafts of sunlight.

His adversary did the same, stepping into the sun's full, dusty beams.

The unarmed stranger moved closer to Charley, meekly, arms still in the air, a haunted, terrified expression in his eyes and face.

Charley also moved out from sanctuary, terrified

himself and hopeful that the stranger's companions didn't have guns trained on *him* from the shadows.

Halfway across, the stranger emerged into the full sunlight afforded by the great circular opening up there in the crown of ringing trees.

Charley stopped abruptly, transfixed. He hadn't seen a white woman in years; this was beyond that, a basic, primal emotion linked by a mist of memory to the rocker he'd seen fleetingly in Nell Joiner's cabin. Images and sensory impressions, vague and wispy and shadowy, then momentarily flowing distinctly before they vanished, swirled through him in a dreamlike gauze; nothing substantial to hold on to. Only the tinted picture in the locket on the stained thong around his neck flashed before his mind's eye. Could it be? Here, in this wild but beautiful place? Could it? A rush of revelation overwhelmed him, its staggering wave bringing reality and relief. And recognition.

It must be.

"Aunt Nell?" he called, almost timidly.

She stopped abruptly, her body reacting with a flinch to the name. Bewildered, she studied him from the few paces that separated them. "Who . . . you—you know me?" she asked, her words soft and halting. Then in a voice racked by waves of emotion: "Wait a minute!" She paused, almost as if searching for her voice. "Charley? *Charley Rogers?*"

# ❋ 18 ❋

**D**ick and Acie, picking their way slowly along the narrow trail, leading the extra horses, straightened in surprise to see through a break in the mesh of trees ahead the forms of Charley and Barney coming toward them, supporting a third person who appeared near some sort of collapse.

"Good Lord, Acie!" Snow's words were gasped. "It's a woman. They found Nell!"

"May the saints be praised!" Acie said, vaulting from the saddle to join Dick, already on foot and headed for the approaching trio.

"She's been out here hiding for days," Barney explained, his voice urgent, as Dick and Acie raced up.

"I found her," Charley said jubilantly. "Aunt Nell practically walked right up to me."

Nell found a last reserve of strength, both physical and emotional, and pulled herself erect and away from Charley and Barney. "I'll be all right," she said, grateful for their help. "So much all at once. I haven't eaten for days." Her voice was soft with exhaustion.

Acie's voice had a ring of command. "Fellas, let's get to a safe place to make a camp. I'll get some food ready for her and for us in short order."

"Better go back down the mountain a ways," Dick said. "Find a place to defend ourselves if Parsons shows up."

Nell's voice was stronger now. "I don't think they've come over the crest yet. I haven't heard them hunting me all morning."

"Parsons? Hunting you, Mrs. Joiner?"

"I escaped four nights ago." She sighed. "They surely have been after me. I've been very fortunate."

"Dick," Acie insisted, "let's get her to a safe camp and some food and rest. Then find out about Parsons."

Charley spoke up. "Aunt Nell, you can ride Dolly, my horse. Here she is."

"You take my horse, Charley," Barney urged. "Dick, I'm going to run on ahead and find a likely spot. You folks take your time bringing the lady down the trail." With that, Barney, rifle in hand, was off at a trot, quickly disappearing among the trees as the trail wended its twisty way downslope.

"We'll have everything fixed up in no time, Mrs. Joiner," Dick Snow assured, holding Dolly and the stirrup to help her get mounted.

"You men must be friends of Charley, my . . . nephew." Her voice sounded tired but trusting as she looked down at Dick Snow.

He smiled back up at her. "Charley? Friends? Indeed we are. We've been friends several weeks now on the trail. Coming here."

"Let's get going, Dick!" Acie blurted.

In little more than an hour they had found a remote

high point, easily defended, and Barney got to work setting up a camp they could use for a day or two until Nell's strength returned.

In no time, Acie had coffee bubbling over a hot fire and was busy preparing a fine noontime meal of cured ham, fresh eggs, and store-bought bread. "While they were in talking to Mr. Bricker at the saloon," he confessed to a famished, exhausted Nell, "I stopped over at the mercantile and got us some fresh groceries."

With Charley's help as his "apprentice," Barney secured horizontal supports for a hasty shade arbor for Nell to four convenient small trees, overlaying them with branches and then boughs. He also created for her a soft bed of thick boughs, overlaid with one of their buffalo robes. For her privacy under the arbor, he and Charley lashed a large tarp from a packhorse load around two of the most exposed sides.

"Ought to be a snug camp before night," Barney remarked, coming to Acie's fire for his plate of food and his coffee. Nell and Charley sat close together, watching each other intently and lovingly, silently mowing away plates heaped with hot, steaming food.

Dick Snow, away to check the perimeter of their camp, strode in to crouch by the fire; Acie heaped eggs, ham, and bread on a plate and handed it across the fire to him.

"More where that came from," Acie said proudly. "And if it's not enough, I'll cook still more. Anybody want more coffee?"

"I think my stomach must've shrunk, Mr. Casey. My first meal in three days, and I feel stuffed. Everything is delicious. I will have some more coffee."

Acie gingerly picked up the hot coffeepot with his

bandanna. "I always like satisfied customers, Mrs. Joiner. But please call me Acie."

She gave him a smile and it was a sincere one. "And I'm Nell, Acie."

Nell looked around at the men, leaned over, and happily hung an arm around Charley's shoulders. "I suppose I'm tired enough to sleep. But . . . finding Charley alive and being among people I know I can trust after so much cruel deception and brutality—and wanting to know how all this happened—I couldn't sleep if I tried."

"I think we're secure enough up here for the time being," Dick said. "We've got a lot to talk about, Nell, if you're up to it. It might help if we heard about Deweese and Parsons, just in case we have another confrontation with his eminence, Mr. Parsons. By the way, I don't suppose anybody's had a chance to tell you. Dave Deweese is dead. Stabbed, I understand, by a woman he'd wronged some time back."

Nell's grimace was noticeable but brief. She looked Dick Snow in the eye. "I'm truly sorry. He deserved punishment for the way he abused people. But not death."

"He deserted you?" Acie asked, his eyes on Nell's, registering a characteristic deep compassion.

"He'd persuaded me he'd been there when Charley and his family died on the trail and that Frank Rogers had entrusted him with the gold samples, which he later sold. His story sounded truthful, and he seemed to have trustworthy ways."

"That lowlife stole our horses when our backs were turned," Barney put in. "Caused us no end of annoyance. Held us up getting here."

"I needed someone to help me find Seth's mine; Dave seemed like such a logical choice. We had such a happy time riding up here. Then this Parsons bunch came to our camp, talking about all manner of evil, unspeakable things to make me reveal Seth's claim. To save his hide, Dave turned me over to them."

"He deserved to die," Charley said angrily. "What he did to you. To us."

Nell reached across and laid her hand over his. "No, Charley. Dave Deweese was totally self-centered. But given time, he might have seen the error of his ways."

"They say a leopard can't change his spots," Dick said, staring thoughtfully into Acie's noontime fire.

"So tell me," Nell broke in, seeing a subject that needed changing, "how did you men get together with Charley?"

With the four of them chiming in, she was told the story of Charley's tragedy, his life with the benevolent Elk Leggins, of Parsons's unwelcome visit and crude behavior, the theft of Charley's ore samples, of their subsequent visit, and then of the web of events on their journey to reunite her with her nephew.

"Now," Dick said. "Here we are. You're safe, Charley's safe, and unless I've been hearing wrong, Simon Parsons still hasn't any notion where your late husband's claim is."

Nell's laugh was like a free, happy chirp. "Why do you think he tried so hard to catch me after I got away?"

Barney cleared his throat, getting their attention. "Looks to me like we've got at least two choices. But first we've got to give Nell time to rest and plenty of Acie's good food to get her completely back on her feet. Then we either go back to town and wait for Parsons to run himself ragged up here and pull out, or when we're ready, we hunt him down and take him on with whatever dangers that'll present.''

Barney looked around at his saddlemates for opinions.

"He could also find out somehow that we're here and attack," Dick said.

"It's about two days back down the trail to town," Acie put in. "He might catch us out there, too, unprotected. Anything's chancy as long as Parsons is around. He could even catch Nell in town when we're not looking and drag her away."

"Seth used to say that the best defense is a good offense," Nell said, her eyes agleam.

Dick Snow smiled at her, admiring her pluck and feeling his heart warming toward the brave woman. "Couldn't have said it better myself. Charley, how about you? You've got a say in this matter, too."

"Aunt Nell would say Parsons doesn't deserve to die—and so would the rest of us. But I think he ought to be made to pay for what he's done to us."

"And if Parsons is persuaded that we mean business and goes on about his and leaves us alone, we can go on to find Seth's claim," Nell added.

"You make it sound so easy, Nell," Dick said, his eyes registering admiration.

Nell looked around her at the four men; "Little Charley" had already proved to her that he was well on his way to a strong manhood, thanks to his three adult partners. "Depends," she said. "If Parsons wants to make it easy on himself."

*     *     *

For two more days they languished in their small, craggy fortress high on the slopes of Spindrift Ridge. They neither heard nor saw anything of Simon Parsons or his men. Acie's coffeepot, always warming beside the fire, become a mecca for relaxed and sometimes serious conversations. Nell insisted she give Acie a hand with the meals, and he happily and gratefully accepted. They chattered over their chores like a pair of old housewives.

In time, they didn't even try to be especially quiet, not caring if gunfire alerted the Parsons gang. To continue his education of Charley in woodslore, Dick took him hunting with the "big two-shoot rifle," the muzzle-loading scattergun barrel ready for birds or small game, the big-bore rifle barrel with patched ball for larger prey.

They'd hardly been away from camp a half an hour when Acie, Barney, and Nell heard the gun's muffled report. "I'm bettin' fresh meat in camp tonight!" Barney said.

In an even shorter time, Charley charged jubilantly into camp, proudly toting the heavy and ornate caplock gun. His eyes were bright and his cheeks flushed in victory.

"Dick let me shoot the rifle when we saw this deer. And ... and I got it!"

Snow came into view right behind Charley, toting a small buck over his shoulders, the legs draped in front of him and held by his arms. He had carted along a small chunk of canvas and had it over his shoulders like a cape, under the deer, to keep blood from soaking his clothes.

Charley chattered about the hunt most of the afternoon. They had returned with enough fresh meat to keep them for weeks. Nell and Acie, both skilled at "jerking" meat, dried much of the tender venison, saving enough in fresh roasts and steaks. Charley watched them work, helping when he could, absorbed in learning more of the process he had seen done by women in Elk Leggins's village.

A mountain stream, crystalline and icy, gurgled and chattered not far from camp. Acie packed a large quantity of the fresh meat in his empty, watertight lard can and dropped it in a small pool. "That'll keep it fresh as the day it was butchered," he told Charley, who had helped him with the meat.

Fully recovered from her ordeal, Nell grew restless and, with Dick Snow as her companion and guard, hiked long hours in the tall, somber forests surrounding the camp. They returned full of small talk and pleasantries, seeming to grow close and contented as friends. Acie and Barney observed it all and exchanged knowing glances. Without a word passing between them, they remembered a conversation they'd had on the prairie about Dick's need of a proper woman to support his fatherly interest in Charley. As Charley's closest living relative, the childless Nell—to them—had no peer.

Midmorning of their third day together found them breaking camp, loading equipment, and girding themselves to take on the risky confrontation with the Simon Parsons gang. They were suddenly alerted by someone hailing them.

"Hello, the camp!" came a voice from below their eagle's-nest stronghold.

"Easy does it," Dick Snow hissed at the others. "This could be a trick." He took command. "Let me handle this."

He moved closer to the edge of the flat camp area formed by huge rocks that had trembled down the mountainside. Keeping securely hidden, Dick called out to the nameless, faceless voice. "State your business!"

"We need help!"

"Do you ride with Simon Parsons?"

There was a long pause, as though several men conferred among themselves. "Yes," came the response from the tangle of trees below Snow. "Who are you?"

Dick took an arrogant approach. "The man Simon condemned to death the night of the raid on your horse herd! Dick Snow. Once again, state your business."

"Simon accidentally shot himself! He's in a bad way."

Snow turned with a puzzled look back at the others not far behind him. "Just a minute," he called down. He turned to Nell and the others. "What do you make of that?"

Barney piped up. "Sounds too real to be a trick. Let one of them come up here and state his case." Snow stepped back to the rim of their sanctuary.

"One of you can come up," he shouted. "But no tricks. We'll level you the minute you make a wrong step."

"No tricks, Mr. Snow. I'm unarmed, hands in the air." A figure materialized out of the dense forest below the ancient rockslide and picked his way up to where Dick and others stood waiting.

"They call me Shorty," he called, his smooth leather boot soles slipping on the rocks as he climbed to them.

Nell immediately recognized his voice as that of one of the men who had rested outside her hiding place several nights before.

"Come on in," Snow called hospitably, and the man drew nearer to him. "Okay, Shorty," Snow said. "What's this all about?" The others stood nearby. Without comment, Shorty observed Nell standing with Charley.

Shorty's face was ashen with concern. "Couple days ago Simon was drunk. Worse than he ever was . . . that—well, the lady there had got away from him, and we hadn't caught her. He hauled off to draw and shoot one of boys, Wild Card—Simon blamed him—and hardly cleared leather. Shot himself through the leg. The wound isn't serious, but it's mortified. Simon's deathly ill and raving like a lunatic. Hard to hold him down. We heard shootin' this way yesterday, and me and Zeb thought to come over here to find help. We sure didn't think it'd be you and your people, Mr. Snow. And that you'd found the lady there."

"Call Zeb up here, Shorty," Dick said decisively. "There's still coffee on the fire. We'll help you out." Snow looked at his friends, who now clustered around him and Shorty. He looked at him. "Won't we?" His suggestion was greeted with murmurs and nods of assent.

"But remember, Dick," Barney—often the devil's advocate—warned, "it could be a trap."

"I've thought of that," Dick responded, his eyes crinkling with shrewd calculation. "We ride in there with guns on these two and others of us ready to spray lead at the rest. I don't think they'll try anything with that display of force."

Dick looked at Shorty, who had just summoned Zeb to join them. "You are telling us the truth, aren't you, Shorty? Because the second I think you're leading us into an ambush, you'll be dead meat. Get that through your head right now."

"I'm not lying to you, Mr. Snow. Simon needs somebody to help him, and he needs it bad."

Minutes later, Shorty and Zeb crouched by the night fire, sipping coffee. Zeb, wide-eyed, was virtually speechless; his expression suggested he expected to be shot any minute.

"We did what we could for him, Mr. Snow, but he just got worse," Shorty said. "We flat didn't know what to do. Now his leg's swole up and bloated and purple, and he's wild out of his head."

"That's all beside the point now, Shorty," Acie put in. "We got to get busy and get over there and try to save your boss's life."

With a frightened look, Shorty regarded Acie, a man he'd only seen fleetingly at their first confrontation weeks before—and whom Simon Parsons had ranted and raved over as a bloodthirsty cutthroat.

"Sir, I'll be mightily obliged," Shorty said, holding hat in hand, sheepish with the realization of what he asked of people Parsons had treated harshly.

"Well, let's go," Nell intruded. "We haven't a minute to lose."

Charley watched them, amazed at the emergency that had galvanized his friends into action; even Aunt Nell, who had every reason to hate Simon Parsons. He realized that hate had suddenly taken second place; a man's life was threatened. Despicable or otherwise, Simon Parsons—the former hated enemy—was a human being in grave danger. With little or no discussion, Dick, Acie, Barney, and Nell were concerned and ready to help.

At the Parsons camp, beyond Spindrift Summit, in the trees at the edge of a sprawling meadowland, Charley watched, trying to keep out of the way as his adult companions took charge.

Parsons's ragtag outlaws stood around the camp, their vacant faces registering concern and helplessness. Parsons, his thin face seamed with agony and illness, lay huddled and stiff under a dingy gray blanket.

He was also helpless—completely.

Snow went directly to Parsons and crouched beside him. "Well, Simon. Sorry this had to happen to you." Charley heard a voice that registered genuine concern; in that moment, Charley learned from Snow a very basic principle—never kick a man when he's down.

"Your boys found us camped on the other side of the ridge," Dick went on. "We'll see what we can do for you and get you to town. Mrs. Joiner tells me they've got a doctor there."

"You've got to help me, Snow," Parsons said, his voice thin and weak.

"We have every intention of doing just that."

Nell had crouched on the other side of the wounded man. "Can I have a look at your wound, Mr. Parsons?" she asked.

Parsons studied her with apprehension in his pain-dimmed eyes.

Dick spoke up. "Simon, bygones are bygones. She and I are here to help you."

Parsons weakly reached out and pulled aside the

blanket. Someone had cut open the leg of his buckskin trousers to expose the wound. Grimy rags, now blood-soaked, had been tied around Parson's thigh to stop the bleeding.

Nell looked at Dick Snow. Charley, along with Acie and Barney, stood back out of the way with the Parsons men. "First we've got to get those awful cloths off there, Dick," Nell said. "And cleanse his wound."

"Likely two wounds," Snow said as Nell began to loosen the rags secured around Parsons's leg. Parsons flinched and screamed out in pain. "Looks like the bullet hit him when he tried to draw. Entered the right side of the right thigh and went out the back. Didn't get the artery, or he'd be dead. And didn't break bone, or he wouldn't hardly be able to talk."

"Let's get busy," Nell said.

# ❊ 19 ❊

As Dick and Nell consulted over the severity of Parsons's wounds and infection and began to do something for him, Barney and Acie took charge of rigging a horse-borne litter to transport Parsons to the help of a doctor in Dalton with as little discomfort as possible.

Anticipating the narrow downslope trail, Barney designed a lodgepole-length lash-up secured on ropes and slung lengthwise between two horses. He hastily stitched bedroll blankets and buffalo robes to the poles for a sufficiently comfortable bed for the ailing man.

"We could try a travois," Barney explained to Charley, who was familiar with the Cheyenne method of dragging belongings from horseback. "But that downhill country is so rough, we'd jar him to death before we got him there. So a travois is out. This rig will be bad enough, but it's better than bouncing him all over the place."

Charley marveled at how Barney thought things through and then got them done. He realized that he—learning from Barney—had begun to look at problems from several angles and not just jump at the first solution that came to mind. Sometimes, his new wisdom taught him, a little extra thought produced a better and easier way.

All this in readiness, and with Nell and Dick having brought as much ease to their patient as their primitive means allowed, the odd downslope entourage began the long, tedious trip to Dalton. Parsons's outlaws rode the trail ahead; Charley's companions clustered near the litter bearing a nearly subdued Simon Parsons; but only his evil aggressions were held in check. Everyone still heard from him. The jolting pain caused by the irregular gait of the horses transporting the litter through rugged country had Parsons—never known for his stoicism—howling in agony and discomfort.

At frequent stops, Nell and Dick cared for Simon Parsons's miseries as best they could; his wound was checked and washed and dressed. Like a hovering angel, Nell bathed Parsons's face and chest, arms and hands with cool, comforting water from the nearby streams.

Dick and Nell, having committed themselves to saving Parsons's life, functioned smoothly as a team; their only actions and remarks to each other concerned the ailing man in the litter. Acie and Barney—as well as Charley—marveled at how skillfully they worked together in the emergency.

They all become so geared to Parsons's crisis and their responsibilities toward the sick and wounded man that time passed, and before they knew it, they had ridden into the head end of Dalton Gulch.

Acie and Barney looked at each other with rolling eyes when Old Bill Wheeler stepped away from his gold rocker in the narrow stream to watch the procession pass by, astonishment in his rheumy old eyes.

"What you got there?" he called, his beard wagging like a billy goat's and his words rapid-fire as Acie and Barney followed Parsons's men just ahead of the horse-drawn litter. Parsons's mouth still spouted mindless drivel associated with intense pain and the rantings of a fevered brain.

Old Wheeler wasn't far behind Parsons when it came to raving. He strung his words together almost breathlessly. "Say," he continued, "that's that jasper I warned you fellers about. The guy in the wore-out leathern clothes. What're ya messin' around with him for? That one is trouble in the flesh, I'm here to tell ya. I'm a man as tends to his own affairs, but if you was to ask me, I wouldn't mess around with the likes of that one. What'd ya do? Shoot 'im? He prob'ly don't deserve better, but you ought to've left 'im back up there. I know his kind. They're backshooters. Hangin's too good for jaspers of that stripe!"

The trail had opened out, and Dick and Nell could walk on either side of Parsons's litter, doing what they could to ease the man's suffering.

"It was an accident," Dick said quietly as he passed the old prospector standing and yammering beside the trail. Dick did not elaborate.

"Well, if it was up to me, I wouldn't waste my time savin' his hide." Old Wheeler turned back to where his gold washer sat at the edge of the stream. "The times, they sure are a-changin'," he could be heard muttering to himself, "when they start mollycoddlin' owlhoots the likes o' that'un. In my day, by God, we got aholt of one like that, and we'd string 'im up quicker'n scat!''

Out of his hearing, Nell grinned across the litter at Dick. "Old Bill Wheeler," she said, a happy tinkle in her voice. "A town character. Swears up and down he doesn't meddle in the affairs of others. Then you can be sure he has something to say about everything!"

They had talked it over as they came down the trail. Nearing Dalton, Acie and Barney spurred their horses to town to locate Rufus Walker, Dalton's local sawbones. When the procession neared the edge of the settlement and Dick and Nell could see Nell's cabin, a chaise with a bay mare in the traces was already hitched out front, along with Barney's and Acie's horses.

Standing with them was a genial-looking, ruddy-faced man with a ready smile, watching their approach expectantly. He had short-cropped gray hair going white at the temples and wore a black hat and suit, white shirt, and black string tie. The trademark of his profession, an ample black valise, was on the ground at his feet.

Shorty, who had ridden the forward horse bearing Parsons's litter, stopped the animal close to Nell's front door.

While Parsons's gang members looked on indifferently from their horses clustered around the buggy, Barney and Dick locked their wrists and hands into a square seat for Parsons—who spewed profanities against the pain—got him hoisted up, and, with his arms around her shoulders, gently carried him into the cabin.

Dr. Walker, smiling benevolently, walked in behind

them, lugging his satchel. As quickly as he was inside, he shrugged out of his frock coat, rolled up his sleeves, and set his medicine bag where it would be handy. The engaging smile never left his face, but he settled down to business the moment Simon Parsons had been made comfortable in Nell's ample bed in the cabin.

"Mr. Snow?" he said, extending his hand. "We haven't met. Walker's my name. Rufus Walker, the only doctor hereabouts. I'd like you and Nell to stay while I examine and treat our patient. The rest of them outside may leave, along with your friends here." He shooed Acie, Charley, and Barney out of the cabin without a bit of discourtesy; no one took exception. The doctor had work to do.

"Dick," Acie called as they filed out of the cabin, "Barney and I'll take Charley down to the beanery for something to eat. We'll be there or around nearby in town if you need us."

Dick waved them on with an acknowledging smile.

Dick and Nell were occupied with Dr. Walker in reducing the danger of fatal infection from Simon Parsons's wounds, and Charley—with Acie and Barney—put away a fine dinner in the Ritz-Dalton, with Charley being effusively made over by Mrs. Mariposa Green, wife of the proprietor. So no one paid particular attention to the dissolution of Simon Parsons's outlaw band.

If anyone did, it was Lew Bricker's bartender, Cecil, a big-boned, heavyset man with a walrus mustache the color of honey. Gang members came into Cecil's bar for whiskey flasks and jugs—depending on their money supply—to take on the trail. Cecil noted that their minds seemed to be made up to ride on even before they wandered into the saloon.

Cecil overheard a Parsons man named Wild Card talking it over with several others. "Even if Simon gets better, and I don't think he will," Wild Card said, "that woman's gonna get the law down on him for what happened, and a lot of other stuff we did'll come out. Won't none of us get off easy. I'm for goin' my separate way. I don't particularly care what the rest of you do." Arming himself with a bottle, Wild Card mumbled his good-byes and rode on. With Cecil as the only witness, one by one or in pairs, the Parsons gang rode off downhill to disappear into the early afternoon sunlight.

Rendered docile by a hefty dose of Doc's laudanum, Parsons had meekly submitted to the physician's examination of his wounds. Nell stood by to hand him instruments or cloths, and Dick Snow was ready to bodily restrain Parsons if the pain of the procedure was too intense.

Walker examined the bullet's exit wound first.

"Hmm," Walker hummed. "Not much infection here. The work of the two of you seems to have aided the healing of that one. Let's have a look at the other wound. Hmmm."

Motioning Nell to hand him a damp cloth, the doctor cleared caked blood away from the wound to expose it; a small, darkened object impacted within the bullet-sized puncture resisted his wiping.

"Aha!" the doctor exclaimed, leaning close to his work. "Nell, in my bag. A set of small tweezers. Pour some alcohol over them, please."

As Nell and Dick watched, absorbed, Walker caught hold of the dark object and gently and gingerly eased it out of the wound that oozed blood and matter. As it emerged, it grew larger. A black and bloodied wafer the size of a small fingernail was withdrawn by the tweezers.

"There's your culprit," Doc Walker exclaimed happily, dropping the darkened relic on Nell's damp cloth. "Seen it a thousand times in wartime wounds. The often irretrievable foreign object. A small shred of uniform, a piece of overcoat, gets carried into the wound with the Minié ball and stays there. Causes a physician no end of frustration when a man fails to respond to treatment. In Parsons's case, nothing more than a shred of that brittle and hideously filthy buckskin of his— loaded with infectious microbes—carried into the wound by the bullet touched off massive infection. If unattended much longer, he stood a very real risk of amputation or death. I daresay now, though, that with good food and rest for a few days, he ought to come out of it good as new."

Walker rinsed his hands with a small dollop of his alcohol and wiped them on one of Nell's dry towels.

"There was extensive muscle damage with that bullet, so he's likely to have a game leg the rest of his life. But with proper care over the next few days, I believe the man has a few more years to live. Nell, change his dressings daily, feed him well, and get me right up here if there's any change."

Dr. Walker climbed into his coat, put on his hat, and, with valise in hand, started for the door. "Funny, isn't it? Tremendous trifles. If any of his gang had seen that scrap of infectious leather sticking out of the wound—had pulled it and laved it with some of their ubiquitous hootch—all his agony could have been avoided, and he could still be up in the mountains raising hell, given appropriate time for the wounds to heal.'' With that, Dr. Walker, like some kind of mystic elf, scampered out the door, leaving Nell and Snow looking at each other over the limp, drugged form of Simon Parsons.

The door hinges squealed again, and Dr. Walker beamed a cherubic smile at them. ''Enjoy your lives together, you two! I predict they'll be long, happy, and productive!'' he said with no elaboration. Just that fast, the good doctor disappeared again.

Dusk was dimming the air of the gulch, and miners were drifting down from the diggings for the day when Dr. Walker, with his perpetual good-natured grin and ever-present valise, climbed into his chaise and clucked the bay mare down the sloping street to his office and living quarters. Dick and Nell watched him leave from the cabin door.

''Well, I don't know what that was all about, but I guess I'd better bandage his wounds,'' Nell said, looking into Dick Snow's eyes as if she'd rather do that than tend to Parsons.

Snow studied her. The tiny scrap of leather Doc had extracted still lay on the damp white towel. ''The water in your wash basin is a little bloody. I'll empty it and rinse it out. It's been quite an experience, Nell, these past few days.'' He looked again at the waferlike scrap of leather. ''Hard to believe,'' he said, ''that such a small thing could raise such havoc—and make such a difference—in his life, as well as in ours.''

''We did what we had to do, what we could,'' Nell

said. She looked sweetly and lovingly into his eyes. "As you say, it's been quite the experience. I've learned a great deal about myself. About you. About us." Nell reached out and gave his hand a squeeze and as quickly released it. They continued to stare intently into each other's eyes.

Nell dozed away the night shrouded in a blanket in the comfortably contoured balloon-back rocker, her ears sensitive to her patient's sleeping sounds or wakefulness. To be close but yet proper, Dick Snow spread his snug bedroll on his buffalo robe just outside the cabin's back door and slept soundly.

In the morning, while Simon Parsons snored contentedly on the other side of the cabin, Dick Snow quietly proposed marriage and joint parenting of Charley Rogers to Nell Joiner.

"I'll say it now, Dick Snow," she said, that merry tinkle again in her voice, but with a sincerity from deep within her heart, "and I'll say it again when the time comes. *I do!*"

# ✷ 20 ✷

It was a long hike for Charley Rogers from the school-house downhill on the flats of Dalton's earliest settlement back up to the cabin he shared with his new parents. Unlike his school friends, he didn't speak of them as Mother and Father, but as Nell and Dick. It was a bewildering situation to the other ten or twelve students in his school; he went by Charley Rogers, and his parents were known as Mr. and Mrs. Richard Snow. Sometimes skipping happily uphill to his home, his books and slate over his shoulder on a leather strap, Charley knew he couldn't have loved them more had they been his real parents.

He was the envy of the other schoolkids, the only one of them to have an extremely prosperous gold mine named for him. He'd lived with Indians, been on horse raids and in gunfights. Rather than have it all turned into bones of contention with the other kids, some older and some younger than he, Charley was shrewd enough to stay willing and happy (whenever he thought of happy, he was reminded of Acie)

239

and gregarious, and it never festered to the point of bullying or threat.

The Little Charley Mine had proved to be the richest piece of real estate anywhere in the vicinity of Dalton.

While Dick and Nell handled the business affairs of the mining activity in a headquarters office in Dalton, Acie and Barney—the on-site managers—with hired crews of workmen had widened and graded the road over Spindrift Summit to accommodate heavy-duty wagons pulled by teams. A giant six-stamp mill of massive metal components and huge timbers designed to crush and separate gold from granite had been laboriously hauled in manageable sections over the widened pass and erected at the bustling mine operation, with its numerous adits, side drifts, tunnels, and vertical ventilating shafts.

Also at the site, gold was extracted from the crushed ore, melted, and cast into ingots for the trip to Dalton and then on to the gold markets in Denver. Charley had counted it as odd at first but got used to the idea after Acie and Barney suggested to Dick that the crippled and jobless Simon Parsons be put on to ride as shotgun guard on gold shipment wagons. Dick called Simon to the office building in Dalton, had a long talk with him, and put him to work at a respectable wage.

In the year that had passed since the five of them made the return trip that rediscovered the Little Charley Mine, Simon Parsons and his characteristic limp had become a common sight in and around Dalton.

Following the lead of his "parents" in forgiving Parsons, Charley quickly got over his hostile feelings toward him, too. His stupid wound, the excruciating infection, and the way Snow and the others had rallied to his side had changed Simon Parsons's attitudes. And after a while, people in Dalton as well came to forget how Si had gotten there in the first place, and what had crippled him, which suited Simon Parsons just fine. He even had a drink now and then at the Pick and Poke with Old Bill Wheeler, who had conveniently forgotten Si Parsons's past—particularly when Si was setting them up.

Charley raced into the office of the Little Charley Mining Enterprises to share his good news with Dick and Nell: he had an excellent school report to show them—high marks in all his subjects.

Nell studied the report, with Dick beaming in pride as he leaned down to peer at it over her shoulder.

"Fine work, Charley. Fine work!" Dick enthused.

"We're both really proud of you, Charley," Nell said.

"We've been talking, Charley. Nell and I," Dick said. "Things are going well enough up at the mine that I think we can leave Acie and Barney in charge of things for a few weeks. Nell and I never had a real honeymoon. I think we can afford it now."

Charley looked at Dick, wondering where he fit into all this.

"Well, don't look so forlorn, Charley," Nell said. "You're going, too."

"Elk Leggins's village will move to the summer camp on Amity Creek soon. We're thinking of visiting them." Dick spoke to Charley in Cheyenne.

His response was in English as his heart leapt. "Won't be long until I'm out of school! Oh, yeah! Let's go!"

Charley's thoughts centered on Elk Leggins's dimly

lit lodge and of grand moments within the gentling medicine to its periphery, the carefully measured words of profound wisdom of Charley's Cheyenne father. He suddenly yearned to be there right away. His mind turned to times at games with the boys of the village. Of nighttimes alone in the grass, staring at a star-encrusted night sky. There'd be moments of reliving his long, solitary, free-spirited runs or thoughtful, serene walks alone on the prairie's vast openness with nothing and no one in sight and the cleansing winds sighing through the yellowed grass and the warmth of sunlight out of a sky blue and cloudless.

And of Dick Snow and Aunt Nell sharing the precious moments with him.

"What do you think Elk Leggins will say when he sees the lady in the locket in the flesh?" Nell asked, her smile and her words loving as she interrupted Charley's reverie.

Charley didn't miss a beat. "He'll say that you are prettier than your picture!"

# Everything Comes To He Who Writes

## Late Career Surge For *Epitaph* Contributor

### by Robert H. Dyer
### Western History Writer

**The Tombstone Epitaph, June 1992**

After struggling in the world of Western fiction for many years, R. C. "Dick" House is on his way to fame with publication of his fourth Western novel—and a three-book contract with Pocket Books of New York.

His first novel, *So the Loud Torrent,* is a mountain-man yarn published by North Star Press (St. Cloud, MN) in 1977. Then came *Vengeance Mountain,* a Western adventure, published by Tower Books of New York in 1980.

His third book, *The Sudden Gun,* published by M. Evans, New York, in 1991, is a marvelous Western that showcases his talent with dialogue and characterization. This book is now on library shelves across the country. His fourth book, *Drumm's War,* a Western army adventure done in collaboration with the late Bill Bragg of Casper, Wyoming, is set for publication later this year.

Then his agent recently sold his manuscript, *Track-down at Immigrant Lake,* to Pocket Books. Officials of this publishing giant were so impressed with the material that they requested two additional novels based on the *Trackdown* characters. The *Trackdown* sequels are in progress as this is being written.

Born some sixty-six years ago far from the West he would come to love and write about—in Ohio—his greatest boyhood joys were reading (emphasis on Westerns and historical adventures, of course) and hiking and exploring the nearby woods and farmlands.

## Muzzleloaders

When he was twelve he bought a much-abused Civil War musket for $2, beginning a lifelong interest in collecting and shooting muzzle-loading weapons.

After army service in World War II he attended Bowling Green State University and Kent State University in Ohio, studying journalism and public relations. His Bachelor of Arts degree was awarded at Kent in 1951. While at Kent he was editor of the *Kent Stater* and elected to the KSU journalism honorary society.

Four years on daily newspapers as reporter, photographer, and editor launched a nearly forty-year career in corporate communications, writing and editing employee newspapers and magazines for such firms as the Ford Motor Company and Occidental Life of California, and then twenty-three years as employee magazine and newspaper editor for the Jet Propulsion Laboratory in Pasadena, California, explorers of deep space, affiliated with NASA and Caltech. From this he has just retired (preferring to call it a "career change.")

**A newly discovered asteroid has been named for him, a co-worker's recognition of his long service at JPL.**

Why did Western fiction and not science fiction become the subject of his freelance writing? "Interpreting science and technology for a very diverse audience was a real challenge," he remarked.

"When I found time to peck away at the typewriter at home I wanted to lose myself in a totally different world. It was there waiting for me in the old West. But one fed off the other; my professional writing style improved as I wrote Western and muzzleloading articles and vice versa."

### Western Writers Stalwart

House is a longtime member of the Western Writers of America, serving as Membership Chairman, Vice President, and then President. He served several terms on the Executive Board and was Editor of the Association's magazine, *The Roundup,* for three years.

House and his wife, Doris, met when both were reporters for the Conneaut, Ohio *News Herald* in 1948. They have two children, Laura and Jonathan.

A man of many interests, House sings with "The Barbershop Four" quartet. He is a "chili head," involved with cooking in and judging chili cookoffs for years. E Clampus Vitus lists him as a member, as do The Westerners and the National Muzzle Loading Rifle Association.

### Prolific Writer

Meanwhile, House has written literally hundreds of nonfiction articles and stories under his own name—as well as his nom de plume, "Beau Jacques"—

for such magazines as *True West, Far West, Western* magazine (in Norway), *Gun Digest, Chili* magazine, *The Buckskin Report, American Rendezvous Magazine, Blackpowder Times, Then and Now, The Trade Blanket, Rendezvous Trails, Muzzle Blasts, Muzzleloader, The Backwoodsman, The Books of Buckskinning,* and, of course, *The Tombstone Epitaph.*

He also was commissioned to write "The Saga of the Cowboy" for the premier issue of *Disney Adventures.*

In addition to writing, he enjoys primitive desert camping, music of the swing era, and traditional and contemporary jazz.

House says he got some of his best advice from the legendary A. B. "Bud" Guthrie, Jr. (*The Big Sky* and many other books).

Over drinks and smokes at Guthrie's kitchen table in his cabin near Choteau, Montana, late one night in 1970, the famous Western writer told him, "You'll never hit unless you swing" (translation: "If you're going to be a writer, write!").

Guthrie also advised: "Write a good scene, and much else will be forgiven you." And "The adjective is the enemy of the noun, and the adverb is the enemy of every other part of speech." (Translation: "Seek until you find the most accurate noun and the most active verb, and you'll seldom need modifiers or superlatives.")

Has he applied the Guthrie principles to his work? If you haven't read a House Western novel, do so. You may soon be a fan.